THE MERCHANT FROM SEPHARAD

James Hutson-Wiley

Published by New Generation Publishing in 2022

Copyright © 2022 James Hutson-Wiley

Front cover design by XXXXXX

First Edition

ISBNs:

Paperback: 978-1-80369-659-1
Hardback: 978-1-80369-660-7
eBook: 978-1-80369-661-4

www.newgeneration-publishing.com

New Generation Publishing

ACKNOWLEDGEMENTS

The Merchant from Sepharad, the third book in the Sugar Merchant series, would not have been written without the patience and support of my wife, for which I will eternally be grateful.

Dr. James (Ted) Blanton once again provided substantial assistance in ensuring that the narrative was as historically accurate as possible. Dr. Blanton also supervised the construction of travel maps drawn by Sabastian Ballard, a cartographer and travel guide writer based in the United Kingdom. Intentional or not, any historical, theological, or geographic errors are entirely my responsibility.

THE AUTHOR'S CONFESSION

In the late twelfth century, the Jewish philosopher, physician, and Rabbi, Moses ben Maimon (Maimonides) wrote in his *Guide for the Perplexed*:

"Do not consider it proof because it is written in books. A liar who will deceive with his tongue will not hesitate to do the same with his pen."

If we are to be serious students of history, this maxim is worth remembering. Many first-hand accounts of the commercial and social revolution of the eleventh and twelfth centuries are biased by both personal and political agendas. Some are pure fiction or, worse, outright falsehoods. Although many characters described in the following pages were actual participants in the tumultuous events of the early twelfth century, we can only guess at their beliefs and motivations.

Notable exceptions exist within the trove of Jewish commercial correspondence discovered in the Cairo Genizah. Scholars have devoted themselves to recovering these documents, which provide a glimpse into what the revolution's participants believed to be true. Examples may be found in Elizabeth Lambourn's masterful work: *Abraham's Luggage, A Social life of Things in the Medieval Indian Ocean World*.

Regarding the commercial revolution of the twelfth century and its transformative effect on the theology of the Jewish faith, I have relied upon translations of contemporary sources. Although Maimonides was only a child during the period covered by this novel, Moshe Halbertal's *Maimonides Life and Thought* was helpful. Jacob Neusner's *Understanding Rabbinic Judaism from Talmudic to Modern Times* was also invaluable.

To the extent possible within a work of fiction, I have attempted to avoid lies and discover the truth. As is the case in the first two books of this series, I have followed the example of the first historian, Herodotus: if the truth is unclear or unknown, fabricate it.

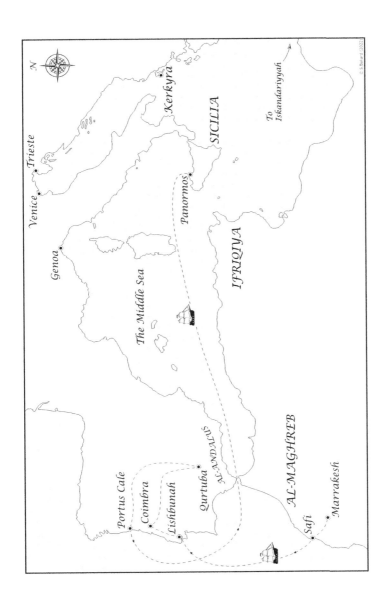

N

Venice
Trieste

Genoa

Kerkyra

The Middle Sea

SICILIA

Panormos

IFRIQIYA

To
Iskandariyyah

Portus Cale
Coimbra
Lishbunah
Qurtuba

AL-ANDALUS

AL-MAGHREB

Safi

Marrakesh

© S. Ballard 2022

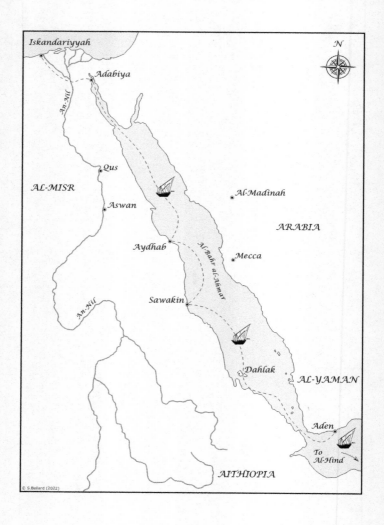

DRAMATIS PERSONAE

The following characters in the novel were actual persons whose existence is well documented in historical sources.

ALFONSO HENRIQUES, King of Portugal

HIYYA AL-DAUDI, chief rabbi of Portugal and adviser to King Alfonso Henriques

YAISH IBN YAHYA, Jewish mercenary and son of Hiyya al-Daudi

TEOTONIO, prior to the monastery of Santa Cruz de Coimbra

MAIMON BEN JOSEPH, Rabbi, and father of the Jewish philosopher Maimonides

ABU AL-QASIM AHMED, chief judge of the city of Cordoba and father of the Muslim philosopher Averroes

GIORGOS OF ANTIOCH, emir, and commander of the Kingdom of Sicily's armed forces

HALFON BEN HALEVI, an Egyptian Jewish merchant, engaged in the India trade

MADMUN BEN HASAN-JAPHETH, Jewish merchant and leader of the Jewish community in Yemen

ABRAHAM BEN YIJU, a Tunisian Jewish merchant in Yemen and India

BENJAMIN OF TUDELA, a Jewish traveler and author

PRAEFATIO
The Kingdom of Sicilia
The Christian year 1148

The story you are about to read was written by my friend, Joshua ben Elazar, a Jew. It is a tale of a journey, both physical and spiritual. At my insistence, Joshua wrote his tale in Arabic, the common language in the lands bordering the Middle Sea. His manuscript followed the conventions of the time, but Joshua refused to write God's full name. If he did so, he explained, his manuscript could never be destroyed.

When Joshua first arrived, al-Andalus, which Latins know as Hispania, was governed by the Muslim al-Murabit dynasty, subservient to the caliph of Baghdad. Al-Andalus has been under Muslim control for over four hundred years. A change in control, however, can be expected. With the success of the armed pilgrimage to the Holy Land, the Pope's legions intend to wrest control of the riches of al-Andalus. Christian armies are making significant gains in the north and west of that land. At the same time, a new Muslim sect, calling themselves the Almoravid, has risen in Ifriqiya and shares the same goals. The Jews, who refer to all followers of Islam as Ishmaelites, are caught between these would-be conquerors. Alliances constantly shift, and the world is in turmoil.

In the Levante, further to the east, the situation is more confusing. The various kingdoms established by the armed pilgrims, called *crucesignati*, are at one another's throats. Taking advantage of the resulting weakness, Muslim armies are forming to drive Christians from the Holy Land. To make matters worse, there is open hostility between western Christians, subservient to the Pope, and those in the east, who bow to the Patriarch of Constantinopolis.

Jews, too, have their divisions. There is a conflict between those who follow the laws set by their Rabbis and a sect known as Karaites, who disavow such rules. At stake for all is not only the matter of faith but the potential advantages from the rapidly growing and highly lucrative trade routes to India (known as *al-Hind* in Arabic), for spices and other precious commodities.

Here on the island of Sicilia, we enjoy a privileged position. For many years we have satisfied the needs of people of all faiths. We are not perfect, but we are a bastion of peace. I do not know how long that will last. Our ruler, King Ruggiero, has his own desire to achieve wealth and power in the Middle Sea.

It is through this maze of conflict and confusion that Joshua must navigate.

William ibn Thoma
Notarius Magistros
Panormos, Sicilia

My heart is in the east, and I in the uttermost west.
How can I find savor in food? How shall it
be sweet to me?
How shall I render my vows and my
bonds while yet
Zion lieth beneath the fetter of Edom, and
I in Arab chains?
A light thing would it seem to me
to leave all the good things of Spain –
Seeing how precious in my eyes
to behold the dust of the desolate sanctuary.

Yehuda Halevi – Tudela 1140

I

MY TALE BEGINS
Panormos, Sicilia
The Christian year 1146

I was in a deplorable state when I first met William. I possessed nothing: no baggage and no coin. My shabby black robe was torn and stained with seawater. My hair and beard were untrimmed, and I was full of rage.

William was resting comfortably in the garden when I banged on his gate and demanded entrance. The servant who answered looked at me with disdain. I am certain he thought I was a beggar; he made to drive me away.

"My name is Joshua ben Elazar," I shouted. "I have business here."

A blond-headed man of my age, dressed in a fine gown of gazz, looked up from the manuscript he was reading and gestured to the servant to stand aside.

"What is your business here?" he asked. "I am William, the son of the physician Thoma. Do you require his services?"

I swallowed my anger and answered as politely as I could.

"Cousin, forgive my appearance, but I am Joshua, the son of Elazar," I said. "Our grandfathers were partners in commerce. Your father, Thoma, knows mine well. I have traveled far and will be making a longer journey soon. I ask if I can rest with you until my departure. My father said he would write to me here and told me to feel free to call upon you."

William was not my cousin, but I called him that. Long ago, our respective grandfathers and their Muslim companion had formed a commercial trading venture to trade in al-sukkar and other precious spices. Each of them had owned one-third of what, under Latin law, was called a *Collegantia*. Together, the partners overcame adversity and achieved great success. Now the Collegantia was owned by my father and William's Muslim true uncle, Abdullah. William's father, the physician Thoma, no longer possessed an interest in the enterprise.

William greeted me gracefully, but I knew he found my appearance distressing. I had not trimmed my beard for weeks. Although my skin was brown from the sun, I knew my face reflected the weariness and anger I felt.

"Forgive me, Joshua," said William. "Sit with me here, and I will have one of our servants fetch your belongings. No letter has arrived for you. Please stay with us until it does."

"I have no belongings, only the clothes on my back," I said. I sat on the bench opposite William. "I would like a cup of wine."

"Of course," William responded, gesturing to a servant nearby. "I will have a cup myself. From where have you come?"

"The land of Sepharad," I declared.

William ignored the sullenness which marked my words. "Forgive me," he said. "I do not know this word. I have never heard of that place."

I was surprised at William's ignorance. He appeared to be an educated man.

"How can you not know this, William?" I said. "I have resided in the cities of Lishbunah and Qurtuba. Those cities are in the land of Sepharad."

William looked at me in puzzlement. "I know Qurtuba is in al-Andalus, and Lishbunah is in the territory called 'Gharb al-Andalus' or, as some would say, Arth al-Bortucal, but what is this land of Sepharad?" he asked.

I shook my head in disgust. "Have you not read the words of the prophet Obadiah? The Muslims claim these cities are in al-Andalus. We disagree. It is the land of Sepharad and has been so since ancient times."

William's face betrayed his confusion. "Joshua, again forgive me," he said. "I do not recall the words of Obadiah. I do not understand."

In retrospect, I should have expected William's response, but at the time, I was incredulous. I did not attempt to hide my feelings.

"Christians and Ishmaelites – you call them Muslims – think the world revolves around you," I said. "You control the world and ignore the heritage of my people, the Jews. None of you bother to learn anything of us or our history. You ask about the land of Sepharad. We Jews arrived long ago in what you call Al-Andalus as slaves of the Romans. According to the prophet Obadiah, who lived long before your own Yeshua of Natzeret, this was the land of Sepharad. Read this yourself in the scriptures. From that time, we have grown in wealth and power. Can you believe that one of our rabbis became a grand vizier to the ruler of Gharnata? Despite our success, no one has attempted to understand us. We are treated as refuse."

William raised his brows and pondered my words. I should not have blamed him for his ignorance. Nothing has changed since my people's exile from Siyyon. Our treatment everywhere has been the same. I did not, however, apologize for my curtness with William and gave him no time to respond.

"If my father permits, I will return to Yerushalayim with my people. G-d has promised through the prophet that we Jews will inherit all the lands of the south. 'The day of judgment for all nations is soon at hand. Evil will be punished, and the righteous renewed,' says the scripture. You do not know this?"

I could see that William remained at a loss for words. The anger which had been building in me since I fled Arth al-Bortucal came to a head.

"Your father, Thomas, spent years amongst followers of Islam," I said. "His mother was an Ishmaelite, and your father was raised in that faith. Now, your father is a Christian. Although you live in Sicilia, where all faiths are welcome, it seems you know nothing about my people."

William now opened his mouth in shock. "Joshua, I am no enemy," he said. "If I have offended you, please accept my apology. And please tell me more."

We conversed well into the evening. After my second cup of wine, my anger began to dissipate. My journey to Sicilia had been profoundly difficult, and the horror of recent events was still on my mind. I knew this was no reason to be rude to William, and I apologized for my behavior. At dusk, his father, the physician Thoma, arrived home, accompanied by his assistant, Roland. Thoma greeted me warmly and seemed delighted to meet me. But before he could speak, Roland had much to say and many questions. From my father's description, I knew Roland found it challenging to speak with brevity.

"Ah, my boy, I see you have had a difficult journey," he exclaimed. "I am Roland, the assistant, friend, and partner in the art of curing illness to the great physician Thomas who stands here before you. Some still call him Thoma. I do not. You should know that I, too, am a physician. You do not look well. Where have you been? Why have you not visited us before? I know something of your father, Elazar. I have heard stories about your grandfather. His name was Jusuf. Is that not correct? I assume that he has passed. Hakim Thomas says he was a great man. Please accept my condolences. But what about you? You must tell us everything! Thomas has invited me to dine here tonight. You are dining with us well?"

William interrupted before Roland could continue or ask again where Joshua had been.

"You are right, Hakim Roland," said William. "Joshua has made a difficult journey and has only now arrived from the city of Qurtuba. I was about to take him to his chamber so he can prepare for the evening meal. He will need to change his robe and trim his beard. His journey has been difficult. We can discuss all this later."

With that remark, William led me away. As he did, William whispered: "Prepare yourself for more questions, Joshua. We love Roland, but he can be tiresome. Having another large cup of wine before we dine would do you no harm. I will give you a clean robe to wear."

I thanked William for his kindness; I did need to collect my wits. During our meal, William prompted his father and Roland with questions to keep the potential inquisition at bay.

"Joshua, so that you may eat in peace, perhaps my father can relate some of his history and recount what transpired between him and your father," William said. I nodded my head in agreement; I understood William's intentions.

William's father required no further prompting and began to speak. Roland, of course, interrupted.

"Hakim Thomas will be too modest. Through his skill, he saved my life and saved Jerusalem from the Turks. He has traveled the world, cured the ill, and is the personal physician to Ruggiero, the King of Sicilia. He even befriended a skilled Hashshashin, who helped him prevail in many great battles."

William's father buried his head in his hands when Roland mentioned the Hashshashin. I learned later that Thoma had never told anyone the true story of how Roland had unknowingly caused the death of his great friend. The memory of this was too painful. Engrossed in his story, Roland did not notice.

"Hakim Thomas was treated poorly in Jerusalem and thrown in prison, and I saved him. I was on the path to becoming a knight. Did you know that? My actions closed that door forever, but Hakim Thomas rescued me again. It was because of him that I became a physician. Did you know that he gave up his rights to the Collegantia and that the Church stole his fortune? I am certain you do. He asked only for support to create our hospice here. You must visit us there, and we will show you what we have done. William here is a respected counselor and scribe. William studied law, both Canon and Roman, at the great institution of Bologna. Everyone respects his wisdom. That is why he is the right hand of our emir. He will tell you more himself. If you need anything on our island, it can be done. Is not that correct, William?"

Roland did not wait for William to respond. He paused to take a breath and peered closely at me. "You do not look well," he pronounced. "We should examine you. Has anyone looked at the color of your excrement?"

Although it was true that I felt unwell, the last thing I wanted was for Roland to conduct an exploration of my waste.

I am not sure that William's father said more than a few words; Roland dominated the conversation until it was time for sleep. Although I listened attentively, I spoke little myself.

Fortunately, over the following days, William's father and Roland continued to spend long hours at the Hospice, and William's duties at court were few, so we had time to talk in private. I remained his guest for the next month, waiting for word from my father. Over that time, I began to relax and shared some of my tales of tribulation in Al-Andalus with William. I believe he tried to comprehend what I had faced.

"William," I said, "you cannot truly understand. You cannot walk in my boots. You can nod your head in understanding. You can offer condolence and prayers, but you will never be able to share my pain. You will never know what it is to be a Jew in the lands of Islam or those under Christian rule. I will do my best to explain, but, in the end, you will still know nothing."

"I will try to learn," William assured me. "I will listen. Better yet, why not take the time to put your story in writing? The letter you are awaiting from your father will take time to reach our shores. Besides, I can see that your soul is tortured. Setting your tale down in script may be of benefit."

William was correct. I wanted to remember all that transpired in the land of Sepharad. The fire I had caused was still vivid in my memory, as was the brutal murder of my dearest friends. I had failed terribly but learned much. Perhaps the exercise of putting my thoughts on a parchment would provide solace. Perhaps I would be better prepared for the task I had sworn to undertake. Thus, I present, in the following pages, all that is still fresh in my memory.

II

MY FIRST LESSON
Lishbunah
The Christian year 1142

Almost twenty-four years ago, my father, Elazar, established a trading venture in the city of Lishbunah, which the Muslims called al-Ushbuna. At that time, Lishbunah was ruled by the Al-Murabit Emirate of Qurtuba. At one time, Lishbunah was one of the largest cities in the world. Even now, it remains an important trading center. Its opulence draws merchants, scholars, and would-be conquerors, all eager to gain from the city's freedoms and wonders.

In the beginning, my father and his Muslim partner, Abdullah, believed that establishing commerce in Lishbunah was essential to the Collegantia's ability to deliver al-sukkar and other spices to the Christian world. My father and Abdullah were correct. Jews in Lishbunah were, at that time, protected by law and free to engage in commerce without restriction, providing they paid their Jizya taxes. That was important to the venture's success.

When I arrived in the Christian year 1142, all had changed. The Al-Murabit rulers were in a state of confusion. Their fear of Christian incursion in the north, coupled with the constant conflict between Muslim Taifas in al-Andalus left Lishbunah without clear leadership. The rulers directed their insecurity at us, the Jews. Everything had changed since my father's time. Those of my faith were no longer free. We could not carry weapons. We could not ride horses. We were forbidden to wear fine clothes. As a Jew, I was required to show deference to Muslims, even those who had nothing. We were forced to bow and scrape to everyone or face severe consequences. This was not the worst of it. No, we were not free.

I was eighteen years of age when my father directed me to travel to Lishbunah and assume control of commerce on behalf of the Collegantia. This was both an honor and a test. If all went well, my position in the Collegantia would be assured, and I would bring credit to my family. I was grateful for the opportunity and the responsibility granted to me. At my age, it was impossible to imagine failure and easy to dream of success. On the two-week journey by sea from my home in Marrakech, I read and reread my father's brief instructions. I was to find the Collegantia's representative, a man called Essua, in the port and present a letter of introduction. Essua would show me a home on a hill above the city center. This abode would be sparsely furnished but comfortable. My first task, which seemed simple to perform, would be to deliver a small box of gold ornaments made by one of the best Jewish artisans in Marrakech to a merchant who would give me a letter of credit in exchange.

The wealthy in Lishbunah coveted such ornaments and would pay dearly for them. Proceeds from the transaction would be sufficient to pay my living expenses. Another vessel, wrote my father, would be arriving soon from Iskandariyyah, loaded with flax to be woven into cloth, and ten sacks of precious al-sukkar. I was told to secure a *makhzan* to store these precious commodities and, under Essua's guidance, pay the fees for their import. My father instructed me to unload the cargo quickly to avoid rot, given the long journey and the damp weather in the city. I had gained some experience in trade working for my father in Marrakech, and these instructions seemed easy to follow. Success, I thought, was assured. I was wrong.

When I arrived at the port, I gave thanks to G-d that I could once again put my feet on dry land. I was thankful that I could now begin my first true adventure as a merchant. The port was bustling with activity, and hundreds of workers lined the docks. I was confident I could find Essua amongst the crowd. Surprisingly, no one stepped forward to greet me. I had no description of Essua and did not know the entirety of his name. I was unsure of what to do. One man stood out from the rest, an official of some kind. Dressed in a robe of gazz, this man wore a white turban and gave orders to workers in the crowd. This man, I thought, must be the functionary who assessed fees for landing at the port. I collected my box of ornaments and pushed through the crowd. As I came closer, I noticed that the official's robe was shabby and his poorly wound turban soiled. I was so anxious that I neglected to give the customary greetings. Instead, I asked the official if he knew a man called Essua who was to have met me. The official looked at me with disdain and spat. His response was terse.

"Have you no manners? Do not address me as you would a peasant. Who are you?"

I came from a wealthy and influential family and was not accustomed to being addressed rudely, "I am called Joshua ben Elazar of Marrakech," I answered with pride. "Please answer my question."

Upon hearing my name, the official shook his head in disgust. "A Jew; that is who you are. What is in the box you are carrying?"

Foolishly, I opened the box and handed it to the official, who gasped at its contents.

"This," he said, "must be valued by the Sahib al-Suq. You may collect it when you pay the fees." The official gestured to one of his armed guards and gave him the box.

My father had always instructed me to respect authority, but I became worried at this point. How could I pay fees? I had expected to deliver the ornaments to the merchant my father had named and collected their price. Without Essua, I had no coin myself.

Holding my anger in check, I addressed the official with greater formality and explained my dilemma. The official waved me to silence.

"That is not my problem, Jew. I know of no one called Essua." He spat again. "I am busy. Seek others of your kind who may be able to help you. You people remain together, don't you?"

With that remark, the official turned to other business.

I was deeply stung by the official's words and knew I was now in great difficulty. After several attempts to secure assistance from others at the dock, I finally obtained directions to the area of the city in which others of my faith lived and worked. There, fellow Jews warmly greeted me. All had questions. What was my name? Who was my father? From where had I traveled? It was not long before a small crowd gathered, and I was asked to repeat my responses. Those in the group spoke amongst themselves and argued about where I could find my missing agent. Following a spirited debate, these men finally nodded their heads in agreement. I should go, they said, to Rabbi Hiyya al-Daudi. The Rabbi would know what to do. One of the older men in the crowd stepped forward and took me by the hand as if I was a small child. "Come with me," he said.

Walking through the maze of winding lanes, I became lost and gave silent thanks for my guide. I thought I was being led to a house of worship. That was not the case. Soon I found myself in front of a high-walled residence protected by an elaborately carved wooden door. Above the door was a stone plaque inscribed with words in a script I had only rarely seen. When I entered, I saw a small garden where a group of young boys listened intently to an old man who sat on a cushion. The old man was reciting a beautifully cadenced poem in Arabic. Without exception, the boys were giving their full attention, nodding together to the poem's rhythm. Upon closer inspection, I noticed the children transcribing the words in the Jewish script. I did not wish to interrupt whatever lesson was being imparted and remained silent. The teacher then began a recitation in another language altogether. Although the cadence was Arabic, it was different and, to me, more pleasing to the ear.

Engrossed in his recitation, the teacher did not notice me at first. When he did, he gestured to a well-built man standing nearby, who appeared to be about my age and height. Without hesitation, the young man approached me with a smile and led me further into the garden.

"Welcome," he said. "Do you have business with my father, the Rabbi? I am his son, Yaish ibn Yahya. Can I help you?"

I thanked Yaish, introduced myself, and told him of my dilemma.

"You say this man Essua is an agent for your father?" he asked. "We know someone with this name, and he is a commercial agent. He assists merchants from al-Maghreb. Essua was taken to prison only two days ago by the authorities on a charge of immorality. Could this be the man you are seeking?"

"I pray this is not the case," I said. "What is this charge of immorality?"

"It is not unusual, I am afraid. Our people are often subject to accusations that have no merit. The rulers here ensure that we know our place. In Essua's case, an Ishmaelite woman reported that Essua stared at her too long in the street and gave her a fright."

I opened my mouth in wonder. "Stared at this woman too long, you say? "What nonsense! The women here are covered in veils and long robes, just as women are in my own country. What is there to stare at?"

Yaish sighed. "You are speaking reason. We are not dealing with reason. We are dealing with power. The woman involved is the daughter of a merchant who engaged in a dispute with Essua. The incident occurred near a mosque. There were no Ishmaelite witnesses upon whom Essua could call to refute the accusation. His only witness is a Jew, and Jews are not permitted to testify against Ishmaelites in court. Essua was in the wrong place at the wrong time. That is his only crime. My father will do what he can, but it will take time."

By now, the Rabbi had completed his lessons. The young boys were collecting their belongings and talking amongst themselves.

"Let us go to my father," said Yaish. "He can tell you more."

Rabbi al-Daudi was heavily bearded. His face was lined with the marks of age and his hair was white. Following the customary greetings and introductions, Yaish repeated what he had imparted to me.

The Rabbi nodded in understanding. "You are the son of Elazar ben Jusuf of Marrakech? I have met your father. He has undertaken sound commerce in our city and has a fine reputation. If I can assist you, I will. Unfortunately, there is little I can do for Essua. If our rulers follow custom, he will be released from captivity in a few weeks. Of course, Essua will be brought before the court, but I doubt his accuser will present herself. This happens frequently; I am sorry to say. Have you any place to stay?"

I admitted that I did not. "Essua was to have shown me the home he found for me, and that is now not possible. Worse, my box of ornaments had been confiscated at the port. To recover it, a fee is required. Besides being homeless, I have no coin."

"Given your father's reputation, we can help you with that problem," said the Rabbi. As you can see, this is a Yeshiva for young students. We also have a beth midrash for older boys, what the Ishmaelites call a madrassa. It is a school of learning. You may stay with us here. Now show me the receipt you were given."

"Receipt? What receipt? I was given nothing," I responded. "The official told me to present myself at the Alcazar fortress with sufficient coin to pay the fees."

The Rabbi and his son raised their brows and looked at each other in understanding. "What was the official's name who took your box and gave those instructions? Do you remember?"

I had been a fool. I had not asked the official's name. I thought I was obeying the port's rules and had accepted the situation as it was presented. It was at that moment that I realized the depth of my error. My face fell. "I do not know," I admitted.

Following a moment of silence, Yaish turned to his father. "I will see if I can discover who was on duty when Joshua's ship arrived."

The Rabbi addressed me directly: "I regret this too is a common occurrence. It would be best to accept that you may never recover your ornaments. Perhaps G-d will aid you, and all will be well. The prophets tell us that we should not complain or be disappointed when we are faced with loss. Your possessions are worldly matters. Is it not sufficient that you are alive? It is best to see the reality of the situation. You may hope to regain what you have lost but be uncertain in that hope. Remember the story of Moses. G-d may show you a new and better path. For now, stay with us until the situation is resolved."

At the time, the Rabbi's words provided little comfort. I was to realize their truth much later. G-d did open a new path for me, but He took His time in doing so.

I was given a room in the Yeshiva that evening and the next. As expected, Yaish could not discover the name of the port official who had confiscated my gold ornaments. After several visits to the Alcazar, we finally met an assistant to the Sahib al-Suq. This led nowhere. This official was gaunt, and his features sharp. He wore a perpetual frown. Wearing a fine robe of blue gazz, he was ensconced behind a large writing desk surrounded by clerks. The official looked up from his work and scowled when he saw us approaching.

"What do you want," he said tersely. Using the most formal language I could think of, I told him. The official smiled and nodded his head in what I thought was sympathy.

"I know nothing of this," he said. He turned to his clerks and asked if they knew anything about a box of gold ornaments taken at the docks. Without exception, the clerks all denied any knowledge. The official looked at me with an evil grin.

"You see, there is nothing we can do. Even if such a box existed, you have not been harmed. All you have lost is the profit you would have made. The fees for gold ornaments of this kind would equal their cost. Of course, the profit you Jews expect to gain on your commerce is, how shall I say it, excessive. Is that not true? Perhaps your loss is a punishment from Allah."

I could not hide my feelings. The official's words were not only blatant lies but an insult.

Seeing the look on my face, the official continued. "I see I have offended you. Am I wrong about the avarice of your people?" The official continued to smile and then continued, "Have you paid the Jizya tax for your residency in the city?"

I said nothing. Under the circumstances, I had forgotten the tax imposed upon Christians and Jews in Islamic lands.

"You do not answer me, and thus I suspect not." Said the official. "We are the ones who should complain, Jew. I expect you back here in a week to pay your tax. Of course, you can always convert to true faith beforehand. Then you would owe nothing. Leave us now. We are busy with important matters."

I struggled to control my anger, but there was nothing I could do.

As we left, Yaish whispered, "As my father told you, this is the reality we face. It is best never to show your true feelings. Many of our faith have converted to Islam simply to avoid the humiliation and cost. We pray for them." Yaish hesitated for a moment before continuing. In a lower voice, he said: "G-d willing, we shall soon be delivered from the hands of the Ishmaelites."

We had better fortune in our search for the missing Essua. He was imprisoned in the alcazar awaiting his appearance before the Qadi. Yaish paid a guard the princely sum of one-half dinar for privately meeting with the prisoner. When we did so, we found Essua in poor condition. His body was thin, his clothing in rags. A purple and yellow bruise marred his face. Essua confirmed he was indeed the Collegantia's representative who was to have met my vessel on arrival. Through tears, Essua begged forgiveness for his failure. He had done nothing wrong and the accusation of immorality was false.

"I argued with an Ishmaelite merchant over the cost of a residence for you, Joshua. This abomination dared to charge me twice the going price, and I called him a thief. That was foolish, I know. The Ishmaelite claimed I looked longingly at his daughter. Can you believe it? No one of a sane mind would look at his daughter. With her girth, she will be fortunate to find a husband. Why would I do such a thing?"

Yaish looked sadly at the poor wretch. "Be calm, Essua. You know as well as I do that this will come to nothing. My father will pay the cost of feeding you properly while you are in this miserable place. Pray and be patient. All will be well."

Once again, Essua began to cry. "Praise G-d for your kindness. I have had nothing to eat for days." Turning to me, he said: "Please forgive me. I was to have shown you to your home and where to take the gold. Now there is nowhere for you to live. Take the ornaments to Isaac ha-Levi, the gold merchant. Isaac will arrange the sale and pay you well. You must pay the fees at the port first. G-d willing, your father gave you coin to do so. The Ishmaelites have taken all my funds until I appear in court."

I told Essua what had happened to the ornaments, which produced more tears.

"Aye, Aye, Aye, your father will never forgive me. That gold was worth at least one thousand dinars. Our brethren in Marrakech are the finest craftsman of gold ornaments in the world. This is all my fault. I have failed in my duties. You have been robbed, and it is my fault. No one will retain me as an agent again." Essua banged his head against the iron bars of his cell and continued to weep.

I was now at a loss for words. Yaish, however, knew what to say.

"Essua, you have broken no law of G-d. Do not feel ashamed. You have made an error of judgment. That does not mean you are evil. When you are released from this place, and you will be, come and pray with us. It is enough that we stand together. We must go now. Have faith. All will be well."

As we returned to the Yeshiva, I kept my head down in silent contemplation. It was true that the fault was not Essua's. My lack of judgment was to blame for losing a small fortune in gold. Yaish guessed what I was thinking.

"Joshua, I must give you the same advice I have just given Essua. What has transpired is the result of your ignorance; that is all. What you must do now is take what steps you can to avoid such an error in the future. Dwelling upon guilt resolves nothing. If there is anger in your heart, pray to remove it. G-d has granted you the ability to see this event in diverse ways. The sages tell us that to dwell on anger is the same as worshiping an idol. Surely, you have studied our faith?"

I had not. Although my father had studied the Talmud, we rarely discussed our faith, and there was no yeshiva in Marrakech. If there had been, my everyday tasks would not have permitted religious study. It was enough that I had learned to read and write Arabic and gained a sound knowledge of numbers. Until my voyage to Lishbunah, my duties for my father and the Collegantia had involved aiding my cousins in collecting salt to exchange for gold in the far south of Ifriqiya. Rather than answer the question raised by Yaish, I changed the subject of the conversation.

"This has been a difficult day, Yaish. I am grateful for your help and offer to shelter me until all is resolved. Are you certain this will not inconvenience your father?"

"Not at all," said Yaish. It is our duty. Stay with us for now. Perhaps we can find some way you can be helpful to us."

Days turned into weeks as we waited for Essua to be released from prison. With reluctance, I wrote to my father and briefly related the disaster which had befallen me. It would be at least a month before the letter arrived in Marrakech. Until it did, and my father replied, there was little to do. Rabbi al-Daudi resolved the problem.

"Joshua, while you wait, join our classes. It will help the young boys see a man your age interested in learning."

"But I do not know the script the children are writing nor the language they speak. I know you are reciting poems, but otherwise, I am ignorant."

"I am not surprised," said Rabbi al-Daudi. "Most of our people speak only Arabic. Other teachers and I hope to bring back the Hebrew language of our forebears in the land of Siyyon. Much of the spoken form of the holy language was lost long ago during our war with the Romans. We call our script 'Ashurit.' Although merchants and scholars write in this script, Hebrew is rarely spoken here. I believe that to maintain our faith's strength, we need a language for everyone, not just for those of us who teach and study. Remember, our people were expelled from their homeland and scattered throughout the world. Our strength and survival depend upon our unity. This truth is what I am teaching."

It would be interesting to learn Ashurit, but I thought my remaining days with the Rabbi and his son would be few. Learning a new language and script could take time. When I raised this issue, the Rabbi nodded his head in understanding and continued:

"It will be easier than you think, my son. The alphabet of Arabic and Ashurit are similar. These languages were derived from the same source. In Qurtuba, a scholar, Judah ben David Hayyuj, developed the grammar of our sacred language. It is not greatly different from Arabic. I instruct my students on both the language and its grammar using verse. Do you know anything about poetry?"

The Rabbi shook his head in sorrow when I admitted I did not. "You are missing much. For years, our poetry was only in the Arabic language. Now, we have borrowed the patterns and rhythm of that language and combined them to create something new. That is what I was demonstrating to the children when we first met. Perhaps you should attend class tomorrow. One of the older boys will help you."

Although joining children in their lessons was embarrassing, I enjoyed my days at the yeshiva. I was diligent in my studies and soon could read and write the characters of Ashurit. Rabbi al-Daudi continued to recite poetry and teach the similarities and differences between the sacred language of Hebrew and Arabic. The Rabbi also read from scripture, what we Jews call the Tanakh, written in Ashurit.

Given the many hours I spent each day in study, I had little time to worry about the situation in which I found myself. Every day except the Sabbath was the same. The young boys would gather in the courtyard on fine days or, when it rained, would meet in a large room within the Rabbi's residence. After prayers, the Rabbi would read aloud, and the boys and I would listen and inscribe what we heard in Ashurit.

On a few occasions, at dusk, visitors interrupted lessons. Dressed in Arab garments, these callers looked as if they had been traveling for some time. One of them was a giant. He must have been over four cubits in height and was proportionately wide. Each time, the visitors introduced themselves in the same way, by extending a greeting from someone named Eugene. Whoever permitted their entry to the yeshiva would look both ways in the street outside before granting them access. When that happened, the Rabbi and his son would excuse themselves from lessons and meet with the strangers elsewhere in the villa. Their absence allowed the young boys to talk amongst themselves and engage in games and general mischief. I was, of course, excluded and used my free time to practice calligraphy. No one ever spoke about these visitors during meals with the Rabbi and his family, and I kept my curiosity in check. Instead, we discussed current events. I rarely left the residence and thus knew little about what was happening in the world outside. When I asked for news, Yaish told me that Christian forces were gathering in the north, under the leadership of Alfonso Henriques.

"He is a clever man,' said Yaish. "Alfonso spread the news that he achieved a great victory over the Governor of Qurtuba at the battle of Ourique. This is false. There was no great battle. It was merely a skirmish, and it did not happen in Ourique. There was a conflict near the city of Santarem, but those who spread the news do not care for the truth. The Christians will believe anything. Alfonso used this so-called victory to proclaim himself the Prince of all Arth al-Bortucal, and many accepted his claim. He has written to the Christian Pope, pledging his allegiance, and asking the Pope to acknowledge his self-proclaimed position. In return, he promises to drive the Ishmaelites from the land.

"Does this make any difference to us?" I asked.

"Indeed, it may," said Yaish. "Our lot would improve."

"How so?" I asked. "The Christians say we killed their messiah. They hate us. At least here, we are free from fear."

Both the Rabbi and Yaish chuckled at my words and shook their heads. "You have much to learn," said the Rabbi. "I do not know how things are in Marrakech, but you have already witnessed how we are not free from fear or anything else in Lishbunah. Our people are called 'dhimmis' – protected people. Under the laws of Islam, we are free to practice our faith and govern ourselves under our laws. As 'dhimmi,' our lives are protected, so long as we are loyal to the rulers and pay the Jizya tax. However, that is just the surface. All is not what it seems."

I had, indeed, witnessed the reality. We were most certainly not protected. "Tell me more," I said.

"You see, our people are supervised by a special official from what is called the Office of Protection. This office is charged with restricting our expansion. You already know we cannot bear arms or ride horses. We can no longer build houses of worship. We cannot marry an Ishmaelite woman or bear witness against an Ishmaelite in court. At all times, we must show deference to our masters. We may not dress in any way as to be offensive. There are other restrictions, and all are intended to keep us in our place, and that place is low. Christians are treated the same, but there are few of them. Our lives are not difficult if we stay together and do not complain. We are not, however, free. In many ways, we are slaves to the Ishmaelites."

I knew the truth of the Rabbi's words but wondered why he thought the Christians would treat us any better.

"But what difference will it make if the Ishmaelites are defeated, and Christians become our new masters?" I asked. "Will that not be the same for us?"

Yaish and his father looked pointedly at each other. "We have reason to hope," said the Rabbi. "As I told you, it is best to be uncertain in hope, but we have faith in G-d and what steps we can take. Let us leave it at that."

From that time forward, discussions at meals were confined to philosophy, poetry, and scripture. No one mentioned the place of Jews in the city again.

After several weeks, Essua was finally called to answer the charges of immorality. As expected, his accuser failed to appear, and thus the Qadi had no cause to hold him any longer. Yaish and I met Essua at the prison gates; we were not permitted in the court. Essua wept with joy when he saw us. Although he was thin and covered with filth, his bruises were gone. His spirits were high now he had finally gained his freedom.

"Thanks be to G-d; I can finally perform my duties for you," Essua said. "Seeing the sky and breathing air is a joy beyond comprehension; but enough of that. We have much to do. I must return to my home to see if there has been any correspondence from your father's Collegantia. I need to find you somewhere to reside while you are here. You must also present yourself to the authorities to pay your tax. I have some hidden funds for that purpose and will pay the cost myself. It is the least I can do."

I told Essua that I had been well cared for at the yeshiva and, if the Rabbi permitted, I would prefer to stay there. I had much to learn and wished to continue my study for as long as possible. Of course, I had forgotten about the tax, so I was grateful for Essua's offer. I was less excited about discovering what correspondence from my father had arrived. What would my father say about the lost gold?

When we arrived at Essua's residence, it was in shambles. Someone had rifled through all his belongings. His ledgers were strewn haphazardly on the floor. Essua looked at the mess in horror.

"What more will these heathens do to me?" he cried. In a panic, he went to his cot and carefully inspected it. He sighed with relief when he saw that the straw covering was still intact. Carefully, he tore a strip of the cloth covering and extracted a bag from the straw.

"This is my coin," Essua said, opening the bag and examining the contents. "At least the Ishmaelites were not thieves. They looked in my ledgers for anything that could be used to prove my guilt. The rulers here claim we are free in this place. What an evil myth!"

Essua's belongings and documents were restored to their original condition; nothing appeared to be missing. Essua eventually calmed, and we returned to the Alcazar fortress so I could pay my tax. Essua said I would owe two gold dinars. Once there, we sought out the assistant to the Sahib al-Suq, with whom Yaish and I had previously met. The official was surprised to see that Essua accompanied us and spoke directly to him.

"I see you have been released from bondage," he sneered. "We have had complaints about you before. This time, I hope you have learned your lesson." The official then turned to me and said, "Are you still searching for your ornaments, or have you come to pay your tax? I was thinking to send someone to fetch you if you did not appear soon. We know where you are staying. Tell me you have the funds we require."

I said nothing. I simply placed two dinars on the writing desk. "This is the correct amount, is it not, Excellency?"

The official scowled. "You have much to learn, young man," he said. "This is not how we do things here. Let me show you how we collect taxes from Jews properly."

With that remark, the official motioned for his clerks to gather around the three of us. Then he stood and, without warning, grabbed me by the throat. I was too shocked to move. In a loud voice, the official chanted so all could hear:

"Oh dhimmi, the enemy of Allah, pay the Jizya you owe us for the protection and tolerance we grant you." The clerks repeated these words in unison and laughed.

"Now, you can hand me the coins. For the present, that is the amount you owe. Of course, you can always convert to the true faith, but I doubt you will do so. Until then, remember your place and to whom you are subservient. Now be gone."

I was so shocked and angered at this barbaric ritual that I began to protest. Yaish and Essua had witnessed this ritual before and knew to remain silent. They dragged me away before I could say or do anything.

"You will gain nothing through complaint or anger, Joshua. This matter is closed. It is best to forget," said Yaish. "Our day will come. Have faith," he whispered.

On the walk back to Essua's residence, Yaish told me more.

"Joshua, it is better in the east of al-Andalus. When your father came here, it was different. The rulers here have, from fear, become rigid in their faith. Many Ishmaelites ascribe to the beliefs of the Almohad, a Muslim sect from al-Maghreb that now rules much of Ifriqiya. The Almohad are warlike people who wish to win al-Andalus and al-Maghreb from the Al-Murabit rulers. We hear rumors that the Almohad demand that Jews and Christians convert to Islam. The penalty for not doing so is death. This tribe believes their leader to be the true Mahdi, the divinely guided lawgiver for all of Islam. Many do not speak in the Arabic tongue. They have their own language."

I knew something of the Almohad. When I was a child, they had attempted to seize Marrakech. Fortunately, the city's rulers soundly defeated the Almohad army in the famous battle of al-Buhayra. Yaish claimed that the Almohad had too much pride not to return. The days of Marrakech were numbered, he declared. Once the Almohad had conquered al-Maghreb, they would direct their attention to al-Andalus. Upon hearing this, I became concerned for my father and my family in that city.

At Essua's home, there was no letter from my father. There was, however, correspondence from the Collegantia. It consisted of only two words in the Ashurit script and a number. When he read the brief note, Essua nodded his head in understanding.

"We are to expect a shipment of flax and sukkar in about three weeks," he said as he handed me the note. It made no sense to me, and I shrugged my shoulders.

"I do not understand," I said.

"You are a student at the yeshiva, said Yaish. "Look again and tell us what you see."

I looked once more and took a moment to think. "The numbers are the date when we are to expect the shipment, counting from the destruction of the Temple. I am familiar with our way of determining

44

time. But the letters I do not understand. I can read them and give their sounds, but I do not know the words," I said.

"These words in our language mean al-kitan and al-sukkar in Arabic," said Essua. We prefer not to inform the Ishmaelites of what cargo we expect, and none of them can read our language, nor do the followers of Islam understand our way of measuring time. This correspondence would mean nothing to them. That is precisely what we intend."

Indeed, this was a clever way to keep secrets. Now I was more convinced of the necessity to complete my studies. Essua interrupted my thoughts.

"Now we have work to do. We must secure a makhzan for storage at the port and hire workers to meet the ship when it arrives from Iskandariyyah. We will also arrange to sell these goods. Of course, we will not inform anyone of what merchandise we are expecting. First, we must explore the market and learn what merchants are paying. If we are fortunate, there is a shortage, and no other shipments are expected. I will make appropriate inquiries. For now, it is best that I do not negotiate for the makhzan myself. Perhaps you can do this?"

"Of course," I said. I was happy to have something to contribute. "But why are you reluctant to secure storage?" I asked.

Essua smiled at this question. "The best makhzans for our purpose are owned by the merchant that I offended. He will not soon forget. He does not know you, so perhaps you can secure an arrangement that is favorable to us. I will provide what guidance I can."

Over the next few days, after completing my studies at the yeshiva, I visited the port at the mouth of the river Tagus. Although there were makhzans close to the quays, the best was owned by the merchant Essua had offended. I found him supervising the discharge of cargo from a small boat. I did not wish to cause any offense this time, so I gave a low bow and greeted the merchant with grave formality. He did not return my greeting and looked at me with disdain.

"You have business with me, Jew?" he asked.

I had taken the time to consider how best to accomplish my task. I knew our vessel could arrive earlier than the expected date or be delayed beyond it. Thus, I thought the prudent course of action was to arrange for storage over a period of time.

"I would like to hire your makhzan, the one nearest the quay, for a month," I said. "I am newly arrived here, but I understand the cost would be two dinars. Is that correct?"

"It is not," replied the merchant. "For you people, the cost will be three dinars. That is my best price. If you want something further away, I can do better. It is your choice."

I did not want to make the same mistake as Essua. To call this man a thief would be foolish. At the same time, I did not want to be cheated. Two can play this game, I thought. I fabricated a look of dismay and fear on my face and answered.

"Sir, my master has only given me two and one-half dinars. If I choose storage further from the quay, I will have to pay for a cart we cannot afford. I beg you to assist me. I have the coin now and can pay you in advance. Would that not be to your benefit?"

The merchant raised his hand to his chin and looked away. He tried but failed to keep me from seeing his grin. Finally, he spoke.

"Since you are new here, I will grant you this favor, but only once. Give me the coin. You can use the makhzan for one month from today, no longer."

I had learned one lesson before. Trust was to be earned, not granted freely. "Please, sir, my master will ask for a receipt to confirm our agreement," I said innocently. "You know how it is. He might think I spent his coin on myself if I have nothing to prove my words."

The merchant frowned and then, reluctantly, wrote the agreement on a scrap of parchment and handed it to me.

"Our business is done, Jew. My watchman will give you the keys," he said. He turned away and returned to supervise the unloading of cargo.

Then, when the merchant could not see me, I smiled. I had been prepared to pay three dinars and successfully reduced the cost without provoking anger. At last, I thought I had done something correctly. My happiness was short-lived. As I turned to leave, one of the common laborers standing nearby blocked my path. I wished for no confrontation, so

I turned to the side, but the man stopped me with his hand.

"You did not bow to me, Jew. Do you not know your place?"

I felt my face turning red with anger. I came very close to making a reply I would regret. It took a great effort to respond. I breathed deeply, bowed, and said, "Peace be upon you. Please forgive my rudeness." That was the best I could do without striking the man with my fist. It was not like this in Marrakech. There, the city's rulers did not treat Jews this way. We engaged in our affairs and were left alone. Many, like my father, had accrued great wealth from the gold trade. Some served as high functionaries at the court. There was a curfew, of course. No Jew could leave their city area after dark, but who would want to do that?

I was still angry when I met with Essua to tell him that arrangements for storage had been completed at a favorable price. All the joy I felt from my success was, however, gone. This was no way to live, I thought.

III

Downfall
Lishbunah
The Christian year 1142

While waiting for the Collegantia ship's arrival, I devoted myself to learning to read Ashurit. It was embarrassing that one of the younger boys had to serve as my teacher, but I came to love the Hebrew language and the poetry it created. Some of these poems, called *piyutim*, were sung during worship. Rabbi al-Daudi, who composed several piyutim, spent time with me studying scripture. "You are a fast learner," he said. "You should ask your father if you could attend the beth midrash in Qurtuba. I cannot devote appropriate time to you, and you deserve more."

One afternoon, Essua gained entry to the Yeshiva and interrupted me in my studies.

"Our ship has arrived! It is entering the port now. Our timing is perfect. There is no al-kitan in the market, and demand is great. The weavers have nothing with which to ply their trade. There is also a shortage of al-sukkar. We will do well with this cargo!"

This news made me very happy. This time, I could achieve success and earn enough profit to compensate for the loss of the ornaments. I had still not received any correspondence from my father, but there had been no other vessels from al-Maghreb.

"This is wonderful news, Essua," I said. "Let us go to our makhzan and make everything ready."

Essua shook his head. "You forget; I cannot join you. I will make all the other preparations. I have sufficient funds to pay the cargo fees and hire workers for the task of unloading our vessel. The weather is changing. You can see the storm clouds forming now. We must act quickly. There is no time to lose."

I almost ran to the port. Along the way, I was careful to bow briefly to the Ishmaelites I passed. Nothing could go wrong. I was breathless when I arrived at the makhzan. To my surprise, the door was chained and secured by a lock. I looked through cracks in the wood siding and saw bales of fabric in the dim light. What is this? I thought. I paid for the use of storage in advance. There should be nothing inside. I wondered if I had tried to enter the wrong makhzan but, on further investigation, knew I had not. There must be some other error, I thought.

I questioned others nearby, but no one had an answer. Instead, one of the merchants directed me to a port official supervising another vessel's discharge. Having learned my lesson, I bowed and gave a formal greeting. When I explained my problem, the official merely shrugged his shoulders. "I know nothing of this," he said. "The Sahib al-Suq is here today. Go to him. His excellency is on the quay next to this one."

The Sahib al-Suq was standing with his entourage on the quay to which I had been directed. There was no mistaking the man. He was wearing a white robe decorated with fine gold thread. His turban was equally adorned, and his beard was perfectly trimmed. With politeness I did not feel, I begged for an audience from one of the retainers and was told to wait. The Sahib al-Suq was busy.

I was now growing angry. It was almost dusk, and the Sahib al-Suq did not appear to be doing anything. He was just watching the bustle of the port. Finally, I could take the delay no longer.

"Excellency, peace be upon you," I shouted. "I need only a brief moment of your time; my problem is urgent, and it will soon be dark."

The official scowled and motioned me to come closer. "What is this problem that requires my attention when I am engaged in other affairs?"

As calmly as possible, I explained that the makhzan I had hired was chained and locked. It contained other goods. The vessel I expected had entered the harbor, I had paid the fees, and a storm was brewing in the west. "What can I do?" I asked with as much deference as I could muster.

The official nodded his head in understanding. "You are a Jew; is that correct?"

"Yes, Excellency," I answered.

"That confirms my understanding," said the official. "A merchant of the true faith needed storage. He has precedence over your needs. I am confident he will remove his goods soon, so you must wait."

Now I was desperate. I tried to keep the anger from my voice. "Excellency, I paid for the use of the makhzan in advance. I have a note to confirm that. An Ishmaelite partially owns the Collegantia, whose cargo is to be unloaded. Is that not sufficient? I need to use my space now."

"Do not be insolent with me, young man," said the Sahib al-Suq. "The rules here are clear. Your note means nothing to me. Do you have anything to support what you say regarding ownership of your cargo, or do I only have your word that someone of the true faith partially owns it?"

Once again, I had made an error. I had nothing to prove that an Ishmaelite partially owned our Collegantia. The only way to prove the truth of my words would be to have a letter from the partners. I had no such thing. I shook my head and admitted I had nothing.

"Then this matter is ended," declared the official. "You must wait. If the merchant who has taken your storage is available, you can ask him to grant you a favor. His name is Mohammed ibn Salah. His rights take precedence. Why don't you convert to the faith of Islam? That would make your life easier."

Tears of fury came to my eyes and I stumbled back to the makhzan. Once again, all I had strived for had come to naught. Worse, I had not only lost the valuable ornaments but now the cargo from Iskandariyyah as well. My father would disown me. That would be the least that would happen. Any dreams I had of success were gone to dust. These calamities resulted from how these worshipers of false prophets treated my people. The more I thought about my situation, the angrier I became; and the more troubled. By the time I reached the warehouse, I was beyond reason. I saw that the watchman had lighted his lantern and left it near the makhzan, presumably as he used the privy. I did not think. I acted.

It began as a waft of lazy white smoke, curling into the evening breeze. Then, a delicate yellow flame crawled slowly toward the dry timber at the base of the makhzan. Heated now to a warm glow, the timber provided fuel, and the flame became a flickering, bright orange. The fire was so small at its birth that the night watchman noticed nothing until it was too late. When he did, the fledgling flame had scrambled up the wooden wall. Before he could cry an alarm, the entire side of the structure was a roaring inferno. Many ells of thin cloth lay behind, and it too caught fire, belching thick black smoke. The watchman screamed for aid but to no avail. Wind from the sea gave breath to the conflagration, and before any help could arrive, the entire makhzan was alight. The only hope was to prevent the fire from spreading to nearby structures. Several laborers finally arrived. Without direction, they stood silently and watched. There was nothing to do except wait for the rain that was sure to come.

Looking on in wonder from his hiding place, I think I smiled at the success of my work. This, I thought, was righteous retribution. Although the weather had been dry, thick black clouds rapidly formed in the west. Soon it would rain, and the cargo my father sent from Aegyptus would lie rotting in the harbor. Now my adversary would suffer as well. I had paid good coin to use this makhzan. All arrangements for unloading the precious cargo that had traveled so far had been made. But I was a Jew. The Sahib al-Suq had made the position clear. The dog had the insolence to suggest I convert to his faith.

"We will see who has difficulty now," I mumbled. "The Book of Leviticus says that for a man who injures his countryman, 'as he has done, so it shall be done to him.' An eye for an eye (ayin tachat ayin), it reads. That is the law. The Ishmaelites know that. Their law is the same as ours. My cargo of al-sukkar would become a worthless moldering slop in a ship's hold, but fire now consumed Mohammed's cotton. Is this not justice?"

It was not long before Mohammed himself arrived to witness the catastrophe. From a distance, I immediately recognized the fat merchant. Mohammed, wearing his usual gaudy blue turban and gaze robe, was trying to run. At best, he could only waddle. The look of horror on his face turned to fury. He shouted at the workers, demanding they bring water to douse the fire. It was, of course, too late. As he realized the extent of the destruction, Mohammed fell to his knees, prayed to Allah, and wept. He had borrowed the funds to bring the fabric to Lishbunah. Who had advanced Mohammed the coin? Jews had done so. And now, the corpulent heathen was ruined, his remaining wealth forfeit. That, too, was the law.

My pride in my righteous revenge was short-lived. What would my father, Elazar, say? For me, assuming control of the Collegantia's venture in Arth al-Bortucal was a great honor. Never had my father given me such responsibility. Never had he granted me such respect. And now, what would happen? There was no way to recover the loss of our precious cargo. That shipment was doomed. I knew that to my father, there was no excuse. I could hear him now. 'Why did you not take the matter to the Qadi of the city?' He would say. 'You paid for the use of the makhzan. We have always paid the Jizya tax. Our partner is a Muslim. You had rights. Did you simply accept the words of the port master?'

Leaving the conflagration and the weeping Mohammed behind, I knew I must avoid notice. My heart was beating fast, and my eyes began to well with tears. It took all my effort to avoid running from the scene. Where would I go? What could I do? All was lost. I could not return to Marrakech. I was a failure. I was close to panicking. The joy I had felt was gone. It was replaced by abject fear. To make matters worse, the expected rain now began in earnest.

Not knowing what else to do, I returned to the yeshiva. I would confess to the Rabbi, I thought. There was no alternative. When I arrived at the gate, I was soaking wet. I did not wait to dry myself. Immediately I asked a servant to find the Rabbi.

Rabbi al-Daudi and his son, Yaish, listened to my confession in horror. For a long moment, they said nothing. The Rabbi was the first to speak.

"You must leave the city, and so must Essua. It will not take the authorities long to accuse you of this. The Ishmaelites know where you both reside. It will soon grow dark. The city gates will close, so we need to act quickly. Gather your belongings, change your robe, and I will send someone to fetch Essua. We need to talk to you before he arrives."

I listened to these instructions silently, went to my room, and stuffed my few possessions into a satchel. I had nothing else. As I returned to the Rabbi's chamber, my remorse was overwhelming. Tears now streamed down my face. I had ruined everything.

"We do not have time for pity, Joshua. Here is what will happen. I want you to go to Qurtuba. There you will find a famous interpreter of the law, what we call a *Dayyan*, and the Ishmaelites call a *Qadi*, named Maimon ben Joseph. You will find him at his yeshiva; he is a dear friend. You are a quick student. Both my son and I have been impressed with your ability. In any event, you will be safe in that city."

"But what about my father, Rabbi? What about our commerce here?" I asked.

"I know enough about your father to believe he will agree with me. I will write to him myself and explain matters. He will understand you have no choice. That I can promise."

I quickly consented as, indeed, there was no alternative. I thought the discussion was over, but I was wrong.

The Rabbi turned to Yaish. "We can trust our young Joshua, I believe. Tell him our plan."

Yaish raised his brows and answered his father. "Everything, father? Tell him everything?" The Rabbi nodded his assent.

"I will make this short, Joshua. We have little time before Essua arrives, and what I tell you must be kept secret. Do you swear before G-d not to reveal what I explain?"

I did not hesitate to make my oath.

"You must have wondered about the men who sometimes visit us. They are friends who carry messages. My father and I have provided information to Alfonso Henriques, who proclaims himself King. We have determined that matters here will become worse. Already, the rulers here have written to the Almohad, begging for assistance in fighting the Christians. The so-called Caliph of the Almohad recruits mercenary soldiers from Catalonia and devotes his efforts to conquering al-Maghreb. The Caliph is planning to foster uprisings in al-Andalus to conquer it as well. Here in Lishbunah, the condition of the walls is poor, and our rulers have expended nothing on defense. We know that a force of crucesignati from England is en route to Yerushalayim. This army will stop for provisions in the city called Portus Cale. That is close to the camp of the King's army. We believe this force will assist Alfonso in taking Lishbunah. Now is the time to strike. I was to have taken this message myself. Now you can do so on our behalf. You will find Alfonso in the city of Coimbra, to the north. It will be a difficult five-day journey, and we will give you funds for this purpose. When you have completed your task, go to Qurtuba as my father has suggested."

I was startled by this request. Performing such a task would only provide another opportunity to fail. I was unsure what I should do and quickly thought of an excuse.

"Of course, I would be happy to aid you, but I do not know the road to Coimbra," I said. "How will I find that city? Is it safe for me to travel?"

Yaish shook his head and dismissed my concern. "Once you leave the city walls and travel for two days, you will be in Christian lands," he said. "The Christians all dress the same, so we will give you a black robe and a yellow cap to be recognized as a Jew. Do not worry about the road. We will send someone with you as a guide."

Then, Yaish looked over my head. "Ah, here is your guide now," he declared.

I turned to look, and behind me, the giant I had seen before stood silently; he had not made a sound when he entered the Rabbi's chamber.

"This is our friend Blazh," said the Rabbi. "He speaks little, but he will be a loyal companion and knows the way. Blazh is a Christian. He can tell you more if he chooses to do so. In any event, you will be safe traveling with him."

To be accompanied by this giant gave me some assurance. Looking at Blazh, I nodded my head in resignation and said, "Peace be upon you, Blazh. I will be glad of your company."

I had no time to consider matters further, as Essua then arrived. His face betrayed both a look of anger and despair. Someone had already told him of the fire and my responsibility for it.

"What have you done, young man? My commerce in this city is ruined. The Rabbi tells me I am to accompany you to Coimbra. I have never been to that place. Everything I possess is here. It would have been better if I stayed in prison." Essua looked pointedly at me, expecting a response.

Saving me from further embarrassment, the Rabbi spoke.

"Essua, I do not have to tell you that your life is in danger. As I have explained to our friend here, you have no choice about what you must do. We have given Joshua a task to perform. You will be safe, and a new and better fate awaits you. Trust me on this. Have you brought your coin?" Essua nodded his head. "Then give it to me. I will deposit your funds with Samuel, the money changer; you know him well. Hurry now and count the coin so I can give you the receipt. You will be able to draw upon your account in Christian lands. There is no time to waste."

Rabbi al-Daudi then began to write several letters. The first, he gave to me. It was written in Ashurit.

Yaish whispered, "Give this to the King and guard it with your life." The second was for Essua, who had finished counting his coin. "Give this to one of our faith in Coimbra. You know what it is." Then the Rabbi wrote another brief message in Ashurit script and handed it to Essua. "Keep this with you. Joshua will tell you to whom it is addressed when you arrive."

Essua had had the foresight to bring a donkey, and, together with the taciturn Blazh, the three of us left the yeshiva and walked towards the nearest city gate. The guards seemed to know Blazh, and we had no difficulty passing through the entrance. For a long time, no one spoke; we trudged slowly away from the city.

Traveling north, through hilly countryside, the going was difficult. Essua's donkey bore our meager possessions, and that was a benefit. Essua complained most of the way, and I said nothing to relieve his anxiety. I was absorbed in my own difficulties. I did not wish to disclose the goal of our journey, as that could only make matters worse. Instead, I prodded Blazh to tell his story. Blazh was reluctant to do so. I realized that one of the reasons for his perennial silence was the pitch of his voice. It was like that of a woman. To hear that voice coming from such a massive man was startling and oddly amusing. Hearing it for the first time, I was tempted to laugh but had the good sense not to do so. Essua, however, was not surprised. He had heard the strange voice of Blazh before. The tale Blazh told was one of tragedy, but at least it relieved the monotony of travel and kept Essua and me from dwelling too long on our own difficulties.

IV

The Tale of Blazh
On the Road to Coimbra

Blazh was born in a land far to the east and north, about thirty years ago. His people were Southern Slavs, who spoke their own language and were considered Christians. When he was a child, strangers raided his village and seized all the women and young boys. They killed the men. The captives were marched north along the seacoast. The captives were given only bread to eat, and some died on the journey. His mother was one of those unfortunate souls. The dead were left beside the road, without ceremony. After many days of travel, Blazh and his fellow captives entered a small town where they were displayed to interested merchants.

"Who captured you? Were they Muslims?" I asked. "Surely those of my faith do not deal in buying and selling human beings."

Blazh gave a squeaky chuckle. "The Jews once did. Ask your friend here. He will tell you."

Essua was quick to respond. "Joshua, it is true that many of our fellow Jews once engaged in this trade. It was profitable. Our people have not engaged in it for many generations now. I suspect the merchants were Muslim and that your captors were Venetians. They have no scruples regarding enslavement. It is old commerce."

These words disconcerted me. I apologized for my interruption and asked Blazh to continue his story.

After considerable haggling, the group was divided. Some went with one merchant, others with another. Blazh was the tallest of the children and attracted much attention. He was subjected to loud dickering amongst the merchants. At an early age, he understood that many coins were being offered for him. Finally, he was sold to a swarthy, dark-haired man who, unlike the other merchants, was dressed in a splendid robe of gazz. As he was led away, the man spoke to his assistant. "This one will fetch a good profit in al-Andalus when he is properly prepared. You can tell he will be tall. Let us hope he lives." Blazh was treated as a mere animal who understood nothing, and these words brought fear to his heart.

Tears welled in his eyes. "I do not like to think or speak of what happened next. You laugh at my voice. It reminds me constantly of what I have lost and what I became."

I was reluctant to press Blazh to continue. "If it causes you pain, I do not wish to cause more. Continue your tale only if you truly desire to do so." Blazh pursed his mouth, wiped his tears, and spoke again.

"It was a long journey, and my captors treated me well," he said. "They gave me food and released me from my bindings. Everything changed when we reached a port town called Trieste. I did not know where it was. They led me to a building made of stone. I will never forget it. I was thirsty, so I was given a flagon of some liquid that tasted strange. It made me feel dizzy, and I wanted to sleep. A wooden table was in the center of the room, and my captors led me to it. Someone removed my clothing and then forced me to lie on the table. I was terrified but could not summon the will to resist. They tied me with leather straps. I remember that a stranger approached. He looked at me carefully and whispered to my captors. I will never forget his words. 'You have chosen well. This one will do.'

Once again, Blazh wiped tears from his eyes as he spoke. "I did not see the knife until it was too late. The stranger leaned over the lower part of my body and worked swiftly. The pain was beyond imagining."

Blazh grimaced and could not go on for some moments. He tried several times to speak but failed. Instead, he sobbed. I had never seen a man cry so openly, much less a man of the size of Blazh. My father frowned on such outward displays of emotion, and I did not know what to do except maintain silence. With a look of agony, Blazh gained control of himself and continued.

"I screamed then. I screamed until I could scream no longer. The stranger was indifferent and continued his work. Next, I remember seeing an iron glowing red from the heat. He applied the iron to my private parts; the pain was so strong that I thought I would die. I do not remember what happened next. Everything went black. When I awoke, my body's lower part felt like it was on fire. Someone gave me more of the liquid, and I fell fast asleep. I knew then I was no longer a boy."

Blazh shook his head in denial. "I cannot go on. I can tell you the rest of the story another time."

I bit my lip and nodded in understanding. "It is enough for now," I said.

For the next three days, we traveled slowly through flat farmland. The fields were fertile, fed by the waters of the river Tagus. With rare exceptions, we travelers were alone on the old Roman road. There were no Ishmaelite patrols. Occasionally, we would meet farmers with carts, but these encounters were peaceful. One look at Blazh and any thoughts of conflict were instantly dismissed. Often, Essua purchased food for our journey and engaged in animated conversation regarding conditions to the north. One of the farmers suggested avoiding the city of Santarem, which had once served as a principal center of learning for the Al-Murabit.

"Are we not welcome there, Sayyid?" inquired Essua.

The farmer looked at Blazh and then at his companions, who silently nodded their approval.

"We have heard of troubles. Everyone fears the Christian army, and the city's rulers are unsure of what action to take. There are Al-Murabit residing in the city and even Mozarab Christians, but I am not certain how you will be treated."

The farmer continued in a whisper. "I will not ask if you are traveling further, but if you do, you will find that the Christians have destroyed most of the fields in the north (may they be cursed). Their armies invade our lands and leave devastation behind. Do not think that, because you are Jews, you will be safe."

After we left the farmers behind, Blazh said he knew how to avoid Santarem. "There is a little-used path through the marshes. It will be wet and slow going. I know the way."

Blazh was correct about the marshes. The muddy track slowed our progress. When we eventually moved away from the river, the countryside was again relatively flat. The few villages through which we passed provided opportunities to restore our dwindling supplies, and, given coin, the villagers were happy to aid us. One evening, I could no longer contain my curiosity.

"Blazh, you say you are a Christian. How is it that you have found company with those of our faith?"

"The Rabbi saved me," he answered without expression. "I owe my life to him and his son."

That response generated more questions in my mind. "If it is not too painful, I would like to know more of your story," I said.

With reluctance, Blazh told the rest of his tale. From Trieste, Blazh was taken by ship on a long journey through the Middle Sea. Because of his size and the removal of his manhood, Blazh was eventually sold to an Ishmaelite in Qurtuba. His new owner sent him to the harem as a servant. He learned Arabic among the women and was treated not as a human being but as a fine racing horse. Often, Blazh was the butt of jokes and teasing.

As Blazh continued to grow taller, his owners trained him in the use of a sword and prepared him to become a guard. Although Blazh had enough food and was never beaten, he longed for freedom. These were not his people. One day was the same as the next. He learned that his best defense against the constant sniggering at the pitch of his voice was to remain silent. His resentment grew stronger as the days, months, and years passed. There was, however, nothing he could do but accept the fate that G-d had ordained. One of the women, sensing his anger, suggested that he convert to Islam. If Blazh did so, she said, he might gain his freedom. Blazh refused. Although his understanding of Christianity was poor, he could not find it within himself to abandon the faith of his parents and homeland. In any event, if he did gain his freedom, where could he go?

Eventually, Blazh became a trusted servant. His master often granted him the privilege of guarding the harem alone at night. On one of those nights, he made the error of falling asleep while on duty. His master happened to pass by and, seeing Blazh asleep, struck him soundly on the back with the flat of his sword. Awaking so suddenly from his slumber,

Blazh's first instinct was to defend himself. He came close to doing so. However, he had the good sense to grovel and beg forgiveness. He promised, before G-d, that this would never happen again.

His apology was not sufficient. His master, red in the face, said, "Dog, you have been given privilege. I paid good coin for you, and this is how you repay us? If you fall asleep during your duties again, you will pray to your G-d to let you die."

Blazh swallowed what pride remained and sought to control his pain from the blow. Again, he begged forgiveness. His master said nothing and turned on his heel and left. When the women learned what had happened, they mocked Blazh for his weakness, and the jokes became more pointed. It was too much. To spend the balance of his days on earth in this condition was intolerable.

Two nights later, Blazh escaped. That was not difficult as there was no one to stop him. He simply walked away.

"I had no plan," he said. "The opportunity to run presented itself. I took it. The problem was where to go. When someone noticed my absence, a search would begin. I knew no one in the city, and if I continued to walk, it was only a matter of time before I was found. I was not certain where I was. I was a fool."

"But you did escape," I said. "I cannot imagine anyone not noticing someone of your size in the city. How did you become free?"

"The Rabbi saved me," said Blazh. "I saw a small Beit Knesset, what you Jews call their place of worship. I could see that candles were burning inside. I thought this might be a place of safety. At least I could ask for help. Thanks be to G-d; I met the Rabbi and his son, and they were kind enough to ask if I needed assistance. When I told them of my plight, the Rabbi did not hesitate. He and his son were planning to leave Qurtuba early the following day."

"I still do not understand, Blazh. Surly, your disappearance had been noticed by then," I said. "You could not have freely walked through the city gates."

"Yaish wrapped me in a large carpet and placed me along with the possessions in their cart. I was afraid that a city guard would demand an inspection. That did not happen. Later, the Rabbi told me he had paid two gold coins to purchase free passage. While wrapped in the carpet, I had an opportunity to think. I did not know the Rabbi or Yaish, and I wondered if I had made a terrible mistake. Why would they not sell me in the next city and take their profit? Had I traded one form of servitude for another? I became obsessed with these thoughts as we left Qurtuba further behind."

Blazh was silent again for some moments. I could see tears welling in the giant's eyes as he remembered what happened next.

"I do not know how long I was carried as baggage. When the cart stopped, Yaish told me it was safe to emerge. When I did, I was certain there would be others to whom I would be sold. I was wrong. The Rabbi just pointed north, gave me four gold Dinars, and said only one word: 'Shalom'."

I was puzzled. "Why did you not go north, Blazh? The Rabbi was granting you the freedom to join the Christians. Surely that is what you most desired?"

Blazh shook his head. "What would happen if I did that? There was no future for me in the north. I would be an object of scorn and had no trade or skill to offer. The Rabbi had saved my life. That was deserving of my loyalty and trust. If nothing else, I was strong and had training in arms, so I thought I might be of use. Thanks be to G-d, I was right." Despite my prodding, Blazh would not speak further of his duties for Rabbi al-Daudi and his son.

V

EXILE
COIMBRA
The Christian year 1142

On the morning of the fifth day of travel, we crossed the river Douro and reached the massive city walls of Coimbra in the early afternoon. It was painfully easy to tell that the city was in the hands of the Christians. The stench was sufficient evidence. My father had told me that the Christians rarely bathed and were prone to throwing their waste in the street. "Where Christians go, so does their excrement," he said. Now, I knew this was true. Ignoring the filth, Blazh led us to the al-Medina Gate, the nearest to the fortress where the King held court. "The guards know me there," he declared.

The guards at the gate greeted Blazh as an old friend. Seeing the yellow caps worn by Essua and me, one of them said, "You have brought more Jews? How many do you have?" He chortled, mimicking the high pitch of Blazh's voice. Blazh said nothing. He just smiled and nodded his head in the affirmative. "And again, you demand an audience with the king?" Blazh nodded again. "You know the way. His majesty is in his audience chamber," said the guard as he waved them through.

I suggested that we visit a hammam first to clean ourselves from the dust of travel. Our appearance was, I said, unacceptable if we were to present ourselves to a ruler.

"There is no hammam," said Blazh. "The world here is different." Blazh motioned for us to follow him up the hill to the fortress. The way was soon blocked by a man in chain mail, wearing a white robe emblazoned with a red cross. "Not so fast," he said. Those guards may know you. I do not. State your business."

I had never seen a Christian warrior before, but summoned the courage to say, "We have a message for the king. Stand aside."

"You order me about, Jew? Who do you think you are?"

I was about to respond, but Blazh held up his hand and moved to the front. He towered over the unarmed man. "Stand aside," he whispered. The knight, for that is what he was, looked up at Blazh and prudently decided not to pursue matters further. He scowled as he made room for us to pass.

At the fortress, the guards also seemed to know Blazh and escorted us into the audience chamber. The king was enthroned on a high-backed chair and surrounded by monks and a few white-robed knights. He, too, recognized Blazh and beckoned him to come forward. "Peace be with you, Blazh. You have news?" he asked.

Blazh pushed me forward. I tried to keep the nervousness I felt from my voice. "Your highness," I said as I knelt before him. "We bring news from Rabbi al-Daudi. We must speak to you in private."

The king waved his hand to dismiss others from the room. When we were alone, he spoke in heavily accented Arabic. "What is this news?" he asked.

Although King Alfonso was in his middle years, he was well-built and appeared in excellent health. Like others of his faith, he wore a ragged beard, and on his head was a gold crown. I did not respond. Instead, I handed him the first of the two letters prepared by the Rabbi.

The king looked at the letter and, without reading it, handed it back to me. "Al-Daudi knows I do not read this script. What does it say?"

I read the letter aloud. It explained that the Al-Murabit were in disarray, fighting amongst themselves. Their forces were spread thin as they attempted to defend their territory. Christian crucesignati had assembled in England and prepared to depart for the Holy Land. Their vessel would stop for provisions at Portus Cale, and they might be induced to aid the king in attacking Lishbunah. The governor of Lishbunah had requested aid from the Almohad in al-Maghreb, so there was little time to spare. Now was the time to strike.

When the king received this news, he smiled. "My friend al-Daudi may be right. The rabbi has never led me astray. To attack Lishbunah, I will need help, and the crucesignati may be the key.

Although the English are undisciplined, their numbers may be useful. But they will demand the spoils of war as compensation. I need to think about this and consult with my new supporters amongst the monks," he said.

The king rubbed his beard. "What about the city walls?" he asked. "I need al-Daudi's wizardly skill for the catapults. My people are not well skilled in the art of geometryah, and he is a master! You know that is the key."

I did know how to respond to this question. As I stood in silence, Essua spoke. "Your highness, neither the Rabbi nor his son, can leave Lishbunah now. You know the story of Yaish, but the authorities in Lishbunah do not, at least not yet. Perhaps the rabbi and his son will be more valuable by remaining in the city?"

The king acknowledged his understanding of Essua's words. "I need to consider matters further. Blazh, take our friends here and show them where they can stay with the other Jews in the city. You know where you can rest here. I will call for you when I have made a decision."

Blazh bowed deeply and turned to leave. I, however, remembered that I had another task. "Your highness, there is another letter. May I read it to you as well?"

The king motioned for me to read. The second letter was an introduction to Essua's skill and honesty. It suggested Essua could be of value as an adviser for commerce. Rabbi al-Daudi begged the king to accept Essua in that role until the rabbi or his son could join them in Coimbra. Without hesitation, the king agreed.

"You are welcome here, Essua. I have promised al-Daudi and his son lands in my kingdom for their assistance. I am thinking of granting his son, Yaish, a lordship, if he acquits himself well in battle and continues to be a trusted adviser. That is an exceedingly rare honor. I do not doubt his ability. If Rabbi al-Daudi recommends you, that is sufficient."

Essua grinned from ear to ear, but my gapping mouth betrayed my ignorance. I had the good sense to wait until we had left the king's presence to ask for clarification regarding the people with whom I stayed in Lishbunah and who had saved my life. "About what was the king talking? I do not understand," I said.

Blazh smiled and answered. "Besides their work at the yeshiva, Rabbi al-Daudi and his son provide the king with information and assistance. Did you not know that? The rabbi is a master of numbers and the art of geometryah. That skill is useful in ensuring that catapults accurately sling their stones at city walls. I do not know how it works, but it does. Yaish was a skilled warrior in al-Maghreb. He has fought the Ishmaelites before and, if you can belief this, he led one of their armies."

I was stunned. A Jew skilled in the arts of war? How could this be?

"I thought Rabbi al-Daudi was a poet and scholar and Yaish the same. Yaish led an Ishmaelite army? That is impossible," I said.

Blazh shrugged his shoulders. "You have much to learn."

Blazh led us down the hill from the fortress to the lower city and the Jewish quarter. There we found an inn near the river Mondego. A breeze from the water dispelled the vile odor permeating the city.

"Stay here," said Blazh. "Do not leave the quarter. That is forbidden."

Despite the king's seeming friendship with Jews, it appeared that the rules in Coimbra were not vastly different than in Ishmaelite lands. When I asked about this, Blazh shook his head and said, "You are wrong. It is not the same." There was no time to ask him to explain as we had just then reached our destination.

The inn was clean and occupied by only a few travelers. None of them wore yellow caps. From their clothing, it was impossible to tell whether these travelers were Jews or Christians. At my insistence, we took the opportunity to clean ourselves and eat a hot meal. A man approached as we sat to eat and asked to join us at our table. He introduced himself as Dayyan Maimon ben Joseph and said he was visiting Coimbra to settle a commercial dispute. He planned to return to his home in Qurtuba when he had completed his task.

I was astounded. This person was the man I had been told to find in Qurtuba.

"Rabbi al-Daudi has instructed me to seek you out in Qurtuba. I never thought to find you here," I said. Much later, I wondered if G-d had led me to this encounter. Indeed, it was not a mere coincidence.

Maimon was equally surprised. "The rabbi is my great friend. How is he? How is his son? You say he wanted you to find me; well, now you have. What splendid fortune! What is it you need of me?"

I briefly told Maimon what had happened in Lishbunah and said that the rabbi had suggested I learn more about my faith and that Maimon was the best teacher he knew.

"I am honored that al-Daudi holds me in high esteem," said Maimon. "Why don't you accompany me on my return? It will be pleasant for both of us... and safer."

Although I readily agreed, I could not contain my curiosity. "Do you find a difference between the treatment of Jews in Coimbra and Qurtuba?" I asked.

"Oh," said Maimon, "There is a significant difference, but all is the same in the end."

"Forgive me. I do not understand," I said.

"In al-Andalus, we are protected by law, providing we pay our tax. You must know that means little, but it is the law. In lands governed by Christians, we are also protected but in a different way. Some say the Christian spiritual leader, the Pope, has decreed that we should be considered equal to Christians. I do not know if this is true, but we are permitted to own land, with the consent of our rulers. We may serve as high officials and engage in trade freely."

"How can this treatment be the same? These people have a vile smell, but from what you say, we will be better off under their rule. Is that true?"

"Our treatment here is not a matter of law, young man. The Christians treat us as equals so long as we are useful. Is it not to their advantage to encourage us to revolt against the Al-Murabit? Do we not provide them coin when they have need? Only thirty years ago, the Christians turned against us in Tulaytula, burned the Beit Knesset, and massacred our people. It can happen again. Do not be fooled by appearances."

"We were told that to leave this quarter was forbidden. Is that what you mean?" I asked.

"It is not the Christians that forbid it. It is our leaders. It would take me too long to explain, but our faith requires us to maintain unity. Our survival and G-d's laws demand it. We must stay together. Think about what would happen if Jews became part of the Christian world. What if Jews converted to that faith for personal gain? What would happen if our young men married Christians? Our faith would die. Our strength depends upon our unity. We are the chosen people!"

I had heard similar words before and chose to leave the subject for later discussion.

"Why are you returning to Qurtuba?" I asked.

"I have a wife and young son in that city. His name is Moshe ben Maimon. We pray my son will become a rabbi. If I say so myself, he will become famous! Already he talks too much."

That night, we slept well on pallets of fresh straw. Blazh came for us the following morning.

"The king requires our presence," he said.

The king was again on his high-backed chair when we were admitted to the chamber. This time, he was accompanied by a tonsured monk dressed in an undyed robe.

"This is Prior Teotonio," he said, pointing at the monk. "You may speak freely in front of him. He is the abbot of the monastery of Santa Cruz de Coimbra and is my most loyal supporter. Of course, I have paid dearly for that support," the King laughed. Teotonio smiled.

"Indeed, His highness has endowed us with considerable lands, providing he can conquer them," said the abbot.

More seriously now, the King explained that if the English crucesignati arrived, he would march on Lishbunah soon. "Prior Teotonio has counseled me to offer nothing to the English for their support. It is sufficient, he says, that those armed pilgrims fight for the glory of G-d. I have written to the Pope. I have pledged allegiance in exchange for his recognition of my sovereignty over all the lands of Arth al-Bortucal. His Holiness will expect me to drive out the Ishmaelites, of course."

"Have you further need of me?" I asked.

"No," said the king. "You may leave the city or stay as you wish. Your companion Essua will remain here to serve me. Unfortunately, Blazh must stay here as well. If anyone witnessed your departure from Lishbunah, he would be suspected, and, as we all know, he is hard to miss!" Turning to Blazh directly, he added, "You know the city. If you agree, I will value your aid."

Blazh bowed his head in acceptance. The risk of return was too great, and he knew he could assist the king.

King Alfonso said he would advise Rabbi al-Daudi of his decisions and provide measures for his safety if an attempt to take the city was made. He thanked me for my assistance and gave me a letter of safe passage. "Go with G-d or whomever you pray to, and thank you," he said.

I departed Coimbra, in the company of Maimon, the following day. I was not sorry to leave the city behind, but I would miss the company of Essua and Blazh. The journey to Qurtuba would take two weeks. Much of it would be along the dangerous frontier between Christian and Ishmaelite lands. On the first day of travel, Maimon asked me to tell some of my story. Not wishing to disclose all of it, I told him that I had a dispute with an Ishmaelite merchant in Lishbunah, which would not have ended well if I had not left the city. I said Rabbi al-Daudi agreed with this decision and asked me to deliver a message to King Alfonso in Coimbra. To change the subject, I asked Maimon why he had made the arduous journey from Qurtuba.

"I have two old friends in the city, distant relatives who begged me to settle a dispute. I owed them a great favor and agreed to provide judgment," he said.

"The dispute must have been serious," I said. "Surely your friends would not have requested this favor from you if the matter was easy to resolve."

"The matter was not serious, but the question of law was important. You see, the two of them equally owned a vegetable garden between their homes. There was a question of who could use the garden for what crops and what rights each had. Each of the parties had different ideas. One of the parties demanded that a wall be constructed to resolve this issue. In such a dispute, our Talmud requires that such a wall have a height of four cubits and that the expense of constructing it must be shared equally. The other refused to pay. The cost of such a high wall was, he said, far too great."

"But that is not a serious matter," I said. "Indeed, such an issue should not require your presence."

"Oh, but it did," said Maimon. "You see, the reason the Talmud makes such a requirement is that one partner, from anger or jealousy, could cast an evil eye on the crops of the other; thus, a high wall was necessary. That would be what we consider to be cognizable harm. Such a solution would be sensible if the dispute was over a common courtyard where people live but not a garden for crops. Is it necessary to compel a four-cubit high wall to be constructed? That is the question I was asked to resolve."

Now I was confused. "I still do not understand why you had to travel for two weeks for something this trivial."

Maimon stopped walking and looked piercingly at me. "You lack understanding of the law, Joshua," he said. "Rabbis such as I constantly render judgment on issues such as this to clarify the law and tradition. We enter a lively dispute. Some scholars will agree, and others will disagree. Often a consensus will be reached. In the end, our Talmud becomes a living document. Change is good so long as it serves the purposes of G-d."

"So, how did you resolve this matter, Rabbi?" I asked.

"The harm of looking into a neighbor's property or worse, of casting an evil eye on it, is different in a courtyard, where anyone would expect a degree of privacy. There is value in protecting the privacy of a space where people live. That is not the case in a vegetable garden. People do not live in such a place. Thus, a low wall is sufficient. It is merely to mark ownership. Of course, no one honestly believes in such a magical thing as an evil eye, but that is another matter. What is important is to avoid jealousy or avarice amongst ourselves. Do you understand?"

I considered his words for a few moments. "What you say is sensible, Rabbi. Will someone record your judgment?"

"Yes, it will be recorded. And another rabbi will dispute my reasoning. That is the way we move forward."

Over the next few days of travel, I took the opportunity to ask further questions, which Maimon was happy to answer. The more I learned, however, the less I understood. Commerce was simple: buy low, sell high, and trust no one completely. The subject of law was very different. There were no simple answers. Everything was subject to change. The rules presented in the Talmud would take a lifetime to understand. Violating the laws would displease G-d, but there were so many. This was what I was to study in Qurtuba? I began to have grave concerns.

We had walked for a week through the borderlands and encountered no difficulty on the road. We paid for passage aboard a barge to carry us across the river Guadiana, bypassing the fortified city of Batalyaws. This city was in the hands of the Al-Murabit. At one point, the road wound near heavily wooded hills, and at the rise of one, we heard shouting.

'Deus Vult,' yelled one voice. 'Allahu Akbar,' yelled another. We crouched at the hillcrest to see what was happening below.

There were two groups of riders. One group consisted of mounted Al-Murabit warriors, waving their curved swords. The other, Christian knights with lances at the ready. Two warriors at a time charged at each other, screaming insults. There was no pitched battle, just single combat where no one was wounded. This battle went on for some time, with neither side gaining ground. Eventually, an

Al-Murabit warrior drove his horse directly at a white-robed knight, who leveled his lance to meet the charge. The turbaned horseman swerved and dealt a heavy blow to the knight's shield at the last moment. The impact was so strong that the knight fell from his horse and lay helpless on the ground. His companions rushed to his aid, and the Al-Murabit wheeled back to his companions. At that point, the knights shouted victory. The Ishmaelites gave a great cry of triumph and then fled down the road.

Thinking that the matter was now over, we continued walking toward the site of the conflict. One of the knights saw us, pointed at my yellow cap, and shouted: "Jews! They warned the infidels. Kill them!"

Maimon did not hesitate. "Run," he said. "Run for the forest." And run we did. The knight arrived just as we entered the densely packed trees. His horse could not follow us; we ran further into the woods. Panting with relief, we decided to remain in the forest for as long as possible. Both the Christians and the Ishmaelites would claim victory in a great battle. Word would spread that war was imminent. That was not true, of course, but villagers would now be cautious of strangers. The rest of the journey would be more dangerous.

Keeping our distance from the main road, it took us longer than expected to reach the great city of Qurtuba. When we did, the tension in the air was palpable. Maimon led me to his home, in the

Jewish quarter, near the fortress but outside the defensive walls. This part of the city was an affluent area and vibrant with activity. There were many places of worship, all competing for congregations. There was a grand bazaar offering everything and anything one could desire. Jewish merchants from around the world, especially al-Maghreb and Palestine, conducted commerce in the market. The noise, colors, and scents were overwhelming.

Although I was delighted to be amongst my people again, I, too, felt the concern of the populous. It was rumored that the city's ruler had requested aid from the Almohad. When I inquired about this, Maimon explained that the worry was not whether the Christians would attempt to take the city, but whether they could do so before an Almohad conquest.

"If the Almohad arrive, they will require us to convert to Islam or face death. That is what they have done in al-Maghreb. Where will we go then?" he said.

VI

THE INITIAL PATH
QURTUBA
The Christian year 1143

The beth midrash in Qurtuba was known all over the world. Established by Rabbi Moshe ben Chanoch, who had come to Qurtuba as a slave, the academy was considered equal to the great school of Babylon. For two hundred years, Qurtuba had been a center of Jewish learning. Now, under Al-Murabit rule, the situation was changing. It was here that I would study for the next four years. It was here that I was to develop the thoughts that poisoned my soul.

For a short while, I forgot the tragedies that befell me in Lishbunah. There was too much to see and learn in the great city. Each day, I attended lessons at the beth midrash. My fluency in written script improved. Because Maimon disapproved of poetry, my studies were devoted to the Talmud. This work provided the basis for all Jewish law. Moreover, these laws were many and complex. It was necessary, Maimon declared, that every Jew follows the prescripts of the law to the best of their ability.

"If we are to regain the favor of G-d, we must stay together even though we are apart. The survival of our faith depends upon it," he pronounced.

When I questioned this assertion, Maimon's response was simple.

"We Jews are trapped between a Christian mortar and a Muslim pestle. If we are not to be ground to dust and discarded forever, we must retain our identity and gain strength from it. We must have a common language, an understanding of G-d's laws, and a common ritual, a tradition, for life itself. Do you know the book of Daniel?"

I was ashamed to admit I had not read this book in the Tanakh. Rabbi Maimon told me to do so.

"You will learn that we are living between Edom and Ishmael," he said. "We believe Edom to be the Christian world. Ismael was the ancestor of the Muslims. That is why we call them Ishmaelites. The Book of Daniel prophesizes that we will be delivered from the clutches of both provided we follow the laws of G-d. Our task is to understand, develop, and enforce the totality of laws that govern how we observe our faith and all matters of daily life. We call these laws *halakha* or 'The Way'. Our fate as a people chosen by G-d depends upon it."

I thought about this and could not but agree. Long ago, Jews had been forcibly expelled from their rightful home and dispersed all over the world. This exile, many thought, was the result of disobeying the laws of G-d. In al-Andalus, which we call Sepharad, some had found temporary shelter. I asked Maimon how this came to be.

"My teacher, Rabbi Joseph ibn Magash, told me a story," said Maimon. "You see, long ago, there were four rabbis who were all teachers at the great academies in Babylon. That was the center of all our learning. These four were sent by ship to raise funds for the dowries of poor brides in the city of Barium. Before this delegation could arrive at their destination, their ship was captured by thieves. The captors demanded a great ransom for the rabbis. The communities of our people in Iskandariyyah, Tunis, and Qurtuba came together to pay the sum demanded, providing these scholars came to their cities and became leaders. The rabbis then traveled to the cities of their redeemers, where they brought the knowledge of Babylon. The leader of the four, Moses ben Hanokh, came here and became the chief Dayyan. That is how the lands of Sepharad became the spiritual center of our faith."

This explanation satisfied me, and over the next few months, I devoted myself to my studies. The more I learned, however, the less I understood. Rabbi Maimon explained that initially, the Talmud was not written. It was passed through the generations orally. When it was reduced to writing, it became the authoritative text for applied law. Maimon taught that the way to distinguish between custom and law was when the latter was written.

"We rely less upon what is called the oral Talmud than we do upon written decided law. That written law, not custom or tradition, is the basis for halakha," he said.

I realized then that reading the Talmud itself was not enough. It seemed that I would also have to read other commentaries and writings. Was the balance of my life to be spent in such an endeavor, I wondered? To clear my mind, I would often go to what to me was the more easily understood world of the market. There the confusion was simple. Either the goods on offer were too cheap or too dear. There was either an abundance of merchandise or scarcity. The quality was good, or it was lacking.

Most importantly, anyone could judge these conditions based on verifiable facts. I found peace in the market despite the noise, the crowds, and the plethora of smells and colors. Best of all, I also discovered inns where other students congregated to drink inferior wine and share their complaints and hardship.

My days of learning were much the same. Maimon or his best students would read and explain laws and their reasoning. A thorough knowledge of the Torah was also mandatory. Thus, we devoted time to reading scripture daily. All of us committed much to memory. Surprisingly, Maimon's son attended class almost every day. This boy put most of the students to shame. At an early age, he could quote scripture, verse by verse, without error. Everyone knew this child would be destined for remarkable things.

Most of the issues decided in court involved commerce. On occasion, Maimon invited the students to attend the *beth din*, or rabbinical court, where actual cases were heard. When this happened, students could ask questions or make comments as if they were Dayyan themselves. Although those rare occasions at court provided a needed respite from the daily routine, many of the cases I heard involved commercial disputes, and these only reminded me of my failure as a merchant.

There was still no word from my father, and this was disturbing. I was a diligent student, but the routine of study weighed upon me. Most days, I could not wait to be released from my lessons to go to the market and the inn. There I found solace in cheap wine and the company of a few students I came to think were my only friends.

Eventually, I felt sufficiently comfortable to share my story with these new friends and express my boredom with the study of the Talmud. My confession prompted the others to reveal their secret.

"Joshua, we think you may be one of us. You just do not know this yet," whispered one of his new companions, whose name was Simon.

I did not know how to respond to his declaration, so I remained silent.

"We are Karaite Jews," he said. "The rabbis consider us heretics. We are not. We believe that our school of law, which we call 'madhhab,' is the only correct path for our people. With their Talmud and legal writings, the rabbis only want to maintain power. It is the rabbis who have corrupted the word of G-d. We call ourselves roses and consider the Rabbis thorns. You are devoting yourself to falsehood, and that is the cause of your confusion."

I had never heard of this branch of Judaism, the Karaites. I had to know more. After several more cups of wine, I swore to keep anything I was told a secret and begged Simon and his new friends to explain their convictions. What Simon was saying could mean all my study was for naught.

"Do you believe that all of the commandments were handed down to Moses by G-d?" asked Simon.

"Of course, I do," I said.

"Then you must agree the Torah alone is the authority for halakha. Anything else is the construct of man, not G-d. If you read the Torah and interpret its words as the ancients did, that is sufficient. It is the only truth. Rabbis are not the authority. Each of us must read the words ourselves and decide their true meaning."

Now I was perplexed. "But if what you say is true, and I cannot dispute you, our way of life is overturned. If we cannot turn to our rabbis, then to whom do we turn? How can we settle disputes amongst ourselves if our courts have no authority?"

Simon smiled. "Now you are beginning to understand. There is a written law. It is the Torah. Anyone can study the words of scripture. Their literal meaning is the sole basis for how we should live. We call that '*peshat*'. Look what has happened to our people when we fail to heed G-d's law."

I carefully considered his words and said, "I need to think about this, Simon. Are there many who share your beliefs?"

Simon's smile grew broader. "Of course. There are many Karaites here in Sepharad and even in Edom. Some of us have obtained high positions under Muslim rule. We are physicians, clerks, and even tax collectors. The Ishmaelites understand that our faith is much closer to theirs than that of the Rabbinates. That is why we have been treated well. Nevertheless, in Sepharad, the rabbis call us heretics. That is not the case in the east. Let us talk no more about this now. We cannot share a meal with you if it contains the meat of animals not slaughtered according to the words of the Torah, but we can drink together. It is time to do just that. Think about what we have said, and we can talk again."

I did not reveal my newfound knowledge to Maimon. Although I continued my studies, I devoted more time to reading the Torah. To relieve my mind of confusion, I also visited the market and the inn more often. All this time, I had received no word from my father. One day followed another. Time began to lose its meaning. But my boredom did not last long.

VII

THE PATH DIVERGES
QURTUBA
The Christian year 1144

It was not until the holiday of Rosh Hashanah, marking the beginning of the new year, that a letter finally arrived. My hands shook as I broke the seal and began to read.

My dear son, word has reached me that our commerce in Lishbunah is ended. This saddens me. Abdullah, our partner, shares this grief. Rabbi al-Daudi says he has arranged for you to study under the direction of Rabbi Maimon in the city of Qurtuba, where you may find the study of the law of greater interest than commerce. I am, of course, disappointed by your failure as a merchant. I am, however, gladdened that you may have found your true calling. I pray this is correct.

There is a great famine in the land here, and we are concerned about the intentions of the Almohad. We hear only rumors, but it may be necessary for me to move our family to Iskandariyyah. To this end, I have taken steps to change our transport routes for gold shipments and to otherwise protect our interests.

It is now difficult for us to correspond promptly. If you wish to respond, it may be best to write to me in the care of Abdullah. Until then, may blessing be upon you.

Your loving father, Elazar

I knew my father enough to interpret these words as a strong rebuke. How could I ever regain his respect or trust? Worse, the letter reminded me of the grave errors I had made in Lishbunah. The more I thought about this, the angrier I became. I had been foolish for not recognizing the degree to which those of my faith were subject to persecution by our Muslim overlords.

My dismay and anger rose further when I learned that King Alfonso had failed to take Lishbunah. The city's rulers had called for aid from the Almohad, and I prayed that Rabbi al-Daudi, Yaish, and Blazh were safe. The English crucesignati who accompanied Alfonso's army left the field when they understood the opportunity for plunder was not part of the bargain. Without these warriors, the King's attempt was futile.

As time passed, my dedication to studying at the beth midrash began to wane. I spent more days in the market, where I continued to find solace. At every opportunity, I drank wine with my new friends. On one such evening, I noticed two strangers sitting nearby. There were always Ishmaelites in the market, but these two were different. The strangers were whispering not in Arabic but in Tamaziyt, the language of my homeland and the Almohad.

Although I had neither heard nor spoken Tamaziyt since I left for Lishbunah, I understood their words well enough. Having spent my youth in Marrakech, I was familiar with this tongue.

"When we take Qurtuba, we will need to clean this market. The Jews will convert to the true faith or die. It is simple," said one.

"It would be best if the Jews do not convert, Nasir. Their goods will fall into our hands. Then we, too, can enjoy the fruits of wealth. You must agree," said the other.

"Allah willing, you are correct. Let us leave this place and continue our duties. The sooner we send our report, the sooner our countrymen can take control."

The two strangers paid for their meal and left. I was stunned. Simon and his companions had neither noticed nor heard them. If they had heard the strangers speaking, they would not have understood the language. There was no time to lose. I needed to discover more about these strangers and their intentions. I excused myself and followed Nasir and his companion south towards the al-wadi al-Kabir and the ancient Roman bridge spanning the river. I had the good sense to maintain a considerable distance between myself and the strangers and walked on the opposite side of the narrow street. When the strangers reached the bridge, they stopped and inspected the Calahorra tower that guarded it. Because the bridge was narrow, the entrance was crowded with people waiting to cross the river. I pushed my way through the bustling hoard to hear what these strangers were saying.

"This barrier will be difficult," said Nasir. "A few warriors could hold it against any attack from across the river. We will need to attack the walls from the north or west. We must tell the others."

I was so intent on listening that I failed to notice the strangers turning away from the bridge. I was too close. One of them looked directly at me. When he did, his face fell in puzzlement. I knew I had been recognized. The only action I could take was to turn away and pretend that I was crossing the bridge with others in the crowd. But I had to learn more. After a few moments, I turned back and saw the strangers moving through the crowd toward the Alcazar fortress. My quarry moved quickly, and, as the street wound west, I lost sight of them. Rounding a corner, I saw a door to a home being closed. The door itself was painted blue. Hurriedly, I walked further. There was no sign of the strangers. I was confident these strangers were Almohad spies.

I did not know what other action I could take and thus returned to the beth midrash to find Maimon.

"Rabbi, the Almohad are here. I have heard them speak," I said. "The Almohad are exploring the defenses of the city. We must inform someone in authority."

Maimon nodded his head. "If this is true, all of us are in danger, and so are our rulers. Let me dress properly. We will report this now." Maimon hesitated and sniffed. "You have been drinking wine, Joshua. Keep some distance when you speak to anyone else."

I assumed that we would go to the fortress. That was not the case. Instead, Maimon led me to the nearby grand Adjama Mosque, where evening prayers were now being completed. As the participants left, Maimon instructed me to remove my shoes, and we entered the grand edifice's patio. The interior was of marble, decorated with exquisite mosaic tiles. The ceiling was at least one hundred cubits high, with golden balls suspended from it. My mouth gaped open in wonder. I had never seen anything like it.

"What are we doing here, Rabbi?" I whispered. "We should seek an official of the city."

"No one will pay attention to us at the alcazar fortress, Joshua," said Maimon. "The Imam here is a friend of mine. He is what the Ishmaelites call a Qadi, a judge. Like me, he is also a physician. He will know what to do."

Sheikh Abu al-Qasim Ahmed was a gray-bearded man dressed in a black robe. When he saw Maimon, he scowled.

"What are you doing in our house of worship, Jew? Have you come to convert to the true faith, or have you come to tell me that I believe lies? Our Qur'an claims your people have confounded the truth; you have hidden and changed the words of scripture."

"Neither, Qadi Ahmed. I have shown this young man the opposite; how you spread falsehood to your ignorant followers. I have told you your Prophet is part of G-d's plan to prepare the world for the coming of the true Messiah."

I was horrified. I did not know what to do. Maimon and Ahmed looked at each other with disdain and then, to my surprise, laughed and hugged each other in a warm embrace.

"My dear friend, it is good to see you," said Ahmed. "To what do I owe your visit? It has been too long since we enjoyed a good argument! And who have you brought to see me?"

When Maimon introduced me, I was still shocked at how the two judges greeted each other. When the rabbi explained the purpose of their visit, Ahmed's smile disappeared.

"Indeed, this is unwelcome news, my friend. The rise of the Almohad in al-Maghreb concerns us. I fear we might be next. Ever since Qurtuba rebelled against Emir Tashfin ibn Ali, this city has had no clear leader. Some say I, as chief Qadi, should fulfill that role, but my power is limited. The Almohad hate us as much as they do your people, and know we are weak. The Christians in the north know that as well. These are dangerous times."

"That is easy for you to say, Qadi," said Maimon. "For us, this is a matter of life and death. You know what those people have done in al-Maghreb. The Almohad will give the Jews only one choice: convert or die."

Ahmed shrugged. "My son, Muhammad, spends most of his time in study, for reasons I do not understand. However, he is quite intelligent, and tells me anything would be better than our current chaos. Our people are killing each other to gain power and coin. Al-Andalus is a kingdom of gangs. The Christians are on our borders. You know they have already conquered Almeria. If it is not the Almohad, it will be these followers of al-masiah Yasu. Our days are numbered. Perhaps he is right."

The Qadi paused to think. "Then again, your fear is justified. We have heard that the Almohad are fomenting civil disorder across al-Andalus. I will do what I can. However, we need to know more."

Qadi Ahmed turned to me and said, "You understand Tamaziyt? Our people also came from al-Maghreb, but no one speaks the language any longer. Do you know where these spies reside?"

I remembered the blue door and answered. "Yes, Qadi, I believe I do."

"Then I will ask you to watch them and learn what you can," said Ahmed. "Whatever happens, we must be prepared."

When we returned to the beth midrash, Maimon gave me formal permission to miss lessons so I could fulfill Ahmed's request. "This is more important than study, Joshua. The lives of our people are at risk," he said. Maimon then added, "It is also more important than wine. Keep your mind clear."

Although I readily agreed to do as Maimon asked, I was concerned.

"Rabbi, I will do what I can, but this task is dangerous. I know nothing about the work of spies.

What if I am recognized? How will I approach them so I can hear their words?"

Maimon smiled. "You must reread the Torah. In the fifth book of Moses, the De'va'rim tells us, 'Do not be afraid of them; the Lord your G-d himself will fight for you.' Where is your faith, Joshua?"

I thought it was easier to recite those words than practice them, but I promised to do my duty. The following morning, I went again to the market. Retracing my steps from the inn, I found the blue door again. I was sure this was where the Almohad had gone. I positioned myself across the lane, where I hoped I could see who left or entered the door but remain unseen by others. Time went by slowly. No one entered or left the house. Perhaps my quarry was elsewhere in the city, or I was mistaken in my assumption. My patience finally exhausted, I abandoned my post and made my way back to the inn.

As expected, Simon and his friends were drinking wine and engaged in their customary debates. They welcomed me and asked where I had been. My company was missed, Simon said. When he ordered wine, I waved him away. "Thank you, but I need nothing to drink today, my friend. I have duties that require vigilance," I said.

"Duties? What duties cannot be enhanced with drink, Joshua?" Simon's laughter halted as he saw my frown. "Is there something wrong?" he asked, now with concern.

"You have trusted me, Simon. I have kept my promise to you," I said. "Now, you must assure me that I can trust all of you. What I tell you must be kept only between us."

Simon and the others all affirmed that my trust was warranted. My friends wanted to know what I had to say. When I related what I had learned about the Almohad spies and the task I had been given, the group began to speak all at once. Simon, as leader of the group, waved them to silence. "Can I tell Joshua?" he asked the others. The others nodded in assent.

"Joshua, this news is not as bad as you think. You are right. We have been concerned about an Almohad incursion in al-Andalus for some time. We should fear them. That is why we have taken steps to protect ourselves and our community. I think you should know of this."

"What have you done, Simon?" I asked.

"We have written to Alfonso Raimundez, the King of Leon and Castile, who calls himself Emperor. Our letter said that Qurtuba is ripe for conquest. We have offered our aid and coin to this end. Some among the al-Murabit secretly support him. As we speak, the emperor is besieging the city of Coria in the west. We know the Almohad covet al-Andalus. It will take time, but the Almohad will be here in force. We told him he must act quickly."

Once again, I thought, Jews were calling for aid from the Christians. I passionately believed my people were merely trading one kind of enemy for another. Once again, my people were between a mortar and pestle. Which was worse, I wondered? My friends had made their choice. Were they correct?

"What makes you think the Christians will treat us better?" I asked.

Simon shook his head in disbelief at this question. "You do not know that the emperor has decreed that Jews are to be treated the same as Christians? His chief advisor is a Jew from Gharnata. How can you ask that question? The Almohad will kill us if we do not convert to Islam."

I kept my thoughts to myself. I was convinced that the Christians would change when Jewish support – and coin – was no longer needed. However, it was true that Christian rule would be better than that of the Almohad. That prospect was unthinkable.

Following further discussion, Simon and his Karaite companions offered to provide me with any assistance I required. It was necessary, Simon pronounced, to learn as much as possible about the spies in their midst. "Pretend you are one of them," he suggested. "You have come here from al-Maghreb and speak their language. That should be easy."

"I am no Ishmaelite and will not pretend to be one," I said. "I will observe and listen. That is enough."

For the next three days, I did precisely that. Every morning, I would go to my position to observe the blue door. I always wore a different robe or turban. Often, I would cover my face with a veil, as did recent immigrants from Ifriqiya. I had almost lost hope when I finally saw the Almohad spies again. They appeared to be returning from a journey this time, as their robes were covered with dust. Where had these spies been, I wondered. I guessed correctly that the two would go that evening to the inn. I found a table nearby and listened.

"The western wall. That is the weakest," said Nasir. "Did you see how it is unguarded?"

"I did," said his companion. "We must tell the others to act quickly. This city is ripe for insurrection. We can begin to spread the rumors now, and, Allah willing, we can provoke the citizens to action."

"Against the Jews?"

"Of course. That will be simple to arrange. However, we must also instill fear of the infidels. We know that some Jews are already seeking aid from the so-called emperor. It would be best if some of the residents in the city asked for our aid. There are no true leaders here. The al-Murabit are not trusted. Our brother, Abdul, will know how best to accomplish this."

At this point, several people entered the inn and sat nearby. Nasir and his companion began talking quietly amongst themselves, and I could no longer overhear anything. I had, however, learned enough. There were more spies in Qurtuba, and, as in other cities in al-Andalus, their mission was to sow discord. I knew I must inform both Maimon and my new friends. As I stood to leave, the spy called

Nasir looked directly at me. I was sure I had been recognized.

I left the inn and walked quickly back to the bet al-midrash to tell Rabbi Maimon what I had heard.

"We should not be surprised," said Maimon. "The Almohad have provoked insurrection elsewhere. Once a rumor begins amongst the right people, it is almost impossible to counter. As you know, the al-Murabit are suspicious of us. They resent our freedom to lend money and our skill at doing so. If we are gone, debtors will be free of their obligations. As for the Christians, that is another matter. The al-Morabit fear them. Well-crafted rumors will only enhance what these Ishmaelites already believe."

"What are we to do, Rabbi?" I asked.

Maimon shook his head. "There is little we can do. Continue to keep watch. I will talk to the Qadi. Perhaps he will have a plan."

I knew I must also inform my new friends. Somehow, the Almohad knew of their activity. They were in danger. I would not find them until later that evening and thus decided to return to my post near the blue door. Perhaps Nasir and his companion would meet their compatriot, Abdul. It would be useful, I thought, to know who this third man was. As I took my usual watching place, I felt a blow on my head. The world became black.

What must have been hours later, I woke to throbbing pain. Touching my scalp, my hand became sticky with blood. I tried to stand and discovered that I could not do so. The pain was too great. I was deep within a narrow alley, hidden from those passing by. On my chest was a small piece of parchment. It was difficult to focus, but when I did, I read the words written upon it: 'Thank your G-d for your life, Jew. Next time will be your last. Do not interfere again.'

That I had been recognized was no longer a question. For the first time, I was truly afraid. I crawled to the main thoroughfare and eventually was able to stand. Covered with blood, I drew the attention of all who saw me. Surprisingly, no one offered assistance. Instead, everyone who passed by turned away, as if I did not exist. My fear turned to anger.

As I entered the neighborhood of the bet al-midrash, I found a different reaction. Several fellow Jews stopped me in the street to help. One of the Jews declared he was a physician and led me to his own home. There, my wound was carefully washed. The physician examined my head, looked into my eyes, and determined there was no severe damage. He bandaged the wound, advised rest, and asked if I required assistance to go to my place of residence. I was embarrassed by the attention and politely refused further assistance. Sauntering to the bet al-midrash, I remained in considerable pain. I told Rabbi Maimon what had happened and showed him the scrap of parchment. As I did so, my anger returned.

"These animals have gone too far, Rabbi. I will return their hurt if it is the last thing I do," I said.

Rabbi Maimon sighed. "My son, it is the nature of man to retaliate against those who do us harm, but we are commanded not to do so. Vayikra, whom the Christians call Leviticus, writes, 'You shall not take revenge.' Do you know why?"

I shook my head. "No," I said.

"I explained that commandment to my son when another child hurt him. Taking revenge is an evil trait. We must learn to rise above our feelings when they arise from worldly matters. Whatever happens to us, whether good or bad, is because G-d wills it to be so. Your assailant is not the reason for your suffering. We must learn to forgive our enemies. G-d himself will deal with those who wrong us. It is not for us to replace G-d's judgment. Do you understand?"

I did not. It was impossible to erase my anger. I could not forgive the Almohad. These Ishmaelites could not be instruments of G-d, I thought. I kept this conviction to myself.

"Rabbi, I will dwell upon your words, but I believe the Almohad wish us harm. We must maintain vigilance. Although I should not follow them myself, I have friends who may help. With your permission, I will go to them now."

Maimon agreed. Indeed, it was too dangerous for me to continue his surveillance. The rabbi did not ask me who these "friends' were. It might have been different if he had.

That evening, I went again to the inn to seek Simon and his companions. My friends were assembled in their usual place and engaged in animated discussions. One look at me with my now bandaged head, and they stopped their talk and asked what had happened. I told them.

Simon frowned. "We have been talking about just this issue. The Almohad are manifestations of Amalek, the enemy of G-d. So, for that matter, are the Christians. They are Edom and Ishmael, our enemies, symbols of evil. Have you not read scripture? We must punish them for what has been done to you!"

"Rabbi Maimon has explained that the commandments forbid revenge," I said. "He has related the words of Vayikra. G-d will punish them, not me. At least that is what he told me."

Taking a deep breath, Simon said, "Joshua, you are being subjected to the teachings of the rabbis. That is exactly what we have been warning you against. Read the plain words of the Torah. The passage Maimon refers to says, 'Do not seek revenge or bear a grudge against anyone among your people but love your neighbor as yourself.' Those are the written words, not oral traditions. Do you think the Almohad are your people? Are they your neighbors?"

I saw his point. "No, the Almohad are not my people, nor are they my neighbors if I understand the plain meaning of that word."

"Exactly," said Simon. His companions all nodded their heads in agreement. "Again, I ask you to read the words of scripture. The ancient hero, Joshua, for whom you are named, was commanded by Moses to fight with Amalek, who offended G-d. G-d commanded a war of vengeance upon his enemies, and His enemies are ours. Read this yourself. We must act."

As I pondered these words, one of Simon's companions, a man called Judah, spoke.

"Joshua, you have been spending too much time debating whether a lender can enforce a judgment against a debtor with no funds. You must study the written words, not the remembrance of what the rabbis call the oral Torah and tradition. The rabbis would have us believe that the wisdom of sages is greater than that of a prophet. Can you believe that? If you wish to understand scripture, read the works of the Mourners of Siyyon. That will help you."

"Mourners of Siyyon?" I asked. "Who are they?"

"They are a group of scholars who devoted their lives to studying the exact words of the Torah, so they might properly be understood. There are scrolls which define each word."

As Judah began to lecture further, I interrupted.

"I will do as you suggest, but how can I take revenge? We are not allowed weapons. We cannot take my assailants to court. There is nothing I can do," I said.

Simon grinned. "I will show you. Come with me now to my home. You say you know where the spies reside?"

"I do," I answered.

"Then follow me. We will act now."

Simon led me to his home, which was nearby. Like other residences, an elaborate wooden gate led to a garden filled with sweet-smelling flowers. Sitting on a bench was the most beautiful woman I had ever seen. She had long, braided black hair and fair skin. She was neither thin nor portly but, rather, perfect in form. Her features were flawless, as lovely as the flowers in the garden. She was reading a scroll and engrossed in her study. She did not notice us as we entered the courtyard. I stopped and stared. I could not take my eyes off this heavenly vision until Simon tugged on my arm.

"That is my sister," Simon whispered. "She is reading scripture; I will introduce you someday. Come, we have work to do. My father disapproves of my friends. Although he is absent now, he may return soon. We have no time to lose."

In Simon's room, I was told to remove my clothing. "Wear this instead," said Simon as he handed me a threadbare robe that looked like that worn by a beggar. Simon pulled off his clothing and donned a similar garment and a leather belt. He wound a dirty cloth around his head and gave me another rag to cover my bandaged head. "That will do," he said. "There is one more thing. We will do that outside. I need some water." He selected a battered drinking cup and filled it with water, giving me no time to ask questions.

When we left, I noticed that Simon's sister was no longer in the garden. Had it been a dream, I wondered? In the lane outside the walls, Simon stopped and poured the water from his cup on the ground, thus making a pile of mud. He dipped his hand in the mixture and rubbed the result on my face, before I had time to protest. Simon did the same for himself. Now we both looked like poor laborers. Simon's final act was to carefully select two stones. Each was smooth and the size and shape of an egg. These he put in the pocket of his robe. "Now we are ready," he said. "Show me the way."

Throughout this process, I remained silent. I was still thinking about the vision in the garden. I had no idea what Simon intended.

I led Simon to my old hiding place near the blue door. "What are we doing here, Simon?" I asked. "You know what the spies told me."

"Be not afraid," said Simon. "You will learn. Your assailants will not recognize you now. They do not know me. Tell me when you see them."

We did not have to wait long. One of the two Almohad opened the blue door and began to walk up the street. The spy was about twenty paces from us.

"That is one of them," I whispered. "He is alone."

"So much the better, chuckled Simon as he removed his leather belt. I was surprised to see that this was not an ordinary belt. It was made of two strands of flax, in the middle of which was a cloth pouch. At the end of one strand was a woven loop. The other strand ended in a flat tab of leather. Simon looked in both directions. People in the street engaged in conversation and trade, but no one looked at us. I opened my mouth to speak. Before I could do so, Simon selected one of the stones and placed it in the pouch. Then, he put his middle finger through the loop on the end of one strand and the flat tab between his thumb and forefinger. He mumbled what must have been a prayer. Simon stared at the Almohad, looked to see if anyone was watching, swung the contraption in an arc, and released his thumb from the tab. The stone flew faster than an arrow and struck the spy directly in the back of his head.

I was stunned. I stood silently with my mouth agape. No one had witnessed Simon's use of his weapon, but everyone in the street now turned to see what had happened to the victim, who lay prone in the road. Simon casually wrapped the belt around his robe and smiled grimly. "G-d was with me," he said. My first inclination when I recovered my wits was to turn and flee the scene. Simon roughly took my arm, pulled me back, and whispered, "No, we cannot run away. We must move with the crowd towards that agent of Amalek."

A crowd assembled around the prone body of the Almohad. Someone cried, "He is dead. Call for help." Simon and I pushed through the crowd to see. A pool of blood ran from the victim's head, which the blow had shattered. I felt sick at the sight. It was not long before soldiers, and a physician, arrived at the scene. The soldiers told the crowd to disperse. We seized the opportunity to slowly walk away.

"I did not intend to kill him," frowned Simon. "I merely wanted to return the blow that Ishmaelite gave you. His death was G-d's will."

I took a deep breath and realized I was shaking all over. Simon's attack had happened so fast I could not find words. I could only stare at him.

"I prayed to G-d that He would direct my stone, if it pleased Him, and was His will," Simon said. "It was. I have no regret."

I still did not know what to say. I had just witnessed violent death. Moreover, the killing blow had been delivered, without mercy, by my friend. Strangely, I also felt joy. Vengeance had been swift. Was it not true that G-d had directed Simon's missile? Were not the Almohad enemies of G-d and the Jewish people? Perhaps, I thought, violence had been justified. As I considered this, I began to calm.

"Simon, I do not know whether to thank or curse you," I said. "What is this weapon you have used to such effect? Are we not forbidden to carry arms?"

Simon smiled again. "We are forbidden to carry edged weapons. Those are the plain words of the law. Was my stone not smooth? Is a braided belt of flax a weapon? This instrument is a sling, the same as King David used to fell the giant Goliath. There is nothing new in the world. What matters is that we have taken vengeance on enemies of G-d. That is precisely what Moses told your namesake. In case you have forgotten, he said, 'Now go, attack the Amalek, and destroy everything that belongs to them. Carry out the Lord's vengeance on them. The

Lord will have war with Amalek from generation to generation.'

Seeing my confusion, Simon continued, "I have followed the commandments of scripture. Think no more about this. Let us go to the inn and drink a cup of wine. I, too, must calm myself."

Upon returning to the Inn, Simon and I found the others in their usual place.

"I see from your face you have succeeded in delivering G-d's wrath on Amalek," said Judah as he looked at Simon. Simon nodded his head in assent but said nothing.

"You need a bath and clean clothes," said Judah. "You look like you have been working in the fields, or the privy."

"Take this cup, drink from the fruit of the vine and let us all give thanks to G-d," said another of the companions. "We have told the innkeeper to bar entry to all strangers until we know more. This place is safe, but you should not stay longer. I agree with Judah. Your appearance does not make for good company!"

Simon and I departed the inn when we had finished our one cup of wine. At the gate to Simon's home, he asked me to wait.

"I must discover if my father has returned. He would disapprove of us in this condition."

Simon opened the gate and, walking into the garden, closed it behind him. It was not long before he returned and beckoned for me to enter. "My father is not here. We must not lose time. Wash your face and change back into your proper clothing."

Upon entering the garden, I once again saw the young woman with whom I had been enraptured on my first visit. This time she looked directly at me and laughed.

"What have you brought to us, brother?" she said. "Look at you! Are you now keeping company with farmers? Have you been tilling the fields as well?"

I was mortified. The best I could do was stammer a greeting.

It took a moment for Simon to respond as his sister continued to laugh. "Sister," he said, this is my friend Joshua. We have been carrying out essential duties. You are embarrassing him!" Turning to me, Simon smiled.

"Joshua, this is my sister Hannah. Forgive her rudeness."

The last thing I wanted to do was forgive this vision of heaven. I bowed my head and summoned the courage to speak.

"It is I who should beg forgiveness. I am ashamed to appear thus before you," I stammered.

I wanted to say more but could not find the words. Simon saved me from further embarrassment.

"Joshua, "he said, "We do not have time for this. Come with me now."

As we cast off our filthy robes and donned our usual dress, Simon looked directly at me and chuckled.

"I see you have become a captive of my sister. She has that effect on men."

The violence of their encounter with the Almohad was, for the moment, forgotten. "I have," I said. "May I speak to her again?"

"You would need to ask my father's permission, Joshua. That will not be easy to obtain. You are not a Karaite, and, as I told you, my father disapproves of me. He spends his time reading the Torah in the Beit Knesset and pays little attention to what is happening in the world. He believes that he and others like him must study scripture every day, or the world might end. My father is, how shall I say, difficult."

"If I must read with your father every hour, I will do so if he grants me permission to speak again with Hannah," I said with conviction.

Donning my proper clothing, I wandered back to the yeshiva. I walked slowly; I had no idea what to say to the rabbi. My mind was in turmoil. It rapidly shifted between considering the implications of the death I had witnessed and my infatuation with Hannah. By the time I reached the gate, I had decided to say nothing at all.

Rabbi Maimon was no fool. When I approached him, he looked intently at me.

"You are troubled, Joshua. What is amiss?

I swallowed hard and took a deep breath. Despite my decision to remain silent, I could not hide my emotions, which the rabbi had so easily discovered. I could not lie to my teacher. There was no choice. I must tell the truth.

"One of the Almohad has been killed," I blurted. "I was there. His death is my fault. And I am in love. I do not know what to think."

Rabbi Maimon said nothing for what seemed an eternity. Finally, he said, "Let us talk about one thing at a time. You say the person you have been watching is dead and that his condition is your fault? There are rumors in the market that G-d struck down a stranger from Ifriqiya. Is it to this event you are referring?"

"Yes," I said and then related what had happened.

Rabbi Maimon frowned as I related my story. I knew that, once again, I was in deep trouble. He shook his head, took his copy of the Torah from its shelf, and motioned for me to sit on a cushion close to him.

Rabbi Maimon spoke softly. "You have been associating with the wrong people, Joshua. I should have warned you about that. Let us discuss matters calmly. First, we will address the death of the Almohad. One of the most important commandments given to us by G-d through Moses is that you shall not commit murder. The word 'murder,' however, requires definition. What does the word in our language mean? Some sages claim the original verb in the Torah means an unjustifiable killing. A correspondent of mine, the great Rabbi Rashbam, argues that the book of Exodus specifically finds a difference between slaying another unwittingly and doing the same with intention. Your friend did not intend to inflict death on the Almohad. Is that correct?"

"That is right, Rabbi. My friend prayed to G-d to direct his missile according to His will," I said.

"Were there any witnesses to this event," Maimon asked.

"No, I am certain no one saw how this death happened."

Rabbi Maimon pondered this response. Finally, he rendered judgment.

"Then I find no fault. Our court would provide a more reasoned opinion, but it is best to keep this matter between ourselves and G-d, the ultimate judge. In any event, you murdered no one. That cannot be disputed. However, study this matter yourself. It is complicated. In Islamic courts, the outcome would be different. Read the law, read the Torah, and tell me what you find.

"Now, what is this about love?"

I proceeded to tell Rabbi Maimon about Hannah. As I recalled and described her beauty, I could not prevent a smile from crossing my face. "Rabbi, I wish to marry that woman. I know in my heart she is right for me."

Rabbi Maimon did not respond as expected. Once again, a frown crossed his face.

"Joshua, I know of Hannah's father and his family. Our custom, and I believe law, forbids marriage between you and a Karaite. That may not be the case in Yerushalayim or elsewhere in the east, but it is true here. Do not see her or her family again. Devote yourself to study, and you will understand why. Your father would agree. Put any thoughts like this behind you."

That was not the response I had expected. Could the law forbid association with other members of my faith, when the only difference was that of opinion? I said nothing to Rabbi Maimon then. I simply shook my head in understanding. I was, however, determined to follow my own heart.

VIII

HOPE
QURTUBA
The Christian year 1145

I halfheartedly participated in the new-year festivities of Rosh Hashanah. Over the weeks following the high holiday, I devoted myself to study. The city authorities ignored the death of the Almohad, despite rumors circulating in the market. For some Al-Murabit, one less Almohad was considered a benefit. Others prayed for more of them to arrive. Every day, there were reports of Christian victories in both the north and west. There had been a great battle, led by a vassal of Emperor Alfonso, near the river of al-Godor. The emirs of both Ishbilliyah and Gharnata lost their lives in that conflict. The heads of these two emirs had been anointed with myrrh and sent to their widows in Qurtuba. Fear spread amongst the city's Muslim populace.

Unfortunately, more spies infested the city and al-Andalus itself. There were uprisings in Ishbilliyah. A group called the Muridun, the 'Disciples', were inciting rebellion against the Al-Murabit. Their imam, Abu al-Qasim, a convert from Christianity, now ruled much of the southwest and he called for open revolt. Pressure from all sides caused the Al-Murabit rulers to become fearful of their position. This strife disrupted Jewish commerce. Merchants began to complain as taxes increased. The Beth Midrash, however, was a bastion of peace. Students spent their days learning and enjoyed a period of tranquility. I was an exception. I could not forget either the killing of the Almohad or my infatuation with Hannah. Rabbi Maimon's exposition provided no relief to me.

One evening, I was reading passages from the Torah to quiet my mind. By accident, I opened the scroll of the Book of Esther, which told how a Jewish queen in Persia thwarted an Amalek plot to kill all Jews. Instead of becoming victims, the Jews killed all those who wished to kill them. The plain words of scripture recited G-d's instruction to "blot out the remembrance of Amalek". The festival of Purim was a celebration of this event. I read the passages many times, until I became convinced that Simon's judgment was correct. This was not a complicated issue. It was simple. Jews had the right, no, an obligation, to kill the Amalek, and there was no question in my mind that the Almohad were indeed the emissaries of Amalek. Was it not true that they wished us to convert to Islam or die?

The answer to my second question, regarding my right to marry a Karaite Jew, was equally simple. There was nothing in the written Torah forbidding such a union. If one studied 'tradition' and the so-called oral Torah, there were many prohibitions, but no words of scripture supported such a law. Rabbis had created it. I concluded that the sages wished to prevent the spread of the Karaite heresy, nothing more.

My faith in Rabbi Maimon and Rabbinates began a downward spiral. Although I continued dutifully attending lessons and engaging in required study, my heart was not in it. Once again, I began to visit the inn to meet Simon and his friends.

Although Simon never mentioned the killing of the Almohad, he did have news. The disruption in trade concerned the Jewish merchants in the market. Many were considering moving their commerce to lands controlled by Christians. When I asked why this was happening, Simon said that Muslim authorities in the city were questioning Jewish loyalty. Many believed the Jews to be actively seeking their downfall. Restrictions were becoming more severe, and taxes increased.

"What I tell you now must be kept secret," said Simon. "My father has concluded that I should travel to Al-Misr before conditions worsen. The Christians may come, and there have been calls for the Almohad to send an army to confront them."

I interrupted. "I do not understand. You have encouraged the Christians to come, Simon. Is that not what you want?"

"That would be best," answered Simon. "Our difficulty is more complex. We are doomed if the Ishmaelites discover that we have supported the

Christians and the Almohad do take control. If we do not help the Christians and they succeed in defeating the Ishmaelites, we will be treated as enemies. Our position is untenable. The best choice is to leave this place. At least in Al-Misr, there are many Jews who share our beliefs, and our people are treated well. We will depart in a few months."

"Then your sister will go as well?" I asked.

"Yes, all of us, including Judah and the others, will leave. My father has decided to remain here. He is too old to travel, he says. But there is more. My friends and I will not remain in al-Misr. We have taken an oath to return to Siyyon and the holy city of Yerushalayim. There, we believe G-d will show us the way to rid our home of the followers of Amalek. We will raise an army from our people and take back what is rightfully ours. As you know, our rebellion long ago against Rome failed. This time, we will, G-d willing, prevail. No longer will we be treated as slaves by either Christians or Ishmaelites."

Simon paused; the others nodded in agreement.

"Join us," he said. "You will not become a rabbi. You must know that. There is nothing for you in Qurtuba."

I considered his words for a few moments. "I will think about this," I said. "I would need my father's consent. He has commerce and friends in al-Misr. I believe he would approve. I do not know what my father would say about a return to Siyyon. I will write to him, but I will say nothing about your plans."

I paused for a few more moments as I further considered my response. There was another reason to join Simon in the journey if Hannah was going too. There were no laws or customs in al-Misr to prevent my marriage to her. "Yes," I repeated. "I will seek approval from my father. I do wish to join you. While I wait for his response, please train me to use your weapon. There may be a need for such a skill."

"Good," said Simon. "We have time, so I will teach you the art of the sling while we wait. Such knowledge may indeed be useful. In the meantime, say nothing about this to anyone."

That evening, I wrote to my father. In my letter, I reported on current events in Qurtuba and my desire to travel to Al-Misr. I confessed that the life of a student of the Talmud was difficult and would not constitute my calling. I begged for the opportunity to engage in commerce once again. Of course, I expected no answer for many days.

Over the following months, I continued to attend lessons at the Beit Midrash and sessions of the rabbinical court. Every day, however, I read the written Torah, and every evening, before sundown, I met with Simon to learn the art of the sling. Simon showed me how to make this weapon and disguise the result as a belt. This training was my most challenging task.

Throwing a stone with the sling was easy. Ensuring that the missile struck its intended target was not. At first, my attempts were disastrous. If I threw the stone at a target, I was fortunate to come within a few cubits. Simon permitted me to make those errors many times before suggesting that the missiles themselves were partially the cause of inaccuracy. I learned that stones should be smooth and oval rather than irregular in shape. That made a difference. Over the many evenings of practice, my skill began to improve. Finally, Simon told me it was time for a test. Taking a small melon from his pouch, Simon placed it on a nearby wall. He then told me to disguise the sling as a belt.

"Step back twenty cubits," he ordered. "Now, I will count to thirty. When I begin, you must convert your belt to a weapon, find a proper stone on the ground, and direct it to the target. Are you ready?"

I walked back the required distance and waited for Simon's signal. At Simon's shout, I removed my belt, prepared the sling, and searched for a correctly shaped stone near my feet. Simon was counting aloud and had reached the number twenty. I took the stone, inserted it into the pouch, swung until the momentum was correct, and released my missile. I smiled when my missile hit the melon and split it in two. "Did I do well?" I asked innocently.

"Not bad," said Simon. "Do it again, and this time your target is smaller. I will count only to twenty."

I did as Simon asked, but I could not quickly find a properly shaped stone this time. Searching for the stone took time. Finally, I chose a fragment from the dirt with a jagged edge. I missed the target by a wide margin. Simon had counted to twenty-five before I was able to release my missile.

"Now you understand the problem," said Simon. "Always carry stones of the proper size and shape with you. No one will notice. Even if anyone does, what harm is there in carrying a few stones? A correct stone will not be affected by wind, and having a few available will save you precious time. Do you think a swordsman will wait for you? You must learn to sling accurately from beginning to end in no more time than a count of ten. Practice each day from varying distances. You do not need me for such an exercise. Let us meet in a few weeks, and I will test your skill again."

Without informing Rabbi Maimon, I continued to meet with my Karaite friends. At each meeting, my friends discussed their plans to leave for Al-Misr, and we exchanged what news was available regarding Christian incursions and the movement of the Almohad. I had heard nothing from my father. I was confident I would soon receive a message as the days wore on.

The eight-day celebration of Chanukah was approaching, and, on one of the occasions when I met my friends, Judah asked if I knew the real story behind the holiday. I knew the traditional stories; of how the Maccabee warriors of Israel had defeated a mighty army, liberated Yerushalayim, and constructed a new altar in the Temple. The pagans had stolen the golden Menorah, so the Jewish victors had to fabricate a new one. The Jews had oil for only one day, but that oil actually lasted eight days. This miracle was unmistakable evidence that G-d had taken His people under his protection again. That, however, was the extent of my knowledge.

The others at the inn knew the whole story, so they waited for Judah to retell it.

"My namesake, Judah ben Mattotyahu, was called Maccabee. That word is composed of the letters of four others: "Mi Kamocha Ba'eilim Hashem' or 'Who is like you, O G-d.' During his time, the ruler of Syria, Antiochus, attempted to destroy our people. He suppressed Jewish laws, removed the High Priest from the Temple, and appointed the priest's brother, who followed Greek beliefs, to replace him. Antiochus imposed burdensome taxes on the Jews, and, when some rebelled, he ordered his army to kill them. Thousands died. He then forbade Jews to worship and confiscated and burned their scrolls of law. Then, his army went from town to town to force all Jews to renounce their faith. Judah gathered his followers and was determined to drive the pagans out. When Antiochus heard of this, he sent his general, named Apollonius, to destroy Judah and his small group of warriors. Judah was clever, and, though his army was small, he defeated Apollonius in many small battles. Antiochus realized that a much larger force was required. Thus, Antiochus dispatched a huge army, as many as forty thousand, to rid the land of the Maccabee once and for all. G-d, however, had different plans. Judah told his followers to fight to the death to defend their souls and the Temple. And that they did. Judah's small army put the massive pagan army to flight. I tell you this so that you can understand."

I nodded my head in agreement.

"You see, Joshua, this is what we also intend," said Simon. "When we return to Siyyon, we will recruit followers amongst the Jews living there. There are many. We will build and train an army. Jews here and all over the world will send us coin to purchase weapons. All can be done in secret. If G-d wills, we can, like the Maccabee, drive out both Christians and Ishmaelites and regain our homeland. It is to that end that we will devote our lives and fortune. Join us!"

I had been enraptured with this tale and was tempted to agree immediately. Indeed, this was a noble undertaking. I expressed my desire but again said I would need my father's consent. Simon and the others understood. They would not depart for some time and thus agreed to wait for me to reach a final decision.

While waiting for my father's reply, I spent my days reading. At every opportunity, however, I practiced with my sling. I habitually wore it and always carried five perfectly shaped stones in my pouch. Every day I practiced, and my accuracy and speed improved. Eventually, I could assemble the sling, aim, and throw the stone within a count of ten, and sometimes faster.

Although I devoted effort to considering the merits and justice of Simon's plan, I could not dismiss his sister from my mind. I dreamed of joining Hannah in al-Misr. Every day, it became more apparent that my calling was not to be a rabbi. I said nothing of this to Maimon, and that prevarication led to a profound sense of guilt. Rabbi Maimon had not only been a kind and tolerant teacher, but had paid my expenses without any certainty of recompense.

A few weeks after the end of the holiday, I received a letter from my father. It was brief, but its contents gave me joy. There was, it said, a need for my presence in Iskandariyyah. My father instructed me to prepare to leave Qurtuba as soon as possible. A Collegantia vessel would arrive in the early days of the month of Tevet and would wait for me in the southern port of Malaqah. From there, I was to travel to Sicilia, where another letter with further instructions would await me at the home of Hakim Thoma. Twenty gold dinars were available for my use through Rabbi Maimon. I was to reimburse the rabbi for my expenses and retain the balance for the voyage. The letter said nothing further. It was impossible that my own letter to my father had arrived, so I thought, this must be simple good fortune. Or, I wondered, was it an indirect message from G-d? I could not wait to inform Simon. First, however, I needed to speak to the rabbi.

"I see the news has pleased you, my son," said Maimon, when I informed him of the letter's instructions.

"Yes, Rabbi, it has indeed," I responded. "I am not destined to become a scholar, and perhaps my father will give me another opportunity to prove my worth in the art of commerce. I pray this is so. You have given me much learning, and I will never be able to thank you enough for your patience and support. Now it is time for me to find a new direction."

"Your words are appreciated, Joshua, but your education has only begun. You are now fluent in our sacred language and writing and have become acquainted with our method of interpreting the law. The path forward is a long one."

Pointing to his son, who was reading at his feet, Rabbi Maimon continued.

"My son will devote his life to understanding our faith and will become a rabbi. Already he knows that. Lately, I have noticed your interest has waned, and I have been concerned. I can see on your face that this news has made you happy. I suspect, however, there is more for you to tell. Is that true?"

I was unsure as to how to respond. I could not disclose my discussions with Simon and his friends. I thought another truth would suffice, although this, too, could lead to contention.

"Yes, there is more to tell, Rabbi. I am in love," I said. "The woman I wish to marry is also traveling to Iskandariyyah, and if G-d permits, I intend to ask for her hand. If I were to remain here, I would never see her again."

Rabbi Maimon nodded his head in understanding. "Who," he asked, "is this woman? Is this the woman about which you have spoken before?"

"I have been afraid to say anything, Rabbi. I have mentioned her to you before. Her name is Hannah. As you know, her family ascribes to the Karaite form of our faith. You have made your disapproval of this association known to me."

Again, the rabbi nodded his head in understanding. "Then that is why you have spent so much time reading the Torah," said Maimon. "There is no harm in reading the words of scripture. These sacred words form the basis for halakha, our law. All of us must do that. The problem is in understanding the words themselves. Properly interpreting what is written requires years, perhaps centuries, of study. That is why we have an oral tradition and the Talmud. The beliefs of the Karaites are dangerous. I warned you about this before."

Maimon put his head in his hands as he thought further. "In good faith, I cannot continue to object to your pursuit of the woman Hannah, but I ask that you do your best to bring her to a better understanding of our Jewish faith. I ask nothing more. Your father has instructed you to leave in any event, and you must obey. I have received his letter of credit, and I will make these funds available to you. We will miss you here."

Rabbi Maimon refused to deduct anything from my credit. The expenses I had incurred were, he said, of little significance. Instead, he gave me the entire amount in gold Bezants. "Keep these safe, my son," he said.

I was relieved that my interview with the rabbi had gone so well. My next step was to inform Simon of my good fortune. I almost ran to the inn.

Simon and his friends were at their usual table when I arrived, panting from exertion.

"Calm yourself, brother," said Simon seeing my condition. "What is your rush? Have a cup of wine and relax. We have good news!"

"Your news cannot be better than mine, Simon," I said. "My father has called me to Iskandariyyah. I will be leaving immediately. When will you depart? Can you do so now? A ship is waiting for me; I am certain you could also gain passage. I must go to Sicilia first, but that should not present a problem."

Simon laughed. "That is the same as our good news. My father has granted me and my sister permission to leave, and our friends here have also gained their family's consent. We will leave from the port of Quadis, and my father has paid for our passage directly to al-Misr. I intended to tell you of this and ask that you join us."

I was delighted. I suggested the group travel together, but Simon said it was too late. The funds for passage had already been paid. It was a much longer journey to walk to Quadis, but there was no alternative.

"Do not worry, Joshua, we will all meet in al-Misr. I will give you the information you need to find us when you arrive. the cities of Quadis and Malaqah are both to the south, and we can walk together for at least the first day. We hope to leave

Qurtuba tomorrow. Can you be ready to go then? We will meet here at daybreak and use the eastern gate."

I enthusiastically agreed and, that night, packed my meager belongings and enjoyed a final supper with Rabbi Maimon and his family. Before I rested for the night, I sewed nineteen dinars into my sling, which I wore as a belt. Although adding these coins would make the sling heavy, I thought it might improve the weapon's accuracy if I ever required it. I kept one dinar in my traveling sack and wrote a brief letter to my father confirming that I would travel to Iskandariyyah immediately. Of course, I thought, there was a good chance that I would arrive before the letter. How wrong I was.

IX

DIVERGENCE
QURTUBA TO PORTUS CALE
The Christian year 1145

That night, I could not sleep. My world had changed, and I was ready to make use of the opportunities that now lay before me. At dawn, I took my leave from Rabbi Maimon and thanked him profusely for all he had done for me. I walked to the inn, where the others awaited me. Simon was accompanied by three mules, two of whom carried the group's baggage. Hannah rode the third animal. My heart quickened when I saw her. I gave a brief bow, which she acknowledged with a smile. At least, I thought it was a smile. I summoned the courage to walk beside her but was reluctant to engage in conversation. I could think of nothing to say. Hannah relieved my discomfort by initiating talk herself. She had many questions. Was I excited about visiting al-Misr? Would I miss Qurtuba? What was my vocation? I did my best to answer them all forthrightly. She was easy to talk to, and my shyness soon disappeared.

Soon, I began asking questions myself, and eventually, our discourse turned into a real conversation. So engaged were we in talking that we almost failed to notice that the group had stopped at a crossroads. It had taken an entire day to reach it. Tired from our first day on the road, we decided to make camp. The following day, the others would travel southeast, toward the fortified town of Istiyyah. I would head directly south, to Malaqah.

We built a small fire at our camp, ate a light meal, and then rolled out our blankets for the night. I noticed smoke from another fire some distance away. At the time, I thought nothing of it. It was just another party of travelers, I thought. The lands south of Qurtuba were safe.

I had slept little the night before and fell into a deep slumber. I dreamed of Hannah. The sun had just begun to rise when my sleep was interrupted by shouts and a scream. Someone kicked me in the side. Standing above me was a bearded man wearing an ill-fitting conical helmet and brandishing a sword. "Get up," he ordered in heavily accented Arabic. Ignoring the pain in my side, I stood. All my companions had been herded to the center of the camp. A least a dozen warriors surrounded us. These were not Ishmaelites; they were laughing and talking in a strange language. One of them was holding Hannah by her hair. Her assailant's face betrayed a look of lust, and Hannah's face betrayed her fear. I was ready to protest when a loud voice shouted what must have been an order, and she was released. Our assailants stopped their chatter and looked expectantly at the man who now appeared in their midst. The newcomer wore an iron-laced hauberk over a dirty quilted robe. His hands were encased in iron greaves, and a diamond-shaped shield was strapped to his back. This man was clearly the leader.

"What have we here?" he asked. "A family of infidels is what I see. If we leave you in peace, you will inform your people in Qurtuba of our presence. I regret it, but we cannot permit that to happen," he said. "Can you tell us anything of value? I suspect not, so make your prayers to your so-called Prophet. We do not have time to delay, so do it quickly."

With that comment, he signaled to his warriors to draw their swords. Two of them, armed with bows, drew arrows from their quivers.

"Wait, Lord," shouted Simon. "We are not Ishmaelites; we are Jews. We have been providing information to your king, and he will be displeased if we come to harm."

The leader smiled and, without warning, struck Simon with the flat of his sword. "Kneel, Jew, if that is what you are. Let me look at you."

Simon knelt and watched as the leader examined each of us. We were unarmed, so he did not search our clothing. Finally, he exclaimed, "All infidels look the same to me. If you are Jews, you are worth coin to us. I would rather gain from your lives than dull the swords of my men on your bodies. For too long, we have made nothing for our efforts. Can you prove your words?"

I knew that taking hostages for ransom was the customary means of gaining wealth for Christian and Muslim soldiers, so I decided to address the leader directly.

"Excellency, we are Jews and are loyal to your king. Our families will pay for our release. Let the woman go so she may obtain the funds you require."

The leader, again without warning, stuck me with his mailed gauntlet. "You can call me Ochoa, not Excellency. That name means 'wolf' in my native language, and that is what I am! Have you not learned to kneel when you address your betters, Jew? I will permit one of you to carry a message to your family. But not the woman. She stays here. You," he said, pointing at Simon. "You will go now and return with one hundred gold bezants before nightfall tomorrow. All your companions will die if you do not return or betray our presence. We might find other uses for the woman first, of course."

The soldiers all laughed when the leader translated his words into their language. Having nothing to bind us, the soldiers kept us together in the center of the camp. I found myself next to Hannah, who was still shivering in fear. I reached out my hand to comfort her, and she took it and held it in her own. Her hand was warm and soft, and for a few moments, I could not think about anything else. One way or another, I thought, we would be free again and travel to Iskandariyyah, where I silently promised myself, I would marry this woman.

The soldiers offered water to us but nothing else. Uncertain as to what we should do or say, we remained silent. In any event, escape or resistance was impossible. Hannah and I held hands throughout the night. The soldiers not on guard duty awoke in the morning, and a small group left camp. They returned just before midday carrying a single chicken and a small sack of olives. Displeased with their meager takings, Ochoa rebuked them in the strange language they spoke. I wished I had some knowledge of whatever this language was. One of Simon's friends resolved the problem.

"These people are speaking a form of Latin, Joshua. The pronunciation is strange. If you listen carefully, you can recognize some of Arabic words. This band has been living off the land, it seems. They are grumbling about their lack of food and the poor condition of the villages around here. Raiding small farms yields little. They all want to leave this place. Their general, Munio Alfonso, told them to scout the environs of Qurtuba. They have been abandoned and fear their leader Ochoa is losing his reason."

The soldiers roasted the chicken on the fire but gave none to us Jews. Instead, we were provided a few olives and water to drink.

Simon returned just as the sun began to set. He was panting with exertion, and I realized he had been running much of the way.

"You have brought the Gold, Jew?" asked Ochoa.

"I have brought you a letter of credit for the amount you asked," said Simon as he handed a parchment to the leader. You can take this to any money changer, and they will give you the coin." Without waiting for a response, Simon directed the others to gather their belongings, untie the mules and leave.

"Not so fast," said Ochoa, his face red with anger. "You think me a fool? I cannot read this. It might entitle us to gold, but it might not. And where do you expect me to go with it? These are not Christian lands. You expect me to go to an infidel city where I can be captured myself?"

This time Ochoa stuck Simon not with the flat of his sword but with its edge. Although Simon continued to stand for a moment, his head fell at a sharp angle from his body, and blood spurted over the ground, quickly turning into a muddy dark red soup. Hannah fell to her knees, sobbing. I looked on in horror.

"Well," said Ochoa, "there is one less filthy Jew in the world." He looked at the others and advanced toward me. His face flushed with rage.

Although I had been paralyzed with shock, I could not contain my anger. "You are a fool," I shouted. "That letter has value in any city, Christian or Muslim. It will exchange us for gold, but only if we are alive. You have just killed an honest man. He was no threat to you. G-d will punish you. I swear that is so!"

Ochoa glared at me. "Jew, my G-d is not yours. And you dare to call me a fool. We will see who deserves that name." As Ochoa raised his sword to strike, one of the soldiers stayed his arm.

"Captain, what if this Jew is telling the truth?" He said. "I have heard of these letters before. What harm is there if we take the Jews with us? When we find Alfonso's army, someone will know what to do. King Alfonso is near the city of Evora. If we kill the Jews, we will never know the truth. Think about it. None of us have gained anything from our service. We can always rid ourselves of them if the letter is false. I beg you to think."

Ochoa remained silent for a few moments while his anger cooled. "Perhaps you are right," he mumbled. "We will take them, and if we discover the letter has no value, the Jews will die. We leave at dawn."

Simon was buried that night. Hannah, who continued to weep, washed his body with water from a nearby stream while the others dug a shallow grave. There was no Cantor to sing or ribbons to tear, but we all chanted the last prayer. Hannah, through her tears, recited the traditional words from the book of Job: 'G-d has given, G-d has taken away, blessed be the name of G-d.' I did my best to comfort her but could not hide my sorrow and anger. No one slept that night.

For the next week, we were led east. Small mountains lay to our right. Hannah was inconsolable. She looked blankly at the path before us and said nothing. I, too, was at a loss for words. Simon's death had happened so fast, and what could I say? On the third day, Hannah broke her silence.

"Where is G-d?" she whispered.

I did not answer. I had the same question. How could G-d permit such a faithful follower to die in this way? I could think of no answer and, thus, turned to tradition. From my study with Maimon, I knew the ritual words of the Kaddish, recited during the time of mourning. Of course, there was no 'minyan' of ten Jewish males. I disregarded this fact and chanted the words alone:

"Glorified and hallowed is G-d's name in the world that G-d created according to His will. May G-d's majesty be revealed in the days of our lifetime and the lifetime of all the houses of Israel quickly and soon. Let us say Amen."

I intended to chant the rest of the Kaddish, but Hannah began to weep. She leaned against me and shook her head. "No more," she said. "I ask again, where is G-d?"

I had no response.

Every few days, the soldiers raided isolated homesteads to steal food. Some of this food was grudgingly given to us Jews. Hannah refused to eat, and each day she became weaker. I begged her to break her fast. "You will die if you eat nothing," I said. She finally relented and reluctantly ate from the meager rations we were given. As we approached the city of Ishbilliyah, which was in Muslim hands, we turned north to cross the mountain range. First, we had to cross the river called al-wadi al-Kabir. The soldiers forced a barge owner to take us across. From the river, the route north was rugged, and with our poor diet, we all became thinner and weaker. Our condition did not concern Ochoa. I continued to hold Hanna's hand. There were no words to assuage either her grief or my own.

As we traveled, I did my best to interpret the words of our captors. They intended to join the forces of King Alfonso and participate in the conquest of Lishbunah. There, it was rumored, all those who aided the king in capturing the city would be entitled to plunder. Our captors were confident that any evil they had done in al-Andalus would be pardoned. I noted that none of the soldiers bothered to pray. They also ignored the Sabbath, both their own and that of us Jews. I continued to grieve for my friend and swore to avenge his death. To make matters worse, I knew in my heart that my father's wishes, once again, would not be fulfilled. The further we traveled, the further away was the ship that was to take me away from this place. It would not wait for me. My only consolation was being close to Hannah and satisfying her need for companionship.

We traveled north and then west again for ten days; then another river blocked our passage. This river was called 'al-Wadi Ana.' The land was barren, only flat fields of dry grass. Convinced that he would find either a ferry or a crossing, Ochoa determined to turn and travel south. His conviction was correct, as we found a ferry in the afternoon of that day.

Ochoa, however, hesitated to approach. A group of horsemen guarded the ferry dock, all wearing robes marked with a large red cross. Ochoa could not hide the presence of his soldiers or us captives. When the horsemen saw Ochoa's band, they galloped towards us with leveled lances, shouting in an unintelligible language. Ochoa lost his nerve and ordered his men to draw their swords. We Jews huddled together, hoping to keep out of harm's way. Ochoa, however, ran to Hannah and, once again, grabbed her long hair. He held his sword to her throat.

"Halt," Ochoa screamed. "We are not infidels, and we are coming to join the forces of your king! Come closer, and this woman will die!"

The riders did not understand Ochoa's words. To them, his language must have sounded strange. That was sufficient evidence of who we were. At an order from their leader, the horsemen began their charge. I did not pause to think. I removed my belt, unwound the sling, and placed a stone in its pouch. Faster than I had ever accomplished the task, I swung my weapon and released its stone directly at Ochoa's face. The stone hit Ochoa's right eye. It made the same sound as when his stones struck a practice melon. Ochoa put one hand to his face and fell crying to his knees. He was still holding Hannah's long hair with his other hand. As his grip weakened, she escaped his grasp and ran to me, weeping. Seeing what had happened to their leader, Ochoa's soldiers threw down their swords and raised their hands in supplication. We Jews remained together.

The riders motioned for all of us to walk to the ferry. Ochoa was now lying on the ground, holding his bleeding head and weeping. His condition was ignored by all except me. I had the presence of mind to remove the letter of credit from Ochoa's robe. Two horsemen dismounted at the ferry and led us onto the vessel. These two looked at me with respect, frequently glancing at my sling. The crossing was swift, and, on the river's far bank, another group of soldiers, wearing red crosses on their robes, but without horses, were waiting. One of these soldiers spoke very rudimentary Arabic.

"Who are you?" he asked.

I was the first to respond. "We are Jews, captive of these thieves. Please help us."

The soldier shrugged with indifference. "Come with us. We will take you to the king, and he will decide what to do with you."

Nothing further was said until we reached a large Christian camp. There we marched to an ornate tent erected in its center. Ochoa's men were ordered to sit on the ground near the tent. My companions and I were led inside.

I could not believe my eyes. There, standing behind King Alfonso, was the giant I knew well.

"Blazh, what are you doing here?" I exclaimed. Blazh looked at me with surprise. He engulfed me in his massive arms.

"My dear Joshua," he whispered. "I should ask what you are doing here. It has been a long time. I never thought to see you again."

"You know this man, Blazh?" asked the king. Blazh released me from his arms, approached Alfonso, and whispered in his ear for some time. The king nodded his head in understanding.

"Joshua," he said. "Blazh here has reminded me of our meeting, so long ago. You brought me information from my friend al-Daudi. I am in your debt, it seems. What brings you here?"

I then related all that had happened to my companions and me since our departure from Qurtuba. I told King Alfonso that I was hoping to travel to Sicilia and that the others were trying to reach Iskandariyyah. All of us had been held captive for ransom by the group outside. I asked him to assist us, as we were now far from the ports from which we could continue our journey.

When the King heard my tale, he acted quickly. "Take the scum outside and assign them to carry baggage," he ordered. "We may have use for them later. I already have enough undisciplined foreigners in my army. A few more will not make any difference." Turning now to me, he said:

"Thank you for removing their leader. That will be helpful. I do have good news for you. Your fellow Jew, Yaish, is here with me. You know him well. Yaish is a commander in my army, and he will know what to do with you. He will have questions about conditions in Qurtuba." The king looked at Blazh. "Blazh, take these people to Yaish."

Blazh nodded his head in understanding and led us out of the tent. As we walked through the camp, he asked me to tell him more about Qurtuba and the events leading up to my departure. Hannah and the others were stunned by King Alfonso's reception and were more surprised at Blazh's voice. They had not expected this giant to speak in such a high pitch. They shook their heads in wonder.

In a tent on the outskirts of the camp, we found Yaish sitting on a carpet. He was dressed in mail and was examining a crudely drawn map in front of him. A knight wearing a white robe marked with a red cross was talking to him, while a black-robed priest stood by. When Yaish looked up, he recognized me immediately and greeted me effusively.

"My old friend," he said as he rose from the carpet. "What are you doing here? Have you completed your studies? Are you now a rabbi?"

I found myself relating the same story I had just given to the king and Blazh, and thus kept my account brief. The others in the tent remained silent until the priest interrupted.

"Commander," he said. "We have work to do. There is no time to waste in idle chat with these Jews. How do we know they are not spies?"

The white-robed knight nodded in agreement. "You are right, Father, he said. "Yaish here has the trust of the king. These others do not. Send them away, Yaish."

Yaish responded with anger. "I am aware of my duties and position. This is my friend. I will not be told what to do by you. Leave us, and I will call for your return when I need you."

Both the knight and the priest bowed in acceptance and left the tent. As they did so, I heard the priest mumble, "Jews – we are ordered about by Jews. What is the world coming to?"

Yaish scowled but ignored this remark. He looked at my companions and noticed for the first time our poor condition. "You need something to eat and drink," he said. "Forgive my discourtesy." With that statement, Yaish called for food and wine and motioned for all of us to sit on the carpet. I then introduced the group, giving special attention to Hannah.

"Yaish, this is Hannah. Our captors killed her only brother, and she was to travel to al-Misr in his company but now is alone." I hesitated for a moment and then continued. "I said nothing to her brother. I had intended to ask for her hand if she would have me. What can I do now?"

Hannah looked at me and smiled. "I would happily accept your proposal, Joshua. You are all I have left," she said as tears formed in her eyes. Yaish frowned and asked a question.

"You say she and the others are Karaites, is that not so? Her father is in Qurtuba?"

I answered yes to both questions, and Yaish thought for a few moments. Finally, he said softly, "I cannot help you with this, my friend. Marriage between you is forbidden here. Perhaps such a union would be permissible in Iskandariyyah. In any event, you would need permission from her father, now that her brother is no longer among the living. Here is what we will do. I will assign an escort to take all of you to my father, Rabbi al-Daudi, in Portus Cale. He can write to this woman's father from there. The city is in our hands, so we can find a vessel to take your companions to al-Misr and another to take you to Sicilia. The voyage will be costly. Do you have funds?"

I unwound my belt and tore the stitches holding my coins. "Yes," I said, "I have gold." My companions were once again stunned. This amount of coin was enough to pay the ransom demanded by our captors. Of course, had I divulged this, the thieves would have taken my coin and killed all of us in any event. Yaish, seeing the dinars, raised his brows and quickly agreed that there was enough to pay for everyone's passage. "Go now with Blazh. He will find you and your companions a place to rest. We leave this camp tomorrow, so come back and see me tonight, when you are rested."

Blazh found an empty tent for my male companions and me and another with some of the soldiers' wives for Hannah. I was concerned fo her safety, but Blazh assured me she would be safe. He swore to take responsibility for her welfare. That assurance satisfied me. In the evening, I returned to Yaish.

"Joshua," he said, "before we talk of other matters, I need to know what you have learned about the Almohad and conditions in Qurtuba."

I told Yaish everything I could remember. There was, I said, no question that the Almohad would take advantage of the disarray amongst the Al-Murabit and attempt to seize Qurtuba and all other major cities in al-Andalus. Yaish said that my concern matched all other reports received. Time, he said, was of the essence, for the Christians to conquer as much land as possible.

"You should know there is a new Christian Pope called Eugene III. The city of Edessa has fallen to the Turks, and the Pope has called for a second armed pilgrimage to retake that city. He intends to drive the Ishmaelites from the Holy Land. King Alfonso believes it is now time to try again to conquer Lishbunah. We are scouting the area now to test the defenses of the Al-Murabit. So far, there has been no resistance. The Ishmaelites are too busy arguing amongst themselves to notice our presence. We will continue our mission for a few more days and then will return to Coimbra."

I listened carefully and had a question. "Who are the white-robed knights I see everywhere?" I asked.

Yaish laughed. "Those so-called warriors are the first of the Christians from England. More are coming here before they travel on to the Holy Land. Their leader is a man called Andrew of Londres. Early next year, this army will be joined by many others. None of the Christians have any military experience. They have never drawn blood in battle. The priests told them their souls will be saved and their debts held in abeyance if they joined the pilgrimage. To be fair, many of the knights are sincere in their beliefs. Others are not. We suspect that the armed pilgrims, who everyone calls the 'crucesignati', will be most interested in an opportunity to gain wealth from their service. Negotiations are occurring as to what the warriors will be permitted to loot from the city of Lishbunah when we retake it."

Yaish whispered, "If our army were larger, we would never accept the aid of these people, but we have no choice. The Pope blesses their mission, and King Alfonso does not wish to disobey the Pope's command. I advise you to avoid these people in the camp. We Jews, some of these Christians believe, are a people of evil and should suffer the same fate as Ishmaelites; we should convert or die. I am only accepted as a commander because I have the trust of the king and now have an exalted position. Alfonso has made me a lord; did you know that?"

"The king made you a lord. How can that be?" I asked.

"That is a long story. For now, King Alfonso values my service and experience. I am now 'Don Yaish, Lord of Unhos, Freitas, and Aldela dos Negros.' That sounds pretentious, does it not? Can you believe it? I, a Jew, am to be granted noble rank and the stewardship of small villages. It is a strange world, my friend."

I agreed. This was, indeed, strange. "Then it is true. The Christians are better for our people than the Ishmaelites. I have been wrong in my thinking."

"Do not be fooled, Joshua. I enjoy my position only so long as I have value, and that is true for all Jews. The Christians tolerate us only to the extent that we are useful. We must stay together, as G-d's chosen people; that is the only way we will survive."

Drinking several glasses of wine, we continued to talk. I confessed my intent to go to Yerushalayim after meeting with my father in Iskandariyyah.

"We must make our homeland in the lands given to us by G-d," I argued. "Otherwise, we will never be left in peace. You know the arts of war. Join us."

Yaish shook his head. "That is a noble pursuit, Joshua, but your plan is doomed to failure. We are too few, and the Amalek too many. You know your scripture. The prophet Isaiah tells us that there will be a day when G-d will raise his hand to gather the children of Israel from the lands to which we were dispersed and lead them back to Siyyon. That time is not now. Continue your studies, marry your woman, and seek a peaceful life for your children and theirs. What is important is for our faith to grow and survive. Have faith in G-d. Our turn will come."

I thought about his words but disagreed. "How do you know G-d has not already raised his hand?" I asked.

Again, Yaish shook his head. "Look around you," he said. "Do you think all Jews have the coin to purchase passage to the east? Do you believe all our brothers and sisters wish to abandon what trades or homes they now have? No, Joshua, when G-d calls us, we will know it. Until then, people like my father and me must remain here to do what we can to protect the people and keep them together in faith through following G-d's law. There is no choice."

I disagreed but kept my thoughts to myself. Scripture was clear. I would, I silently vowed, take what action I believed correct. There was no merit in continuing to argue. I would follow my father's direction and travel to Iskandariyyah by way of Sicilia. Somehow, I would find means for Hannah to journey there as well. I prayed that my father would bless my goal. "When can we leave for Portus Cale?" I asked.

"Tomorrow," said Yaish. "I will ask Blazh to lead you there and assign a few soldiers to give you protection. We can spare a few horses for your use as well."

We left the following day, led by the massive Blazh, and accompanied by four mounted soldiers who did not bother to hide their displeasure with the task to which they had been assigned. These soldiers rarely spoke to us for the entire two weeks of the journey to Portus Cale. At the evening camp, they kept well apart from us. Blazh, however, remained close. He wanted to know the story of each of the Jews, and, over time, they all became used to the pitch of his voice. When we finally reached our destination, Blazh led us to a stately, walled villa near the port, which served as the temporary abode for Rabbi al-Daudi.

Rabbi al-Daudi was reading a manuscript when Blazh ushered me into his chamber. He looked up when he heard the door open. "Blazh, you know not to interrupt me when I am reading. Why are you here?" It was then he saw me and, for a moment, was speechless. "Joshua, is that you? Why are you not in Qurtuba?" The rabbi stood and held out his arms. "Come here. Let me look at you."

I was delighted to see my old teacher once again. Briefly, I explained the reason for my presence and asked if I could introduce Hannah and the others. "Of course, bring them in, Blazh," he said.

Hannah was the first to be introduced, and Rabbi al-Daudi immediately realized this woman was special. He looked at me, looked again at Hannah, and said, "Joshua, you are in love, are you not?" I nodded my head.

"I will tell you everything, Rabbi. First, let me introduce my other friends," I said. When this had been accomplished, Rabbi al-Daudi ordered a servant to prepare rooms for us and bring food and drink.

"You have a long story to tell, Joshua. Let us eat together, and then I will put aside my studies so I can hear all of it."

My tale took the rest of the day to tell. It had grown dark by the time I finished. Rabbi al-Daudi listened intently and did not interrupt. When it was clear that all had been said, he suggested that we all go to our beds. He said he would like to speak to me alone in the morning.

Although I needed the rest, I woke early to meet with the rabbi in his chamber. Al-Daudi had awoken earlier and was waiting for me.

"I wanted to talk to you alone," he said. "Your companions are Karaites. That poses a problem for me; our survival depends upon unity, and their beliefs run counter to mine. My views are not shared by those in the east, so I agree that the men should continue their journey to al-Misr. A commercial vessel in the port can take them to Iskandariyyah. If your companions do not mind sleeping on deck, the cost will be little, and I understand that you have sufficient coin to pay for their passage. Is that correct?"

"Yes, Rabbi," I said. "But what about Hannah and me?"

"That is a more complicated issue, Joshua. Your father has instructed you to go to Sicilia, and that is what you must do. I will inquire to discover what arrangements can be made."

"But I wish to travel with this woman, Rabbi," I said as tears threatened to emerge from my eyes.

"Alas, that will not be possible. Her brother is no longer with us, and the law is clear. She must seek guidance from her father in Qurtuba. He must consent to your marriage, even if it was arranged in al-Misr. In any event, as an unwed woman, she cannot travel alone or in your company. That is not permitted."

To my embarrassment, tears now ran freely. "Surely, there can be an exception, Rabbi. I love this woman, and my intentions are pure; I must find a way for us to remain together. Please reconsider."

"Joshua, that I cannot do. However, do not abandon hope. I told you this long ago. G-d will show you the way if you are sincere in your faith. I will write to Hannah's father and present your case. If her father agrees, he will accompany her to al-Misr or permit her to travel with other women of our faith. You, however, must do as your father has commanded. 'Respect your parents as you respect Me', says G-d; 'everything your father says to you, you are obliged to obey.' That, too, is the law. As I said, I will find you a passage. Hannah can stay with my wife here while we await a response."

With some effort, I swallowed my anger, but I thought this was just one more example of how the rabbis created G-d's law. What if my father said I must not marry a woman I had chosen, if such a marriage was permissible by Jewish law, which would be the case in al-Misr? Would I still be obligated to bow to my father's command? I decided not to argue. There was no point, and there was no question that Hannah required permission from her father before anything further could be resolved.

"I understand, Rabbi," I said. "I will do as my father asked, but I beg you to write to Hannah's father quickly. Please protect her and do all you can to send her to me in Iskandariyyah. I will wait for her there."

X

EXILE REPEATED
PORTUS CALE TO SICILLIA
The Christian year 1146

Two days later, my friends boarded a ship bound for al-Misr. We had all forgotten to celebrate the new year, and I was sorry to see them go. I promised to find them when I, too, could travel to that place. I wrote a letter explaining the delay in my travel and asked that it be delivered to my father. Rabbi al-Daudi did as promised and sent a message to Hannah's father in Qurtuba. I spent the next week waiting to learn if a vessel in port could take me to Sicilia.

Growing frustrated with the delay, I finally asked the rabbi if I could enquire myself. I had sufficient gold to induce a ship to change its route so that I could fulfill my father's command. The rabbi consented to my request but insisted that Blazh accompany me to the port.

"The city is not safe for us," said al-Daudi. "Crucesignati from England are arriving now, and they are a rough lot. Why the king permits this, I do not know. You must be on your guard. Many hate us."

At the dawn of the following morning, accompanied by the massive Blazh, I walked towards the port. The streets were quiet, with only a few shopkeepers now opening the shutters to their stalls. Most were closed. The English, it seemed, were already causing trouble, and the city's merchants were afraid. As we walked, I asked Blazh why the rabbi seemed so unconcerned about my safety.

"Rabbi al-Daudi is an important man," squeaked Blazh. "Everyone knows that he is an advisor to the king and is vital to the eventual conquest of Gharb al-Andalus. He is the first Jew appointed as an Almoxarife, a bailiff, in a town here. He is also a great landowner. No one will touch him."

"So," I said. "That is why the Rabbi wishes to remain here under Christian rule."

Blazh shook his head. "No, Joshua. Others might think just that, but that would not be true. The rabbi is permitted to rent or even sell some of his lands to other Jews, and that has never been the case before. He says his purpose is to ensure that all people of his faith stay together. That, he says, is imperative for the survival of his people. He is offering land to as many Jews as he can."

We had almost reached the port when a group of soldiers emerged from an inn nearby and blocked our path. These soldiers were all armed with swords. None wore mail. Their robes were filthy, and anyone could tell they had been drinking heavily all night. One of them staggered closer and looked up in wonder at Blazh. This man spoke to the others in a strange language, and whatever he said provoked laughter. He then looked at me. "Ludeas," he shouted with a scowl. Without warning, two soldiers drew swords, and one pulled a dagger.

"Retraindre," commanded Blazh. The sound of his voice brought forth more laughter. "What did you say?" I whispered.

"These soldiers must be English," said Blazh. "I told them to stop in their Norman language. I only know a few words. We had best move away ourselves. These people have had too much to drink."

We turned to go, but the soldier with a dagger had already moved behind us. We were trapped, and the situation was becoming dangerous. Perhaps these assailants were thieves. I unwound my sling and drew a stone from my pocket. The soldiers did not notice this. They were still laughing and pointing at Blazh. With the encouragement of his companions, one of their assailants advanced on Blazh with his sword. He was muttering something. He drew closer and raised his weapon. Once again, I did not stop to think. I would protect my friend. I stepped back and swung my sling.

The stone hit the soldier in the chest and knocked him backward into the street. This attack enraged the remaining soldiers. One of them raised his sword to attack me, but Blazh was too fast. His massive, closed fist struck the swordsman's arm like a hammer, and the weapon fell to the ground. Blazh then seized the assailant's hair and casually threw him bodily into the others. I placed another stone in my sling. That was enough. The English helped my victim to his feet and ran. Turning to thank him, I saw that Blazh had a strange expression on his face.

"Blazh, what is the matter? Our assailants are gone, thanks to you." I was preparing to speak further when I noticed Blazh eyes glazing over. The giant began to fall, and I tried to keep him upright. It was no use, he fell to the ground, and blood began to bubble from his mouth. It was then that I saw the dagger wobbling in his back. We had forgotten about the Englishman at our rear, who was now running to join the others. I knelt beside Blazh and listened to the giant's chest. He was still breathing.

"Help," I shouted. No one responded. If there were witnesses to the altercation, they were now gone. The street was deserted, and I could hear windows in nearby buildings being closed. I did not know what to do. Blazh was too heavy to lift, and blood was now flowing freely from his mouth. He tried to speak but could not do so. I held him in my arms as he breathed his last. I left his body there and ran back to the rabbi's home, shaking with horror and sorrow. Was G-d punishing me for all my failures? How could G-d take the life of a faithful follower like Blazh, as He had done with Simon? What could I say to al-Daudi? Was there no end to the evil that befell me? My news would be the second time I had come to the rabbi in shame and sorrow.

Rabbi al-Daudi received my news with sadness. "Blessed are You, Lord our G-d, King of the universe, the True Judge," he recited. I knew the proper response was, "This is also for good," but I could not. How could this be for good? I thought. I said nothing but saw tears in the rabbi's eyes. Blazh had died for no reason, and it was other Christians who had attacked him. His death was only one more example of the scourge of Amalek. Al-Daudi sighed and instructed four servants to take a litter and collect the body.

"Take Blazh to the church of Santa Maria," he ordered. "The priest there is a friend of mine. Ask him to give him a proper burial. I will pay whatever cost is involved."

"I wish to go to his burial, Rabbi," I said, brushing away my tears.

"That is not possible, Joshua. We are not permitted inside the church. Blazh was a dear friend and a loyal companion, but he was a Christian, and we must ensure that he is treated according to his faith. I have done what he would want me to do."

I could not contain my feelings. "Rabbi, how is it that G-d permits such a thing? I know the proper response to your blessing, but I could not say it. The Torah commands us to love G-d. How can I find such love in my heart now?"

"Joshua, we bless G-d for joy, do we not? How can we not thank G-d for the evil that befalls us? He is the true judge. It is not for us to question His ways. Do you know the sayings of the famous sage

Akiva, who lived long ago in the East?" I admitted that I did not.

"Once, Rabbi Akiva arrived in a city where he could find no place to lodge for the night. He knew that Scripture says that all G-d does, He does for the good. Rabbi Akiva slept in a field accompanied by his few possessions: a rooster, a donkey, and a lamp. After he had gone to sleep, a strong wind blew and snuffed out the candle. In the dark, a cat came and stole his rooster. Then, a lion attacked and ate his donkey. The rabbi had the same question as you. How can it be that all that G-d does, He does for the good? Rabbi Akiva had no choice but to sleep on the ground in the dark. Now His rooster was gone, and a dangerous beast had devoured his prized donkey. The next morning, he discovered that an army had attacked the city that night and captured all its residents. The rabbi was saved because he camped outside the walls; no light, no braying of the donkey, no crowing of the rooster betrayed his presence. Thus, he was saved from enslavement. That, concluded Akiva, is why we must thank G-d for all that happens in our lives, whether good or evil. G-d does nothing without reason."

I pondered these words and did my best to acknowledge their truth. Silently, I was uncertain how this parable could apply to the death of Blazh, but I swallowed my doubt.

"Thank you, Rabbi," I said. "I will keep Blazh in my heart and try to accept what has happened.

Should we report this to the authorities? Why should his assailants escape punishment?"

Rabbi al-Daudi sighed. "The authorities will do nothing, Joshua. We do not know who attacked you. Even if you could identify those crucesignati, we only have your word for what transpired. They would claim that you attacked them first, and there is no way to refute that charge. Leave it be, accept G-d's judgment, and consider how knowing Blazh blessed your life. That is what I will do."

I nodded in acquiescence and deep sorrow. "I will consider your words, but now I must leave this place. I must follow my father's instructions and find a ship to carry me to Sicilia. I am already late, and he will be worried."

Rabbi al-Daudi smiled. "That is the only good news I have. I have found a vessel. It departs tomorrow. The captain has asked ten dinars for your voyage but assures me that your accommodation will be comfortable. His ship is sailing to the Levante. It will stop at Panormos, the capital city of Sicilia, to re-provision."

"Excellent, Rabbi, I said through my tears. "I will be ready."

The rabbi sighed. "There is only one problem, Joshua. This ship carries crucesignati to fight the Ishmaelites, and three priests will accompany them. You would be the only Jew, and we know that could lead to difficulties."

I frowned. "I do not know if this would be wise, Rabbi. You know how I feel."

"I thought about that," said al-Daudi. "You will wear a black robe and a turban, as is worn in the far north. I told the captain that you are carrying a private message from Alfonso VII of Castile to King Ruggiero and that you are mute. Your home is in Leon in the north. You will need to wear an iron cross and pray with the Christians. Besides maintaining silence, I do not think this will be an undue burden. The crew and passengers are all from the land of Frisia. They speak their own language. You are not a priest, so no one will expect you to understand Latin. This will be the safest way for you to travel. Can you do this?"

I had to think about this. Maintaining silence for two weeks or more would be difficult. There would, however, be no one with whom I wished to speak. I would devote my time to reading. Wearing a cross was different. Would G-d forgive me for that? I asked the rabbi that question.

"First, Joshua, you cannot take any fine clothes with you in case anyone looks in your belongings. I see no difficulty with taking a few scrolls of scripture so that you can continue your studies. Do not concern yourself with the cross. Think of it as an ornament, not something to worship. Of course, the priests will insist that the soldiers and crew pray every day. You can join them but make your prayers silently. You must, of course, keep the Sabbath yourself. That is G-d's commandment."

I departed the morning of the next day. As expected, a group of forty soldiers and three priests boarded the vessel, a heavily laden cog with a single sail. When I arrived, the captain greeted me and held out his hand for the ten gold coins promised. The captain smiled and gave me a low bow upon receiving the coin. He shouted to the other passengers in his strange language, pointed at me, and presumably explained my inability to speak. Following that introduction, he led me to a small cabin under the rear fighting deck. This confined space would be my home for an exceedingly long journey.

Indeed, it was a lengthy journey. We traveled south along the coast through the heavy seas that were common at this time of the year and then rounded the cape to enter the narrow passage to the Middle Sea. When the wind rose and waves swelled, the priests would shout their prayers. In the early days of our voyage, several of the priests could not complete their supplications without heaving the contents of their stomachs over the side. G-d was not making it comfortable for them.

The food provided did not help. The priests and the crucesignati were fed stale bread, water, olives, and strips of dried meat. On occasion, honey and cheese were provided. Ale was watery but plentiful. I feared that the meat was from pigs and thus subsisted on bread, olives, and cheese alone. The captain did provide me with wine from his private stores.

Every day was much the same. The priests would call for prayer in the morning, noon, and night. I joined in these prayers but silently recited my own. I secretly observed the Sabbath and devoted myself to studying my scrolls. The only excitement came when arguments and fights broke out amongst the armed pilgrims, or another sail was sighted in the distance. Because the others believed I could not speak, they left me alone to my thoughts and study. As the days wore on, my beliefs became more solidified. I would honor my father's demands, whatever they were, but somehow, I would travel to Yerushalayim and join my friends to regain the lands G-d had granted us. I trusted that G-d would bring Hanna to me, and I would ask for her hand in marriage. These were the commitments by which I lived.

When I arrived at the port of Panormos in the spring, my anger and sorrow were still fresh in my mind. My dear friends had suffered horrible deaths. There was little chance I could see Hannah again, and I had, once again, failed my father. My position as a Jew amid the evils of Amalek was clear. Was there no end to my pain? The council the rabbis had given me provided no relief.

While I waited for my father's letter, I followed Williams's advice to commit my story to writing. In the mornings and evenings of each day, except on our respective Sabbaths, William and I met to talk. Thankfully, Hakim Roland and William's father were fully engaged in his work at the hospice and thus did not disrupt our discourse. I had not finished transcribing my tale when I finally received the long-awaited letter from my father. His message was brief. The vessel which brought the letter was waiting for me at the port. I was instructed to board it and travel to Iskandariyyah at the earliest possible moment.

The following day, I took my leave from William and his family. I thanked them profusely for their hospitality and friendship. I had been treated well, and Sicilia had, indeed, been welcoming. When I boarded the ship to Iskandariyyah, I had regained a semblance of peace; but I wondered what new challenges G-d had planned for me. William's suggestion to write a journal of my experience brought forth a clearer recollection of all that had befallen me. I determined to continue setting forth my story in writing so that I would never forget it.

XI

SICILIA TO ISKANDARIYYAH
The Christian year 1146

My voyage south across the Middle Sea was uneventful. The crew and the ship's captain were all Ishmaelites, but were kind to me and treated me with deference. On occasion, we sighted a sail in the distance. Because we were far from the coast of the Levante, there were few reports of pirates in these waters. One crew member was a skilled player of the instrument called an 'ud. He knew most of the songs in the famous Kitab al-musiqi al-Kabir, the Grand Book on Music. Some sailors knew the words. Many were the evenings when the sounds of their singing floated through the breeze. I stood by the rail and listened.

The captain asked if I was familiar with the songs, and I admitted I was not.

"Then you have much to learn, Joshua. There is a rich heritage. We Muslims have taken much from Greek knowledge to develop unique patterns and structures. What is called musiqi is based upon numbers and, when properly performed, can bring us either joy or sadness. You Jews know of this art in the form you call 'pizmonim,' chants to praise God. Christians do the same."

When I arrived in Iskandariyyah from Sicilia, my condition was somewhat better than when I left Sicilia. I was, however, not looking forward to meeting my father.

As we passed the famous lighthouse of Iskandariyyah, I noticed that one side of the tower was crumbling from neglect. This world wonder was falling apart, and I thanked G-d that I could see it before it fell into the sea. The port was bustling with activity. We were fortunate to find a berth amongst the many ships already there. When we tied the cog to the dock, we were immediately accosted by an official, who demanded to know from where we had sailed and what cargo we carried. Several attendants, some of whom were armed, accompanied this official. He offered no greeting. The tone of his voice was that of annoyance. This man was, I assumed, the Sahib al-Suq, the chief of the port. My experience in Lishbunah came immediately to mind. William had told me I would be treated differently in al-Misr, but I now wondered if that was true.

I spoke to the official as authoritatively as I could.

"Excellency, we are from the Kingdom of Sicilia, and our captain will inform you about our cargo. On my part, I am seeking my father, Elazar, and his partner Abdullah ibn Khalid. Perhaps you know where I can find them?"

The man's demeanor changed at once. "You are the son of Elazar? That is a different matter. Let me welcome you to our port. I will not hinder you with official matters now. Feel free to discharge your captain and crew, and we can deal with the inconvenience of fees and taxes later. There is a clean and comfortable Funduq nearby." He motioned one of his attendants forward. "Mohammed here will direct them," he said. Then, pointing to a large building nearby, he continued, "Should you wish to see your father, may peace be upon him, you will find his partner, Abdullah, in that makhzan. Please give him my best wishes."

I was anxious to see my family after so long, so I directed the captain and his crew to follow Mohammed and told them I would find them later.

There was no missing Abdullah. My father had told me that Abdullah's girth was vast. His clothing was always of the finest materials and in the latest style. Such a gray-bearded man was directing some workers to move heavy sacks from one side of the makhzan. At first, he did not see me. When he did, he smiled and wiped the sweat from his face.

"Have you been standing there long, my friend? What can we do for you?"

I returned his smile and bowed. "I am Joshua, the son of Elazar. For all my life, I have wanted to meet you."

Abdullah's surprise registered on his face. He looked me up and down and smiled more broadly. Then tears began to fall, and he engulfed me in his arms. "Thanks be to Allah," he exclaimed. "I knew you were coming, but this is a surprise. Welcome, welcome; let me dry myself, and we will find somewhere to talk. Your father will return soon, but now I have an opportunity to learn more about you."

I started to answer, but Abdullah waved me to silence. "Wait, not now, come with me to my home. I will leave word as to where your father can find us. You must be tired from your journey."

We walked in silence through the crowded streets to what I thought was a grand palace of many stories near the port. Liveried servants bowed to Abdullah and opened the gate. Inside was a garden full of flowers and in the center was a large bubbling fountain. Abdullah motioned for me to sit on a bench near it and ordered his servants to bring refreshments and wine. When I expressed surprise at his request for wine, Abdullah exclaimed:

"I know we Muslims should not partake of the wine, but my grandfather believed the admonitions of our great poet Umar on this subject, and, after all, you are my guest."

A servant brought a platter of dried dates, fresh fruits, and a large earthen jug of wine. Abdullah served me a cup and said, "Now, tell me everything!"

And so, I did. I told Abdullah about meeting William, and my journey. He listened intently and asked many questions.

I had not spoken for long before Abdullah interrupted my tale. "Forgive me, but before it is too late in the day, I think we should deal with the cargo brought by your ship. I will take care of that now."

Abdullah clapped his hands to call for another of his servants. The man that appeared was finally dressed and carried a small pouch. Abdullah whispered an order. The man nodded his head, bowed, and left immediately.

"Now, that is taken care of," declared Abdullah. "Tell me more of your tale. Then again, we should wait for your father as I know he will wish to hear everything himself, and there is no point in your telling your story twice. Have some more wine, and I will send someone to fetch him."

While we waited, another concern came to mind. "Abdullah, what about the Sahib al-Suq? Is it not necessary for me to pay my entry tax?"

Abdullah shook his head and sighed. "William, that is not an issue. Do not concern yourself with such detail. That official earns his bread from us and will do as we ask. Have some more wine. All will be well."

It was not long before my father appeared in the garden. He was thin, and his countenance severe. He did not greet me with enthusiasm. Looking at me carefully, he smiled thinly and gave me a cursory hug.

"It has been a long time, my son. Your journey must have been difficult, but we expected you long ago. Now, there is little time to waste. Abdullah has, I am certain, already asked many questions. I am very busy now and cannot remain here. Abdullah's servant will show you to my home, and we can talk later."

This reception was deeply hurtful. I had expected anger or disappointment, not indifference.

"Father, I am sorry for my late arrival. You know my delay could not be helped," I said. "I faced many difficulties returning to you, but I have tried my best. It is good to see you again. Please forgive me."

Elazar stroked his beard and looked directly into my eyes. "There is a difference between trying your best and doing your best, my son. Go to my home, clean yourself, and then we will converse. For now, I must talk to Abdullah alone."

Abdullah was equally surprised at how my father had greeted me but said nothing. He motioned for one of his servants to show me to my father's house, which I soon discovered was as grand as the home of Abdullah and was not far away.

Much later that day, I met my father in the garden. He was alone. Desperate for his approval, I attempted to explain all that had transpired in al-Andalus. I expressed my regret for losing the gold ornaments and the cargo sent to Lishbunah. I told at length of the tribulations I had faced in Qurtuba and my journey back to Gharb al-Andalus. My father listened attentively. Otherwise, he made no comment. What I did not and could not do was explain my newfound beliefs and the resulting commitments I had made.

My father stroked his chin, sighed, and nodded his head when I had completed my tale.

"I understand the difficulties you have faced," he said. "But there is more to your story. Rabbi Maimon wrote to me after you left Qurtuba. He told me that, at the beginning, you were an excellent student. I understand you provided invaluable service to the city's rulers. However, Maimon believes you have fallen into bad company and have somehow lost your vision of yourself and your calling. He is concerned for your soul; he thinks the evils of anger and pride have afflicted you. You are my only son, Joshua. I feared that you could not follow me as a merchant and thus allowed you to become a scholar or a rabbi yourself. You have failed on both accounts."

I stood and paced nearby for a few moments to control my emotions. "Yes, father, I am angry," I said. "I cannot forget how we are treated in the land of Sepharad. I cannot forget the deaths of my friends. Look what has happened to you in Marrakech. Does it not make you angry that the Almohad have forced you to choose between exile and conversion to their faith? Does it not make you angry that our holy city is now at the mercy of the Christians, that the lands granted us by G-d are no longer ours? We live between Edom and Ishmael, and unless we resist, our people are doomed."

My father rose from the bench where he sat and shook his head in despair.

"G-d decides all, Joshua. I do not wish to pursue this subject any longer. I am going to our makhzan now, as I have matters to which I must attend. We can talk tomorrow. "

With that remark, my father turned his back and left the garden. I knew I had spoken insolently, but what was done was done. Perhaps, I thought, tomorrow would be different. My thoughts were interrupted by a smiling Abdullah, who entered the garden from the street. His smile fell when he saw the expression on my face.

"What is wrong? He asked. "Have you argued with your father?"

"Yes, Abdullah, I lost my temper. I tried to express my feelings, but I spoke in anger."

Abdullah nodded his head in understanding. "You have studied your faith, Joshua. Did you forget the commandments? These commandments are the same in your Tanakh as in our own Quran. Honor your parents, obey them, and respect their opinion. We call this obligation 'silat ar-Rahim,' which means upholding the ties to your family. That is one of the most important obligations we have. I suggest you think about this. Allah willing, tomorrow may be different."

The next day was, indeed, different. Both my father and I had tempered our feelings, and we ate our midday meal in peace.

"Let us forget our disagreement for now," Elazar said. "We will not be long together as I have a mission for you, and I do not wish animosity to exist between us. Let me tell you more. You know that conflict has disrupted our trade. No longer do we have freedom of the Middle Sea or access to the markets of the Greeks. For many years, merchants of our faith have traveled to al-Hind through Al-Bahr Al-Ahmar, to bring spices and cloth to al-Misr. It is time for our Collegantia to engage in this trade directly. Abdullah and I have decided to establish a makhzan and a permanent representative in the land of al-Yaman and, G-d willing, in al-Hind itself. There is a correspondent in the city of Aden with whom we have dealt for many years. His name is Madmun ben Hasan-Japheth, and he holds a prominent position in that city. He will know what commodities will bring us the greatest value and, we hope, will aid in establishing our venture. We have no one else to send on such an important mission. Abdullah's son is too young. It will be a long and dangerous journey, and I think you will learn much."

My father did not grant me an opportunity to refuse. That I would go on this journey was not in question. I gave a low bow and promised to carry out my mission to the best of my ability. I did have one more comment to make.

"Father, I have met the woman I wish to marry. If G-d wills, she will escape from Sepharad and travel here. Her name is Hannah. If I am successful, and if she does arrive, I beg your approval. She is a Karaite Jew."

For the first time, my father smiled. "You wish to marry, my son? This is welcome news, and, of course, I would agree. If she is a member of our faith, I do not care if she is a Karaite. I do not agree with their beliefs, but I see no harm so long as you agree to raise your children as your mother and I have raised you."

I thought to bring forth one other matter. "Father, when all is done, I have promised to go to Yerushalayim."

My father's smile quickly disappeared. "To whom did you make such a promise, son? To G-d or yourself? He shook his head and thought for a few moments before he continued. "Regardless, we will discuss that when you return. Now, Abdullah and I must plan for your journey. I suggest that you visit the city here and learn what you can. Make yourself comfortable in my home and meet me here in two days."

For the next few days, I wandered through the magnificent city of Iskandariyyah. My concern about the reception given to me by my father weakened as I visited the city's marvels. Most buildings were of several stories, and there were many places of worship for all faiths. What the people in the city call the 'Pillar of Columns' particularly impressed me. This edifice, towering high above the city, and built entirely of marble, inspired awe. It was constructed of a single block of stone amid a date-palm grove. No one knew how or why it was made, but I did hear a fantastic story. One day, a famous archer was discovered sitting at the very top of the column waiving to the crowd below. The column was too high to reach by any known means. How did he get to his perch? To me, such a feat was impossible. When I asked Abdullah about this, he gave me a simple explanation. The archer was famous for his skills, and, what he did was shoot an arrow tied to a long thin cord over the top of the column to the opposite side. Then, the archer attached a rope to one end of the cord, pulled this over the top, and anchored it firmly in the ground on one side. He used that rope to ascend to his perch and drew it up after him so that no one could see what he had done. Of course, the archer had an accomplice to assist him in his feat.

As promised, my father summoned me to the makhzan two days later. Abdullah was with him, and they instructed me to sit.

"It is time for you to begin your journey, my son," said my father. "I want you to meet your traveling companions." With that remark, he motioned a servant to bring others into the room.

Two men entered, each giving a low bow to both my father and Abdullah. Abdullah made the first introduction.

"This is Abdul Hamid," Abdullah said as he pointed to the smaller of the two. "Abdul Hamid has come to us from Tunis. He fled that city one year ago. A good friend of ours recommended Abdul Hamid for his knowledge of numbers. Although he has not been in our employ until now, he is highly qualified to keep ledgers and is willing to remain in al-Yaman as our clerk. He is, as you can guess, a Muslim."

Abdul Hamid was in his middle years. His features were sharp, and his beard well-trimmed.

It was his small eyes that concerned me. They constantly darted back and forth and appeared almost feral, as if he were searching for danger in every corner. I disregarded my misgivings and wished him peace. Abdul returned this greeting without expression. Abdullah then turned to the second man, whose girth matched his height.

"This portly gentleman is Nikos," he said. "We call him the Monk. Nikos has agreed to become our representative in al-Hind and promises to decrease his consumption of food for the duration of your journey."

Nikos had a broad smile and laughed at his introduction. I liked him at first glance and gave him the greeting of peace. "Why does Abdullah call you the 'Monk'?" I asked.

Nikos chuckled. "Because that is what I almost became! For three years, I studied at the monastery of Saint Macarius in the eastern desert. I never took vows, and I have yet to convince Abdullah of that fact. I am joining you because of my knowledge of the desert tribes and my skill with languages. I have nothing to keep me here and, in any event, cannot return to Constantinopolis, where I was born. I hope you will find me a useful companion on our journey."

I smiled at Nikos and welcomed him. "I will value your company, Nikos," I said. Before I could say more, my father motioned for someone else to approach. This man was as black as night. He was not tall but was wiry and thin. Stepping forward, he moved like a cat, silent and graceful. He extended no greeting. His expression was blank. He did not look directly at me, but through me, as if I did not exist.

My father smiled as he handed me a parchment. "This is my gift to you," he said. "This person is called Wallo and is of the Galla tribe in the far south. He has made this journey before and will be of value to you. Although Wallo's Arabic is not the best, he is quick to learn. Are you pleased?"

Wallo, who had remained silent, said in a toneless voice. "Sayyid, my people, are not called Galla. That is a bad word in my language. It is an insult. We are the Oromo."

I immediately thought of Blazh. "Father, this man is a slave?"

"Of course, I purchased him for you. His cost was high, but I wanted only the best for you," my father responded. "He can be insolent, but he is worthy of trust."

I shook my head. "Father, I cannot accept. Nikos and Abdul Hamid are welcome but not this man. I cannot; I will not keep slaves."

Both Abdullah and my father were puzzled by this reaction. "I do not understand," said my father. "Everyone keeps slaves. That is the way of the world. How can you refuse?"

I held up my hand to beg silence and summoned my courage. "Father, I have learned something of servitude in al-Andalus. To me, that condition is wrong. Our people were once in bondage. G-d saved us. How can we do unto others what we will not do to ourselves? I am sorry, father. I cannot accept. If you wish Wallo to accompany me, he must be free."

My father and Abdullah looked at each other and shrugged their shoulders. "You are making an error," said Abdullah. "But if that is what you wish, take the parchment your father gave you and go to the Qadi. Wallo must go with you. You can grant him his freedom and ask that the fact be properly recorded. Mark my words, however. That will be the last you see of him. Why should Wallo accompany you on a dangerous journey as a free man? There are safer alternatives for him here. Perhaps he will even want to return to his home in the south."

Wallo looked at me with a blank expression and said nothing. Abdullah had spoken as if Wallo was a mere chattel.

My father stoked his beard. His face betrayed his displeasure. "You can deal with that matter later today," my father finally said. "There are two others I want you to meet. They are outside now. Your journey may involve risk, and Abdullah and I want to take precautions. We have retained two skilled warriors to secure your safety. It would not be wise to travel with any more protection as you will not want to draw attention to your party. You will not be carrying anything of real value. It is prudent, however, to be cautious. Nikos has advised that you travel south to the port of Adabiya, on the western shores of the sea. We have chartered a ship, and it will be waiting for you. Although this is not the standard route, it will, he claims, be safer than following the pilgrim's path on the eastern bank."

"I know nothing of the route, so I will do as Nikos suggests, but how am I to purchase anything, father, if I have nothing to exchange?" I asked.

"I will explain later," my father said. "For now, you should know that gifts will be expected by all you meet. In your grandfather's time, we brought the parchment called 'waraq' from the East. Now we make this excellent product here in al-Misr. It is scarce and highly prized in al-Hind and al-Yaman. Our correspondent tells us that he needs a small quantity to write his poetry. It is not heavy, but you must exercise care that it does not become wet. We have packed the sheets in oiled skins for that reason."

I wondered how to conduct trade when I had nothing else to offer. My father said that all would be explained, so I let the matter rest. "If we are done here, father, I would like to take Wallo to the Qadi."

My father told me to wait and dismissed Abdul Hamid and Nikos. When we were alone, he said:

"Son, I did not want to divulge our plan to others in the room. As I said, it is prudent to be cautious. Besides the waraq, you will be carrying one hundred twenty gold dinars and a letter of credit for another eight hundred eighty, which you can present in al-Yaman. We have already placed that amount in our agent's account here in Iskandariyyah. Now, do what you must with Wallo and prepare to leave. We have already lost too much time."

When Wallo and I presented ourselves at the office of the Qadi, we were forced to wait. When we were finally ushered into the presence of the Qadi, I worried that my treatment would be the same as in Lishbunah. That was not the case. I was received with grace and polite salutations. When I handed the Qadi the parchment proving ownership of Wallo and explained my intent, his demeanor changed.

"You want to free this slave?" he asked. "Why? This man has been captive for many years, and, I see, he has already had two owners who have paid a significant sum for him. He has no coin to purchase his freedom. I do not understand."

I thought quickly. "Excellency, this man has done great service for me, and this is his reward. Does not the Quran say that if others have been kind to us, we have no choice but to return what we have been given?"

The Qadi shrugged and asked one of the attending scribes to write a parchment granting Wallo freedom. When we left the office, I gave the document to Wallo and smiled. "Peace be upon you, Wallo. Our business is done." As I turned to leave, Wallo lightly grabbed my arm.

"There is nothing for me in this place," Wallo said. "I will go with you."

I opened my mouth in surprise. "You are free, Wallo. You owe me nothing. I am certain you can find your place in al-Misr, or, if you wish, make your way home. Why would you put yourself at risk just to accompany me?"

Wallo looked at me, this time in my eyes, not through them but directly into them. "You are a good man, Sayyid," he said without expression. "You will become lost on your journey without me. I will go with you. I heard what you said to the Qadi. I have no choice. I will return the kindness you have given to me."

I sighed. There was nothing more I could say to change Wallo's mind. "Very well, let us return to my father and prepare for our departure. I welcome your company."

I spoke truly. There was something about Wallo that gave me comfort. It was how Wallo carried himself. He had an aura of nobility and strength. Whatever it was, I was pleased with his commitment. He was not a Jew, but, without reason, I believed I could trust him on the long journey to come.

Both my father and Abdullah were astonished when I gave them the news that Wallo would join my group of travelers.

"Thanks be to Allah," declared Abdullah. "He is the only one who knows the whole route. I did not expect this result, but I am most pleased. Your father and I were concerned about the wisdom of your decision. We were wrong. When you are ready, I will accompany you to the caravan sari where you will begin your journey."

XII

ISKANDARIYYAH TO AYDHAB
The Christian year 1147

Six camels were waiting at the Sarai, kneeling in the dust. Abdullah had chosen well, and each animal appeared healthy and well cared for. All of them smelled of must. The two guards, Mohammed and Rafiq, who would accompany us, were already present and loading provisions for the long march through the desert. Three camels carried only empty goat skins, which we would later fill with water. Nikos and Abdul Hamid brought their provisions in small woven satchels. Nikos had a small box which he carefully inspected and then placed in his robe. Wallo had made this journey before and slid into the saddle carpet of the smallest of the camels. His belongings were packed in a rolled carpet. Nikos chose the largest of the animals because his weight was too much for any other. Abdul Hamid watched with his beady eyes and then chose his own beast. I was the only one who had never ridden a camel and was nervous when I approached my mount. I wondered if it could turn its long neck and bite. I climbed carefully into the saddle and then almost fell from my saddle when it rose, groaning from its kneeling position.

When I had recovered my balance, I asked Nikos, "For how long will we ride?

"Six or seven days," Nikos said. "It will be slower going than traveling through the desert to the sea's eastern shore, but this route is far shorter and safer."

I did not find it comforting to know I would be riding my animal for many days. Of course, it might be better than walking, I thought.

For four days, we rode through the date palm orchards and cultivated fields south of Iskandariyyah. Mohammed led the way, and Rafiq took the rear. I soon became familiar with the rolling gait of my camel and discovered that riding could become soothing. With the plodding rhythm of the journey, I often lost myself in thought. Could I finally succeed and regain the respect of my father? Would I go to Yerushalayim when my task was completed? Would G-d deliver Hannah to al-Misr?

Traveling south by day, we found a place to rest each night near one of the many small villages. With one of my coins, Rafiq purchased water to fill the goat skins at the last of these inhabited places. The fields eventually gave way to a rocky, barren landscape marked only by low-growing brush. Travel was difficult for the plodding camels as many dry wadis and deeper ravines had to be crossed or bypassed. Because it was spring, the days were not unbearably hot, and the nights were cool. At dusk on the fourth day, everything changed.

Abdul Hamid was the first to see the red-orange cloud moving toward us. "Khamsin," he cried as he pointed to the cloud. Everyone but me knew what that meant and hastily covered their faces with the tails of their turbans. I did not know what was happening, so I followed the example of the others. Mohammed passed me a long thin rope from his saddle and instructed me to hold it part way and then give the balance of the rope to Wallo. Wallo did the same and then passed it to Abdul Hamid and then to Abdul Hamid, who was riding alongside Rafiq in the rear. Now we were all connected by the long thin rope. "Stay in line," shouted Mohammed. I still did not know what to expect.

The strangely colored cloud moved quickly and soon enveloped our party in blinding, fine dust. I could not see beyond the head of my camel. Were it not for the rope, I would be lost in the swirling maelstrom. For what seemed an eternity, the wind howled, and the grit of the dust stung my face. It was hard to breathe. So thick was the sand and so strong was the wind that I thought it would dislodge me from my saddle. Then, as fast as it appeared, the storm was gone, and the air cleared. I sighed with relief. Mohammed turned and smiled.

"Now you know something of the desert, Sayyid," he said. "The khamsin does not last long, but these storms have led to the death of many. Thanks be to Allah, we are safe."

Mohammed looked back and saw Wallo and Abdul Hamid holding the guide rope. Nikos and

Rafiq were nowhere to be seen. Abdul Hamid was puzzled when he pulled the rope given to Nikos. It was loose, its end frayed.

"Where is Nikos? I shouted. "Where is Rafiq?"

Abdul Hamid raised his arms in the air, a look of fear on his face. "I gave Nikos the rope, Sayyid. Nikos was to pass his end to Rafiq," he said. "Perhaps the rope was old, and it broke in the wind. If Allah wills, they will find us."

I turned to Wallo and the no longer smiling Mohammed. "We will wait here," I said. "We cannot leave them behind."

We dismounted from our camels and made camp amongst the rocks. It was not long before Nikos appeared, alone.

"What happened, Nikos?" I asked. "Where is Rafiq?"

Nikos shrugged. "My rope was broken when the winds struck. I tried to give another to Rafiq. He must not have taken it. I found you, and G-d willing, Rafiq will do so as well. We cannot have traveled far."

That Nikos could treat such a matter so lightly surprised me. Perhaps, I thought, this was not an uncommon event on such a journey. The sun was beginning to set in the west, and it would soon become dark, so I asked Wallo and Mohammed to build a fire. As the only light in the desert, it would act as a beacon for Rafiq. When all of us except Nikos lay in our blankets for the night, there was still no sign of Rafiq. Nikos said he would stay awake.

I had fallen into a deep sleep when a scream suddenly awakened me. Rubbing my eyes, I saw Mohammed leap from his blanket.

"Allah, Allah," he wailed. "I have been bitten! My arm is on fire." Mohammed wept as he writhed in pain. When Wallo and I went to his side, we saw a giant black insect with a fat tail creeping away from Mohammed's blanket in the firelight. At the end of the insect's tail was a sharp needle-like protrusion, and near its head, two outstretched claws. Wallo did not hesitate. He stamped on the insect and ground it into the desert floor. "What is that?" I cried.

Nikos, who also saw the insect, shook his head. "That is called an 'al-eaqrab'. The black ones are dangerous. There is no cure for their sting. We can only pray for G-d's mercy. Wallo cradled Mohammed in his arms, mouthing words in a strange language. There was nothing to do but wait. When the sun had fully risen, Mohammed gave a loud cry, and his body began to shake as if possessed by an evil spirit. Froth appeared on his lips, and he then became rigid. Mercifully, he then lost consciousness, and just as the sun reached its highest point in the sky, Mohammed breathed his last. Wallo and I carried his body to a nearby wadi and buried him under stones. Abdul Hamid chanted a short prayer while Nikos silently stood by.

As we returned to camp, Abdul Hamid, shaking his head and quaking in fear, whined:

"We must return to Iskandariyyah, Sayyid. We have no guards to protect us. It is dangerous, Sayyid. I am afraid. I beg you. Let us go back!"

To fail again to meet my father's expectations once again was impossible. "No," I said. "We must wait for Rafiq. This is a tragedy, an accident. We must be patient. We will remain here until tomorrow and pray that Rafiq will find us."

That night, Wallo took me aside and whispered, "Sayyid, this was no accident. I have seen aleaqurab before. Black ones do not live in this eastern desert. The kind residing to the west of the sea is yellow and does not have a fat tail. Something is not right."

"Wallo, you need not call me 'Sayyid,'" I said. "My name is Joshua, and you should call me that. You are a free man and have joined me not as a servant but as a companion. I know nothing about this place, but perhaps you are mistaken. If Rafiq returns, he will know for certain."

Wallo raised his brows but said nothing. When dawn broke the following day, there was still no sign of Rafiq. Once again, Abdul Hamid begged me to turn back. We had no guards, he said, and were defenseless if thieves or wild beasts attacked. I remained steadfast in my decision to proceed. Whatever the risk, I was determined to fulfill my father's charge. When asked, Nikos confirmed that my judgment was correct.

"There is no cause for concern," he said. "Rafiq may have abandoned us for his own reasons, or perhaps he became lost and now will follow the path back to Iskandariyyah. Who knows? There is no danger here. We have water and food. We have come too far and must continue. Have faith that your G-d will protect us. What happened to Mohammed saddens me, but we truly have nothing more to fear."

We left camp shortly after dawn. The water supply was diminished, as two of our goat skins were carried on Rafiq's camel. Nikos claimed this was no cause for concern, as reaching the seacoast was only a journey of two more days. There we would find a small oasis where more water would be available. That day, we traveled until the sun began to fall and again made camp. Nikos was in a joyful mood that night.

"We are almost at Adabiya," he said. "From there, we will take a ship to al-Yaman. The end of our journey is a cause for celebration. Look, I have been saving something to mark the occasion!" With that remark, Nikos pulled a small goatskin from his pouch. "This," he said, "is one of the better fruits of the vine available in al-Misr. I hope the heat has not damaged it." Nikos then produced four leather cups and poured the contents of the goatskin into each one. As expected, Abdul Hamid refused.

"I cannot drink this," he said. "It is forbidden."

"Nonsense," said Nikos. "Many of your faith drink wine; even the Qadi in Iskandariyyah does so now and then. A small sip will do you no harm."

Again, Abdul Hamid refused. Shaking his head, Nikos gave me a cup, and I readily drank from it.

Wallo accepted his portion and took a small sip. I noticed that Wallo grimaced when he tasted the liquid. Nikos dominated the conversations that night, telling rollicking stories of his time in the monastery and life thereafter. The wine made me drowsy, and soon I fell into a deep sleep.

Long after sunrise the following day, I woke with pain throbbing in my head. I rubbed my eyes, and when I looked for Nikos, Abdul Hamid, and Wallo, I found myself alone. Panicking, I called aloud. There was no response. As I stood to survey the surroundings, I discovered that not only were my companions gone, but so were the camels, all of them. How can this be? I thought. There must be a reason. Would Wallo abandon me? Abdul Hamid was too timid to venture far without company. I had no water, and all my possessions were gone. Surely, I thought, the others would return.

The day wore on, and the sun beat down. There was no shade in the barren desert. What had become a mild inconvenience now became torture. I did not know where I was or what direction to take, if I did choose to walk. I could live without food for a few days. Without water, I would die and I was very thirsty. As I thought about my condition, I became ever more despondent. Once again, I thought, I had failed. What would my father say? I still had the letter of credit and the gold dinars, but what good would that do in an empty desert? I did the only thing I could. I prayed to G-d and begged for mercy. I heard no reply, only silence.

The sun had just begun to set in the west when I saw three plodding camels on the horizon. I wondered if G-d had heard my prayer. I stood and waved my arms, hoping that I would be seen. Of course, these riders might not be friends, so I unwound the sling I used as a belt. As the animals came closer, I signed with relief. The first rider was none other than Wallo. Abdul Hamid followed, holding the rein of the third camel, which had no rider. I wept with relief at the sight.

"Where have you been," I cried when Wallo and Abdul Hamid drew near. "I have no water! Where is Nikos?"

"Allah be praised," said Abdul Hamid. "Nikos is no longer among the living. He would have killed me if Wallo had not stopped him. He was evil. He was a spy for the Emperor of the Greeks."

Wallo dismounted and took me in his arms. "Sayyid, I am happy you came to no harm," he said. "I tried to do what is right."

My emotions were in turmoil, relieved that I would not die in the desert from thirst, relieved that Wallo had not abandoned me. At the same time, I was confused. What had happened? The tale took time to tell.

What happened was this. During the evening of the celebration, neither Abdul Hamid nor Wallo had partaken of the wine offered by Nikos. Abdul Hamid had refused outright. After his first sip, Wallo found the taste of the liquid odd and poured the contents of his cup onto the ground. He did not let Nikos witness this as he had no wish to offend the Greek. Seeing that I had fallen asleep, Wallo and Abdul Hamid also decided to rest. Nikos said that he would stay awake and act as a guard. He produced a long dagger from his pouch and said he would keep it ready in case of an attack.

Wallo had found this strange but chose to say nothing, and he, too, fell fast asleep. When he woke, it was still dark. Wallo thought to relieve Nikos from his duties, but the Greek was nowhere to be seen. It was then that Wallo noticed that the camels were gone and that Abdul Hamid had also disappeared. Wallo attempted to wake me but without success.

"I knew then there was something wrong with the wine you drank, Sayyid. I thought it tasted odd, so I did not drink it. I was certain that Abdul Hamid and Nikos had betrayed us and left us to die in the desert."

"What did you do, Wallo?" I asked. "It was still dark."

"I ran after them, Sayyid. It was not difficult to follow the camels. The light from the moon and stars was enough for me to see their tracks. I did not know how far they had gone, but I can run much faster than a camel can walk."

"But you were unarmed, Wallo," I said. What did you think to do if you found them?"

Wallo gave a dark grin. "Oh Sayyid, I was not without a weapon," he said, producing a short spear, its iron point slightly bent. "It is not well constructed, but it was good enough."

I examined the spear. "From where did this come?" I asked.

"I made it," said Wallo. "I brought it in my carpet when we first loaded the camels. Now it has been damaged. I will need to make another."

"Thanks be to Allah," said Abdul Hamid. "If Wallo did not have his weapon; if he had not thrown it straight, I would be dead. Wallo saved my life."

I still do not understand," I said. Abdul Hamid sighed and attempted to explain.

"Nikos was evil," he said. "I had just fallen asleep when Nikos awakened me with a dagger digging into my throat. Look, you can see the mark here." Abdul Hamid lifted his chin to show me. "Nikos whispered that I must remain silent. He forced me onto a camel and tied me to the saddle. When we were distant from our camp, I asked Nikos why he was doing this. I remember he laughed as he answered. He was, he said, loyal to the Emperor of the Greeks. His task was to disrupt any attempt by the Jews to develop the trading route to al-Hind. Your family's Collegantia had grown too strong. The prospect of your family gaining strength in the trade with al-Hind had to be stopped, he told me. I had value for my skill in numbers, so he planned to take me to his monastery in the Eastern desert to serve the needs of his compatriots. Without water, Nikos said, you and your companion would die. No one would know of your fate. We had ridden until dawn when we heard a shout from behind."

"Then my fate changed," said Abdul Hamid. "Nikos turned to see that Wallo had followed. The Greek pulled my camel close to his and pointed his dagger at my side. He shouted to Wallo, 'Return to your master, or this infidel dies.' I prayed to Allah. I was sure that I was breathing my last. I thought my prayer had been heard when Wallo turned away. Nikos, too, believed that the matter was settled, and he turned his head away."

Abdul Hamid paused and began to tremble. "I will never forget what happened. Wallo threw his spear. It struck Nikos in the back. There was blood everywhere. You can still see it on the saddle. Nikos fell like a stone. Wallo said something like, 'I have no Master, Greek.' Nikos was not dead then. He was in great pain, and blood was coming from his mouth. I hope never to see anything like this again. We took the camels and left him there to die in the sand. That is what I remember."

I nodded my head in understanding. "Wallo, you took a great risk. Abdul Hamid now owes you his life, as do I," I said solemnly.

"Sayyid, I learned to use such a spear when I was a child. It has been a long time since I have practiced, but I trusted my skill and that my G-d, Waaqa, would guide my throw. There is something else. I do not know for certain, but I believe Nikos put the insect in Mohamed's blanket. Do you remember the small box he valued so much when we departed Iskandariyyah? I also think that he killed Rafiq during the Khamsin. Nikos was evil, Sayyid."

"Please do not call me Sayyid," I said. "I owe my life to you. I told you, my name is Joshua. I beg you to call me that."

Two days later, we reached the shores of the sea called 'Bahr-i-qulzum.' A fisherman told us that the town of Abadiya was only a short distance away to the south. Abadiya was only a tiny village, and a single vessel was drawn up on the marshy shore. This ship, called a dhow, was long and thin, with a single sail. Its timbers were held together by greased rope. The master of the vessel ran to meet us.

"Allah be praised. We had given up hope of meeting you," he cried. "My name is Ahmed." The shipmaster did not wait for a response. "If you are ready, we would like to sail south now. There is nothing in this place to keep my crew content. There is no mosque in which to pray, and food is scarce. I do not know why your relatives chose this place. Everyone else departs from the town of Aydhab, much further south. If it pleases you, we will sail there to load provisions. I have made space for you in the bow of my ship."

I was only too ready to embark and readily agreed. I asked what to do with the camels.

"A man in the village will buy them," said Ahmed. "He will pay less than your camels are worth, but you will not need them until you return. There will be many such beasts in Aydhab which you can hire for the journey back to Iskandariyyah." Ahmed bit his lip, unsure whether to comment further. After a few moments, he continued. "I must ask," he said.

"Why did you choose this route? Everyone else travels from Iskandariyyah to the town of Aswan on the river an-Nil and then across the desert by camel. That journey is much safer. Aswan to Aydhab is a journey of just a few days."

"We wished to find a new route," I lied. "We hoped to save time."

Ahmed shrugged his shoulders and said nothing.

Abdul Hamid offered to conduct the sale of the camels and soon returned with the proceeds. For once, he was smiling as he handed me three gold dinars. "Our steeds were more valuable than we thought," he said. "We only paid two dinars for them in Iskandariyyah, so the journey is already profitable."

While Abdul Hamid consummated this transaction, Wallo and I had loaded the waraq and our meager possessions, and soon, we set sail, leaving the village behind.

The sea was calm and the wind favorable, and thus, the voyage to Aydhab took only five days. Aydhab was no small village. Providing a transit point for both al-Yaman and the holy city of Mecca, it was a bustling metropolis. Ships of all kinds were tied alongside the docks. Most of these were ships known as jalabah and were much larger than Ahmed's vessel. One of these massive vessels had recently arrived, carrying eighty bails of lax, used for woodworking in al-Misr, small iron ingots called bayd, which were used to make the finest swords, and sixty large sacks of cinnamon. This cargo had an extraordinary value, and the ship had a crew of thirty. Muslims from al-Qahirah owned many of these larger vessels. Ahmed said they usually traveled together in a convoy known as the Karim fleet and were protected by a few Fatimid war vessels. It was always safer to join such a fleet for the journey further south to al-Yaman.

"You must pay the tax on your cargo, Sayyid, and we must provision our vessel for the journey to the port of Aden," said Ahmed. "You should also ask Ibn Najib for permission to travel with the Karim fleet. Those ships will depart two days from now."

"Who is this man, Ibn Najib?" I asked. Ahmed opened his mouth in surprise.

"You do not know who he is? Ibn Najib owns many of these ships and is close to the Grand Vizier of al-Misr. Nothing happens in Aydhab without his consent. He has no quarrel with Jews. He will, however, require payment."

Following Ahmed's counsel, we found rooms at an inn reserved for foreigners and enjoyed a hot meal for the first time in many days. There were many guests, some of whom were Jewish merchants. The inn provided no bedding or any other comfort. Besides the merchants, others who stayed at the inn were Muslims from al-Maghreb. These travelers were making their pilgrimage to the holy city of Mecca, which was only a two-day sail across the sea from Aydhab. There was one man who attracted my attention. He was seated on a cushion at a wooden table, surrounded by others who wished to hear the story he was telling.

"Who is that man?" I asked the serving boy.

"Oh Sayyid, that is Rabbi Benjamin of Tudela, the famous traveler. Everyone gathers around the rabbi each night to hear his tails. He has been everywhere!"

I moved closer to hear the rabbi's tale.

"It is true," said Benjamin to his audience. "I have seen it with my own eyes! "You can read about it in my *Book of Travels*."

"Impossible," said one of the onlookers. "You say that these people you call Falasha are all Jews?"

"Indeed, the Falasha are Jews. They live in a land far to the south called Thelasar. High mountains mark that place, and many Israelites live there. The Falasha are not under the rule of the Christians and have castles on the mountaintops. Yes, there is danger, but our people are strong. Often, these Jews raid the towns below and take the booty to their fortresses. No one has ever prevailed against them!"

Another of the onlookers shouted over the others so as to be heard, "This cannot be true, Rabbi. I have traveled to Aden in al-Yaman many times and have never heard of the people you call Falasha."

"That is because the Israelites live far away in the mountains. Yes, there are Christians and many people of no faith. The infidels have black skin and go naked and eat herbs like cattle. Do you know what happens to them?"

Many in the crowd nodded their heads in unison. The audience had heard the story before.

"The Christians and sometimes the Muslims raid into the lands of the plant-eaters. The raiders take bread, grapes, and figs and throw them to those people. When their victims run to take the food, they are captured and sold to the market in al-Qahirah."

Wallo, who was standing next to me, grimaced but said nothing.

"There is more," the Rabbi continued. "Many Christians near Thelasar know of the Israelites. Our language is used in their rites. Do you not know that the son of King Solomon and the queen of Sheba, Menelik, came to that country and brought with him the Ark of the Covenant? It is kept in a secret place, and even now, the ark is attended by Israelites who are descendants of King David."

This last remark caused consternation amongst the listeners, and several began arguing amongst themselves. Rabbi Benjamin used the turmoil to go to his room without speaking further.

Wallo and I returned to our wooden table, where Abdul Hamid had remained to keep our place.

"Wallo," I said, "why did that tale distress you?

Wallo frowned. "We do not eat plants like cattle, Sayyid. We do not run about naked. He knows nothing. He lies."

Once again, I reminded Wallo not to call me Sayyid and asked for further clarification. Wallo refused. "Another time, Sayyid. I cannot speak of this now. Let us find Ibn Najib before the sun sets.

Aydhab is a dangerous town, and we should not be walking at night."

"You know Aydhab?" I asked. "You have been here before?"

"Oh yes, Sayyid. I know this town well. Long ago, I met Ibn Najib under different circumstances. He will not know me, but I know him, and I can lead you to his place of commerce."

Once again, I begged Wallo not to call me 'Sayyid,' and together, we entered the busy street outside the inn. There seemed to be no reason to the labyrinth of dusty paths in the town, but Wallo knew the way. There were crowds everywhere. Merchants, sailors, soldiers, and veiled women and small children went about daily business. There were shops offering provisions for the ships. Others specialized in hempen lines, sailcloth made of palm leaf, and odd bits of timber. Amongst the crowds were rough-looking characters, eager to snatch an unattended satchel. Wallo, carrying his makeshift spear, led the way, and the crowd parted to let us pass. No one dared accost Wallo.

I thanked G-d for his presence as a guide. Without him, I would not have known the way. I did have a question.

"You carry your weapon openly, Wallo? Is that permitted?"

Wallo shrugged. "Here, anything is possible, Sayyid. Many of your faith, and even Muslims, have lost their lives in this place. Everyone knows the wealth made through trade with al-Hind, and newcomers are often the victims. With me leading the way, we will not be bothered."

Eventually, we arrived at a mud-built gated structure surrounded by a high wall. Nearby, a man was announcing the arrival of what he called 'new stock' and pointing further down the street. "What is this new stock?" I asked.

Wallo grimaced. "People like me," he answered. "Go inside the gate. I will stay here. I cannot look upon Ibn Najib. Your business will not take long. It will be best to return to our ship as soon as possible."

XIII

AYDHAB TO AL-YAMAN
The Christian year 1147

B eads of sweat dripped down the unsmiling, round face of Ibn Najib. There was no place to sit; I stood in supplication before the great man. Not only was Ibn Najib great in power but also in girth. I had never seen anyone so fat. He put the late Nikos to shame. There had been no formal greeting or wishes for peace, only silence when I entered the dark hot chamber in the single-story mud building. Clearly, Ibn Najib expected me to speak first.

"Excellency," I said. "I wish to join the Karim fleet. I understand that a fee is required."

Ibn Najib wiped the sweat from his jowls and nodded his head. "The fee is one hundred bezants," he said without expression.

I was shocked at this outrageous demand. "Did I hear you correctly, Excellency? One hundred bezants are a fortune!"

Ibn Najib sniffed and gazed at me with beady eyes. "You heard me correctly. You are a Jew, are you not? If you convert to the true faith, the cost will be less. Otherwise, the fee is as I have stated. Do not waste my time haggling. You have a simple choice. Pay the fee or sail to al-Yaman alone. To me, it is a matter of indifference."

I knew there was no alternative. To sail this sea without escorts would carry too much risk. Ahmed had told me that ships traveling alone were often subject to attack. An argument would not be prudent, I thought.

"Very well, Excellency," I said. "I only have gold dinars, so how much of that coin do you require?"

For the first time, Ibn Najib smiled. "That is unfortunate. We use bezants here. The cost will be eighty dinars. You may pay my clerk. We sail in two days. Make your ship ready. There will be no delays. Now leave me. I have other business to which I must attend. New slaves have arrived, and I must supervise their sale. Perhaps one of them would be of interest to you?"

"No," I said, trying to keep anger from my voice. "I have no interest in slaves."

"Then be gone from here. Pay my clerk."

I reluctantly paid the fee to a waiting clerk and left Ibn Najib's chambers. My store of gold dinars was rapidly disappearing. When Wallo and I returned to the Sari, Abdul Hamid was horrified at the price I had paid to join the fleet.

"Sayyid, you have been robbed. Gold Dinars are worth one and one-half bezants. You should only have paid sixty-six. This place is a den of thieves. I should have gone with you."

Two of the Jewish merchants seated nearby laughed when they overheard.

"You are new to the trade," declared one of them. "Your companion is right. Ibn Najib constantly subjects newcomers to pillage. You have much to learn!"

I hung my head in shame. Once again, I had failed as a merchant. I should have known the proper rate of exchange. It was, of course, too late to correct my error, so I only nodded my head and instructed Abdul Hamid to prepare for departure. I prayed to G-d that I would make no further errors.

Abdul Hamid chose to ignore my distress. "Sayyid, you are right to pray. Allah knows what is best for us. Have patience. Our captain Ahmed has already done what he must. We will be ready to depart with the fleet, and Allah willing, all will be well."

I had heard similar words before. The virtue of patience and hope was easier to consider than to practice.

Two days later, we boarded our small ship and commenced the long journey south down the Al-Bahr Al-Ahmar. The day was hot, and the breeze was a relief when we entered the sea with the other vessels. Perhaps twenty jalabah traveled together, accompanied by two Fatimid warships, one of which was a fire thrower. Archers manned the other. Our vessel was one of the smallest in the fleet. Because the winds were favorable, the journey to the dusty town called Sawakin, on the sea's western shore, took only one week. In Sawakin, Ahmed and the other captains provisioned their ships, and the fleet continued its voyage further south.

As we sailed, I noticed that Wallo spent long hours gazing at the distant shoreline, a wistful look on his face. When I inquired as to the cause of his strange expression, Wallo shook his head.

"I heard Abdul Hamid's words, Sayyid. All of us must have hope. Who knows what the future will bring?"

After another week at sea, Ahmed shouted and pointed to a group of islands directly in our path. "We have arrived in Dahlak," he said. "The waters here are dangerous, so we must take great care following the fleet. There are reefs everywhere. Many ships have been lost to their clutches. Now we will furl our sail and row."

The largest of the islands, Dahlak Kabir, provided a port capable of accommodating the entire fleet. Wallo had visited the island before.

"This place was a source of precious pearls and other shells since ancient times," Wallo said. "Fortunes were made in that trade. Now it is different. The people here make their living by providing provisions for ships bound for al-Yaman."

As the fleet landed at the port, the two Fatimid warships turned away and sailed north. The crew tied our dhow to the dock, and Ahmed, with Abdul Hamid in tow, went into the small town to purchase provisions for our final sail to Aden. Wallo and I remained at the ship, as did most other merchants. There was no inn on the island.

Ahmed and Abdul Hamid returned with our provisions later that day, bearing news that the fleet would sail in the morning. There had been a shipwreck two days ago. A vessel had attempted to sail through the reefs at dusk. The master of the fleet was now concerned there might be another accident if precautions were not taken and gave strict instructions that the fleet should follow closely. The winds were now calm and would be favorable for the journey. I had my own worries, having seen the Fatimid war vessels turn away.

"Our protectors have left us," I said. "Are we to be left alone?"

"No, Sayyid, there is an agreement," Ahmed responded. "The Sultan of this island will now provide his ships to keep us safe. You can see them at the entrance to the port. The fee you paid to Ibn Najib has covered the cost."

At dawn the following day, the crew was busy untying the lines binding our vessel to the dock. Wallo and I were watching the other ships make similar preparations when Ahmed came to me and spoke.

"I apologize for disturbing you, Sayyid. There is an old man who claims he is a follower of your faith. He asks to join us on our final sail to al-Yaman. This man insists he can pay for his passage, but from his appearance, I have doubts. Will you meet with him?"

There was little time, but I saw no harm in bringing another Jew on board. Perhaps this man could provide helpful information, and, in any case, it would be a relief to have another Jew with whom I could talk.

"Bring the old man to me, Ahmed. I am certain that we can provide for another passenger."

"As you wish, Sayyid. Please make your decision quickly."

The man who presented himself was old indeed. His gray beard was untrimmed, and his robe was torn and looked as if it had been immersed in water and then dried in the sun. He had no belongings.

Ahmed frowned as he presented the prospective passenger. "This man says his name is Abraham ben Yiju and is a Jew," Ahmed whispered. "As you can see, I doubt his ability to pay anything. I have not planned for another mouth to feed, and there is no place for him to sleep. "

I looked carefully at my visitor. Indeed, he did look like a beggar. Wallo, who was standing nearby, arched his brows. My anticipation of having another Jew with whom I could converse faded. I did not wish to make another error in judgment.

"You wish to travel with us?" I asked.

The old man smiled thinly. "Yes, I wish to join you. I must return to Aden in al-Yaman, and none of the other vessels have accepted my plea. Their captains claim I will bring bad fortune upon them. You are my last hope until another fleet arrives. As you can see, I have nothing to offer now. I can pay you for the passage when we reach Aden. That I can promise."

What was I to do? Bringing this man on board would involve an additional burden. Provisions purchased with my scarce cash were sufficient only for the crew, myself, and my two companions. Could I tell an old man that the only sleeping space was on deck?

Abraham saw my hesitation. "I confess my appearance is rather shabby. Did you see the wreckage on the reef when you entered the harbor? That was my vessel. I could swim. The others could not. Thanks be to G-d, I survived. I lost all my possessions. I swear I will pay you in Aden. I beg for your aid."

Ahmed heard this and shook his head. "It is bad luck to accept someone who has escaped a wreck in this way. Who knows what ill fortune he might bring to us? Please say no. He can always find passage on a ship in the next fleet."

Words of scripture came to my mind. 'Open your hand generously and extend to your needy brother any credit he needs to care for his wants.' That was the law of G-d.

Wallo, who was standing nearby, added his confirmation. "This man has suffered enough, Sayyid. I will sleep on deck, and we can all eat less. Our journey to Aden will take only another week."

I considered my response for a few short moments. I would ignore Ahmed's superstition.

"Very well, Abraham. You may join us, but I do not expect a fee. You owe me nothing. Let us depart."

Ahmed scowled at this decision, but there was nothing he could do. I was certain I had done what was right. I had followed the law of G-d, and indeed that act would counter any ill fate. Of course, Wallo was correct. Sharing their provisions with this ragged beggar would cause no actual harm, and an act of charity was called for.

Given the delay in accepting Abraham as a passenger, our ship was the last to leave. However, the seas were calm, and the wind was light as we threaded through the dangerous reefs. The other ships in the fleet were still within sight, and all was well. I was happy that there was another Jew on board with whom I could converse.

"Tell me what happened, Abraham. What were you doing on the ship that was lost?"

"That," said Abraham, "is a long story. I should not have left Mangalore in al-Hind. Our new factory had just produced its first lot of bronze, and it was thought prudent for me to accompany the shipment through Aden to Dahlak. You see, our captain was new. He lacked experience, and I have traveled these waters before. I tried to tell that fool not to cross the reefs in poor light, but he failed to listen. You know the result. I was foolish to go."

"So not only was the crew lost, but all of the cargo?" I asked.

"Yes, all of it. One hundred *bahars* in weight. It would have fetched a great price in al-Misr.

"Then your master will be furious," I said. I remembered the words I had been told when I lost my cargo in Lishbunah. "At least you are alive," I said. "What will you do now?"

"There is no reward without risk, young man. We will make more of the metal and make another attempt. What else can we do?"

I was surprised at Abraham's seeming indifference to the tragedy. He must be a clerk on the verge of retirement from trade, I thought. His master should have chosen a younger man to accompany the shipment. News of such a valuable cargo being lost through error would not be received with kindness.

"What plans do you have?" I asked. "Will you settle in al-Yaman or return to al-Hind?"

"I have many friends in Aden, but I will return to Mangalore. That is my home. I am married, you see. My wife, Ashu, and my grown children will be waiting for me, and, of course, that is where our factory has been built. I love the land of al-Hind and have done well in that place. Do you intend to go there from Aden?"

"I do not know," I said. "This is my family's first venture in this trade. I will meet someone named Madmun. My father claims this man will help us."

Abraham nodded his head in understanding and smiled. "You must mean Madmun ben Hasan. He is a rabbi and, indeed, enjoys considerable power. Your father has chosen well."

For the next three days, we sailed through calm seas with the following wind. Although we remained far behind the main fleet, this did not concern Ahmed.

"So long as there is no storm, we are safe," Ahmed said. "We can see the fleet on the horizon. All will be well."

The slow, steady travel provided an opportunity to learn more about the new passenger. Abraham had come from Tunis long ago, and, following a few years in al-Qahirah, he had seized an opportunity to visit Aden. It was there that he learned the art of trade.

"Although my sojourn in Aden was of great benefit, I had, shall I say, a problem with the local ruler and found it necessary to travel further. Thanks be to G-d, I ended my journey in the city of Mangalore. Have you heard of this place?"

I admitted my ignorance of this place but wondered what problem forced Abraham to leave Aden.

"Mangalore is an ancient city," continued Abraham. "It is an ideal port on the coast of al-Hind and has enjoyed a thriving trade with the west for over a thousand years. The local inhabitants accept Muslims and those of our faith. We all are treated with fairness. There is both a mosque and a place of worship for our people. Of course, there are difficulties, but I love the city. I did well there."

Wallo interrupted Abraham's tale and pointed to a small ship in the distance. "Look, he said, someone on board is waiving to us for aid."

Ahmed had also seen the ship and steered towards the other vessel. As we drew closer, I saw a small, single-masted ship resting motionless in the water. A man on the prow continued to wave his hands in the air. There was something amiss.

I thought that the distressed vessel must have been a member of the fleet. Ahmed, however, was not so confident, and Wallo advised caution.

"Let us sail closer to better see the cause of their distress," Ahmed said.

Because the wind blew from the north, Ahmed circled the smaller vessel and headed into the wind to slow our progress. As we approached, it appeared that only one person was on board. He was standing at the bow. There was cargo on deck covered with woven hemp. Ahmed called to the man and asked why he needed aid. Instead of responding, the man pointed to his ears and shook his head. Abraham, who had joined the others, said: "He tells us he cannot hear. The wind is blowing against us. Perhaps we should move alongside."

Ahmed maneuvered our dhow to within ten cubits and again asked the cause of distress. Instead of responding, the hemp cover was thrown back, revealing at least six armed warriors. One of them jumped to the rail, drew back a bow, and aimed it at Ahmed.

"Lower your sail," shouted the man at the bow, who was the leader. "Do it now, or you will die." Seeing this, Ahmed ordered his crew to comply and raised his hands in surrender. Both ships were now motionless in the water.

My hands were not visible to our assailants, so I carefully withdrew the sling from my belt and placed one of the several stones I always carried in its pouch. A glance showed that Wallo had taken Abraham by the arm and was walking to the stern. The crew, as ordered, lowered the sail and gathered mid-ship. Abdul Hamid cowered on the deck with his hands covering his head. The attacking vessel maneuvered alongside, and I heard a grappling hook landing on the rail. One of the warriors climbed the side of our vessel and, without hesitation, struck down the nearest of our crew with his curved sword. Another warrior followed and, ignoring Wallo, grabbed Abraham by his hair. The archer continued to aim his arrow at Ahmed. The attack had been quickly made, and if we did nothing now, all would be lost.

I did not think. I acted. I made one swing with my weapon and cast my stone directly into the archer's chest. The force of the blow was such that the archer fell into the crowd of assailants who were preparing to board. The archer's fall caused the smaller vessel to rock violently, and the leader of their assailants lost his balance as well.

"Hold," screamed the man who was holding Abraham. His sword was at Abraham's throat. The warrior started to say more, but his mouth opened wide as the point of Wallo's spear emerged from his stomach. Blood poured from the wound and he fell to the deck in agony. Wallo extracted his weapon and held it ready. Seeing what had transpired, the other warrior raised his sword and rushed towards Wallo, who quickly pushed Abraham aside. Wallo shifted his grip on the spear and casually brushed his assailant's sword aside and then, faster than the eye could follow, reversed his weapon, and thrust the point into his enemy's chest. One of our crew members had the sense to pick up an abandoned sword and cut the line attaching our vessels.

"Raise the sail,' ordered Ahmed. "Turn away from the wind!"

Once again, I aimed my sling and threw. Due to the rocking of the smaller vessel, I missed my intended target, and my stone hit the leader's upper thigh instead of his head. That was sufficient. He cried out in pain and fell to the deck of the smaller craft. A few moments later, our vessel pulled away. With the following wind and the sail fully raised, we soon left the attacking vessel behind.

"Now you see what ill fortune brings," muttered Ahmed, as he ordered the crew to throw the bodies over the side and clean the deck of blood.

Still quaking with fear, Abdul Hamid protested that the bodies should be appropriately buried on land, as Muslims. The laws of Islam, he said, prohibited burial at sea.

"Nonsense," said Ahmed. "For all we know, they were Greeks. Regardless, they were thieves." Ahmed then turned to Wallo and me and praised us for our courage and quick action. "Thanks be to Allah. You saved us all."

Abraham, who had remained silent during the cleansing of the ship, placed his hand on Wallo's shoulders. "You saved my life. I can never thank you enough." Addressing me, he said:

"You are blessed to have such a slave, Joshua. Thanks be to G-d, you permitted him to carry arms. And you, I never expected you to have such courage and such skill with an ancient weapon. I will repay you. That I swear before G-d!"

I smiled. "Wallo is not my slave, Abraham. He is my companion. We are all blessed by his presence."

Abraham was surprised at this response. He stroked his beard.

"You gave him his freedom?" Abraham asked. "You have done what is right. I did the same for a slave woman I acquired in al-Hind. She is now my wife and the mother of my children. G-d blesses those who do good."

Ahmed, accompanied by the still-shaken Abdul Hamid, gathered his crew, and together, they prayed to Allah for their deliverance from certain death. As they did so, I began to pray as well. I could not avoid thinking about the events that had transpired. Was it true that bringing the sole survivor of a shipwreck on board brought ill fortune? The Muslims certainly believed that. If I had done what was right by offering my hand to a needy brother, how could G-d then punish me for following the law? Perhaps G-d had aided my stone to be thrown true. Was that my reward? And then there was the fleet. I had paid most of my coin to join it, only to be left behind defenseless. Was that G-d's plan? These thoughts swirled through my mind. I prayed for an answer but received no response; only the sound of softly lapping waves on the ship's hull.

XIV

ADEN IN THE LAND OF AL-YAMAN
The Christian year 1147

The journey to Aden took another six days. By the time we reached the port, our provisions were virtually gone. The other ships in the fleet had already arrived and were now anchored in the harbor. All of these ships were busy unloading their cargo onto smaller boats. There were no docks for large vessels. A large crowd of laborers had gathered on the shore, ready for the arrival of the Karim fleet. Food stalls with fresh fruits and meats to serve the visiting seamen lined the shore. No one noticed our late arrival, and we had to wait for some time before one of the ferry boats came alongside. The port itself was filled with ships from al-Misr and from al-Hind itself. There were Persians, Arabs, and Jews. Strangest of all were the merchants and sailors from al-Hind. These people had darker skin and wore strange costumes. The language they spoke was unlike any other. We gathered at the rail as the smaller boat was tied to our ship.

Abdul Hamid was mesmerized by the bustle in the port. "I did not think anything could compare with Iskandariyyah. I was wrong," he said. "How can we succeed in commerce when there are so many merchants?"

"All will be well," answered Abraham. "Have patience, and you will see."

I asked Ahmed to wait at anchor until we confirmed our plans. Ahmed had no issue with my request, as my father had paid in advance for a return to Aydhab. As we prepared to disembark, I assumed that was the last I would see of Abraham. "Where will you go now?" I asked.

"You said you planned to visit Madmun. I will take you to him. This is the least I can do. You must also pay the port fees, and I can help you with that."

I did not believe Abraham could help with port fees and thought it would be ill-advised to present myself to Madmun in the company of a beggar. I began to protest. Abraham held up his hand.

"Do not be concerned about my appearance. Madmun is a friend, and unless you have forgotten, I owe you for my passage and my life. Have faith and follow me."

Wallo shrugged, and I shook my head in resignation. The idea that Abraham could or would pay for his passage, much less the fees for landing at the port, was ridiculous, but, I thought, it would do no harm to have assistance in finding Madmun. Abraham could remain outside when we visited Madmun's place of business. Thus, Wallo, Abdul Hamid, and I disembarked on the shore and followed Abraham out of the port. As we pushed through the crowds, I noticed many common laborers' mouths were painted red. When I asked Abraham about this, Abraham smiled.

"That color comes not from paint but from their habit of chewing a nut from a special palm tree called 'faufal.' Many people claim it provides strength and energy. Chewing it becomes a habit. Supplying this nut is good business."

Passing through sores of huts made from palm leaves for the common workers and stalls filled with spices and cloth, we followed a dusty street up a small hill into the city's heart. There were many two-story mud-built buildings that appeared to serve as both living accommodations and storage places for merchandise. A short distance from the port, space opened for larger villas made of stone. One of these, surrounded by a high wall, was our destination. Two soldiers guarded the entrance. To my surprise, both bowed deeply and opened the gate when they saw Abraham. A servant inside bowed as well and ushered us into a lush garden. Seated at a bench was a gray-bearded man who, when he noticed us, stood, opened his arms, and laughingly embraced Abraham.

"What are you doing here, you rascal? You look like you have been rolling in the mud. Did you receive my letter? You have swindled me for the last time, scum. I should have you placed in prison. From the look of you, that is where you have been."

Abraham laughed as well. "I did not receive your letter, Rabbi. You must have sent it to Mangalore. I assume you are complaining about my last shipment of faufal nuts. One cannot always expect the best of the product, and you know the Muslim seller Mansur in al-Hind is not to be trusted. Were the nuts too red for your liking? In any event, I am confident you sold them, regardless of their condition, and made a great profit, did you not? Returning the embrace, Abraham continued to laugh.

"With great difficulty, I did sell the nuts to local merchants. Next time make certain they are white, not red. However, I cannot complain about profit. However, my friend, you smell rotten. Who are these companions you have brought to me without ceremony? Do these gentlemen know what a scoundrel you are?"

Abraham gravely bowed. "Forgive me, Rabbi," he said. "These are my friends. They saved my life. Joshua here is the son of one of your correspondents and has traveled from al-Misr just to see you. Where are your manners? We are hungry and in need of a drink. Is this how you greet members of the faith?"

Abraham turned to me. I had been staring open-mouthed during this interchange.

"This rude Jew is the famous Rabbi Madmun ben Hasan," he said. "This rabbi complains about me, but he is the richest amongst us all. Madmun is the Nagid, the leader of the Jewish community of merchants. He owns many ships and is the supervisor of the port. I would have nothing to do with him if it were not for his position. Of course, the rabbi is my friend and teacher of our faith, so

I forgive his transgressions. Introduce yourself, Joshua. Perhaps you will find his favor."

For a moment, I was at a loss for words. Finally, I said, "Rabbi, my name is Joshua ben Elazar. My father has corresponded with you and told me you might assist us in establishing commerce with al-Hind. These are my companions, Wallo and Abdul Hamid. I am honored to meet you."

"I do not know why you accompany the thief Abraham, much less why you saved his life, but yes, I have received letters from your father. We have done some small commerce together. Please, welcome to you all, and let us go into my home. I will call for food and drink. You have a long story to tell, do you not?"

With that remark, Madmun took Abraham by the arm and motioned for the others to follow. Inside the villa, we were led to a grand salon filled with cushions, low tables, and a large desk covered with documents. Madmun whispered to one of his servants, and soon plates of fruit and rice with meat were brought. Rabbi Madmun asked Abraham to relate his tale when all had been fed.

Well into the day, Abraham related all that had transpired since his departure from Mangalore. He provided vivid detail about the loss of his ship and the attack they had suffered at sea. Madmun listened intently and nodded his head in understanding.

"So, your friends here gave you free passage and saved you from certain death? They deserve a reward, do they not? G-d put them in your path."

Madmun turned to me and pointed his chin at Abraham. "Your new friend is rich, you know. He may be the wealthiest of us all. He was clever enough to construct a great factory in Mangalore to produce brass and iron. The rulers of al-Misr need his product to defend against the Christians. Did this habitual liar tell you all this? By the look on your face, I gather he did not."

Indeed, I was shocked at this information. My assumption about Abraham had been very much wrong.

"I think G-d will bless you," said the rabbi. "You risked your lives to save a man you believed to be a beggar. The question, of course, is whether this thief will honor his words to you. What do you say, Abraham?"

Abraham did not respond for some time. "Let me think, Rabbi. I have questions for Joshua and his companions. But first, can you tell me if any of my ships have arrived?"

"Not as yet," said the Rabbi. "I understand that we are expecting several ships from al-Hind to arrive soon. I was hoping you had sent me more nuts, white ones this time."

Abraham then turned to me. "What cargo did you bring to Aden? I have never asked you that question."

"Only sheets of waraq for you, Rabbi Madmun. That is a gift from my father. I also have a letter of credit for eight hundred eighty dinars my father asked to present for exchange."

Madmun smiled at this. "Waraq, you say? I am pleased. My stock is finished, and it is the best means of recording my poetry. I did not know how to obtain more. In exchange, there will be no port fees for you. Of course, I will honor your father's letter of credit and will exchange the amount for Maliki dinars, the currency we use here."

Abraham was still thinking. He turned to me and asked, "What are your plans now that you have arrived in Aden?"

"My father instructed me to ask Rabbi Madmun for his advice," I answered. "Our Collegantia wishes to establish a permanent presence here and in al-Hind. Abdul Hamid has agreed to be our agent. If I must travel to al-Hind, I am prepared to do that."

Abraham stroked his beard. "I think the rabbi would give you the same advice as would I. You see, there are only a few times during the year that the winds are favorable and safe enough for travel to al-Hind. If you are determined to go, you must plan for a sojourn of at least two years. Is that what you intend?"

I was not happy with this news. Two years? If Hanna arrived in al-Misr, how could I ask her to wait that long? I had expected to comply with my father's instructions in much less time.

Before I could answer, Rabbi Madmun interjected. "I see from your face that this news is a disappointment. You do not need to travel so far, providing, of course, that Abraham does the right thing. You could not have a better representative in that country. We will aid Abdul Hamid in establishing a makhzan here. What do you think, Abraham?"

Abraham smiled. "Oh, great Rabbi, we welcome your wisdom and kind offer of my services. However, I agree. That is the least I can do. These people saved my life. Here is what I suggest. I will represent their interests in al-Hind and advise what commodities to purchase. However, there is more I must do to better express my thanks and repay the cost of my passage. I will now visit my agent, who has most likely written a letter to my family to notify them of my death. That thief is thinking of how he will dispose of the cargo on my next vessel. And you, Rabbi, I am certain you will also offer your hospitality. My companions must need rest."

Rabbi Madmun laughed. "Of course! I have no choice in this matter. I will have someone show you to your rooms. We can speak again in the morning."

The next few days passed quickly. With the help of one of Madmun's staff, Wallo, Abdul Hamid, and I were shown the city's sites and introduced to various purveyors of merchandise from al-Hind. The town itself was surrounded by mountains and was exceedingly hot. I was amazed that water was supplied from huge cisterns constructed on the side of one of the mountains. No one knew who had built these basins to collect rain from the seasonal storms. They were the city's sole source of fresh water. The port was well situated in a large estuary filled with ships.

"Is trade the only activity in this city? I asked.

"Indeed, it is," answered Madmun's assistant. "There are only three kinds of people here: merchants, porters, and fishermen. Most of the porters are slaves."

Wallo glanced sideways at the man's comment.

"We depend upon cities further inland for most of our food and drink. Let us go into the port, and I will show you how we have become rich. Our product here is trade," the assistant continued.

In the port, ships from everywhere in al-Hind were anchored. I asked which ones belonged to Rabbi Madmun and was shown at least ten of them. The rabbi was certainly wealthy! All the inbound ships brought cargos of spice, cloth, iron, and forest products. The aroma of the spices in the market was overwhelming. I was particularly interested in goods I had never seen before. One of these was a crystalline substance called *kafur*, derived from tree bark. These trees did not grow in al-Hind but in a place much further east. Many of the ships from al-Hind unloaded their cargo into smaller boats, which were rowed to the shore, and then transferred to booths from which the goods were immediately sold. Abdul Hamid was fascinated; many of these booths posted signs showing prices.

"Sayyad, look at these prices," Abdul Hamid exclaimed. "Kabbaba is selling for twenty-three dinars per bahar. That could be sold in Iskandariyyah for three times that amount. And can you believe it? One bahar of cardamom is selling for forty-eight dinars. Do you know what that would fetch in al-Misr? I would wager that the cost in al-Hind is half the cost here."

Abdul Hamid was so excited that he lost interest in anything else and wanted to purchase merchandise immediately.

"Wait," said Madmun's assistant. "These are prices for the unwary. The good merchants will place their commodities in makhzans and negotiate the price with those they trust and know well."

I noticed that many Karim fleet ships were loading cargo to return to al-Misr. They had not wasted time. I asked Madmun's representative why everyone was acting so swiftly.

"The winds are favorable," he said. "The storm season is approaching, so the wise merchants complete their commerce quickly. You, however, should be patient. You should first hire a makhzan for your commerce. Abdul Hamid will need a place to do business and stay. Shall I show you what is available?"

We immediately agreed with this sound advice. Thus, we spent the balance of the day searching for a storage place and an appropriate residence for Abdul Hamid. As evening approached, we had accomplished this mission. The makhzan was small and far from the port, but the cost was reasonable. There were two rooms above the makhzan which were suitable for Abdul Hamid's residence. Abdul Hamid was happy with both his proposed accommodation and the makhzan.

"It is prudent to be modest for now. Let us see what we can do, and if we are successful, we can hire better facilities."

Wallo, who had silently observed all that was happening at the port, finally spoke.

"Sayyid, many of the porters are slaves. Some look like me. There must be a market for captives, and I do not wish to go anywhere near it. What if the paper you gave me in al-Misr is not recognized here? Am I safe?"

"Wallo, I owe you my life," I said. "I will not permit anything to happen to you. You need not stay in this place. Let us see what G-d plans for us. And please stop calling me Sayyid."

Wallo reluctantly accepted my assurance, and together we returned to Rabbi Madmun's villa. Along the way, we saw many similar grand estates owned by Muslim and Jewish merchants who had become fabulously wealthy from the al-Hind trade. Abraham explained that the best homes were close to the port where they could be cooled by breeze from the sea. Most of the workers, he said, lived in small valleys further away. I began to dream that I, too, could one day join the ranks of the successful merchants.

What is becoming of me? I thought. I have a duty to G-d, and that obligation has nothing to do with accumulating wealth.

As we visited the market and explored the surrounding area. Abdul Hamid met other Muslim agents and merchants, and I met other Jews who were active in trade. Each evening, we ate meals with Rabbi Madmun, and I told the tale of my adventures in Sepharad.

"You say you studied with Rabbi Maimon?" said Madmun. "He is a great man. You are privileged to have such a teacher. Why did you not complete your studies? Not many are granted such an opportunity. Of course, G-d has blessed you. The Almohad have captured the city, and we hear tales of terrible persecution. I pray the rabbi is safe and has escaped Qurtuba by now. Do you intend to continue your studies, or are you now a merchant?"

By this time, I felt comfortable enough to explain the dilemma I faced. I had sworn to G-d that I would join my friends in Yerushalayim and free it for the people of Israel. I confessed that I wished to marry a woman whose father was a Karaite. My father, I said, had agreed to that union, providing that I successfully established a venture to trade with al-Hind.

Rabbi Madmun listened intently as I spoke. Eventually, he held up his hand and motioned me to silence.

"Do you believe the Karaite to be correct in their interpretation of our faith?" Madmun asked. I answered truthfully.

"Rabbi, I no longer know what to believe. We Jews are treated like dirt everywhere. I have seen this myself. G-d granted us dominion over all of Israel, and infidels now occupy our land. How can we survive without a home? How can we fulfill the laws of G-d if we are caught between the oppression of Ishmaelites and the Christians? Is it not our obligation to fight against the Amalek? Nevertheless, I am in love. I want a family. I must honor my father's wishes as I have so often failed him. I do not know what to do."

Rabbi Madmun nodded his head in understanding. "Let me tell you a story," he said. "Once long ago, the people of this land worshiped many gods. They engaged in trade with lands all over the world and controlled the spice trade with al-Hind. The Greek Christians coveted this trade, and they still do to this day. Fearing conflict, the people here began to worship only one creator called Rahmanan, the Lord of Heaven. That satisfied the Greeks for a while. Then, a king from Arabia named Tub'a Abu-Kariba arrived as a conqueror. I assume you know there were many Jewish tribes in Arabia at that time. As King Abu-Kariba traveled south, he came upon a city called Yathrib, which the Muslims now call al-Madinah. He passed through the city without resistance and left his son as governor. However, the people of Yathrib did not accept this new young ruler and killed him. Abu-Kariba returned and laid siege to the city when he learned of this. Many Jews joined the king and fought well. Unfortunately for the king, he became gravely ill after his conquest. His followers called two Jewish physicians to cure him, and they did. The king was so grateful that he converted to our faith then and there. So convinced that our faith is true, the king required all his subjects to convert. That is how the kingdom of Himyar was founded. All the lands of al-Yaman became Jewish, and that kingdom survived for three hundred years, until the arrival of the Muslims."

I could not hide my surprise. "Al-Yaman was a Jewish kingdom? No one ever told me that!"

Rabbi Madmun smiled. "There is much to learn," he said. "It is a fact that this land belonged to our faith. How that came to be is another matter. I have told you one story. There are many more, and all are different. What is certain is that our people have been here for over one thousand years and ruled this land for at least three hundred of those. If you venture north, you can find inscriptions in Ashurit attesting to our presence and rule. Greek Christians also lived nearby, and there were many wars between us. The last of these wars involved Christians from the north and from the land the Greeks called Aithiopia. We sought aid from the Persians and defeated them. And then, the Muslims came."

"Rabbi, I do not understand why you tell me this," I said.

"I am addressing your concern, Joshua. You said that you wished to free Yerushalayim and that you had sworn to do so. Therefore, is it not true that you commit to a task that rightfully belongs to G-d? Once, we ruled this land. Now we do not. Who are we to question the will of G-d? What we must do is maintain our faith and follow the laws.

For the moment, we live peacefully together with the Muslims. We work together in harmony and worship in our ways. As you know, I am the Nagid, the leader of the Jews in al-Yaman. We do our best to maintain our traditions and nurture relations with Jews all over the world. I enjoy great privilege and have done well. Will that last? Probably not. Even now, there is conflict amongst the Muslim rulers, and rumors circulate that we will be subject to forced conversion. The ways of G-d are mysterious, Joshua. We must open our hearts and minds to all possibilities and, above all, have confidence in Him. G-d will reward the good and punish the wicked. That is a basic tenet of our faith."

I pondered the rabbi's words. There was no easy answer. Rabbi Madmun recognized the turmoil in my thoughts and suggested that, for the moment, I concentrate on my duties as a merchant. That was the task that deserved the most attention. "You must do what is right in the eyes of G-d," he said.

Following this advice, we went into the market again to learn more about trade with al-Hind and the opportunities it presented. Several days passed, and there had been no word from Abraham. I began to wonder if I would hear from him again.

One morning, as my companions and I were preparing to revisit the market, Abraham finally appeared.

"I have good news," Abraham declared. "My ship has finally arrived. Call for the rabbi. I want him to examine the manifest."

When Rabbi Madmun arrived from his workplace, he looked through the document and said nothing was amiss. "Do you wish me to calculate the tax on this shipment?" he asked.

"Not yet," said Abraham. "I want you to attest to its accuracy. First, however, I would like to ask Abdul Hamid for his opinion," he said as he handed the document to my agent.

Abdul Hamid scrutinized the manifest and gasped. "This is a valuable cargo indeed," he exclaimed.

"That it is," said Abraham. "As you can see, my vessel is carrying three bahars of Cinnamon, three bahars of al-Luban, two bahars each of azafran and zanjabil, and five bahars of kabbaba." My cost in al-Hind was equal to five hundred dinar. Do you agree, Abdul Hamid?"

Abdul Hamid nodded his head in agreement. He was still awed by the value of the cargo. What was the purpose of this ritual, I wondered?

Abraham turned to me and said, "I owe you for my passage and my life. Here is what we will do. For your first venture into trade with al-Hind, I will accept payment of five hundred dinars, and the cargo is yours. It would be best if you had a bigger ship, so that is yours as well. Do you accept?"

Abdul Hamid could not contain himself. "Sayyid, this is extraordinary. This cargo will fetch a far greater sum in al-Misr. And the ship as well?" Allah be praised. Our venture will be a success, and we have done nothing."

Again, I was lost for words. "That is too great a gift, Abraham. I only followed our law when I accepted you as a passenger. I did not expect a reward."

"That," said the rabbi, "is to your credit. Following the law is blessed by G-d. My friend Abraham is merely returning your favor. He may be a thief and a liar, but he is no fool. If your first venture is successful and your father's Collegantia becomes fully engaged in trade, Abraham will make a proper return on his generosity."

Madmun continued, "I will follow his example. The tax on this cargo would be almost one hundred dinars. I will waive that for this one time. As I said, we will all profit from your success. Not today, of course, but next time and thereafter."

"There is something else," said Abraham as he turned to Wallo.

"You, my friend, saved my life at the risk of your own. I have thought of a small gift, but you must wait another day or two. The sailing season is ending very soon, so I advise you to prepare for your return to al-Misr. In the meantime, I am certain that the rabbi will be kind enough to assist in disposing of your ship and in the transfer of ownership. Is that not correct, Rabbi?"

"Of course," said Madmun. "I will be happy to assist.

Still staggered by the magnificence of his gift, I again began to protest. "Abraham, I cannot thank you enough for your offer. The ship is another matter. I do not own the vessel in which we came to Aden. My father only hired it for this voyage and the return."

"Come now, Joshua," said Abraham. "Do you wish to become a merchant? Think like one. I will leave it to you and your companions to resolve that matter. What is true is that your vessel is too small for the cargo you now have. My agent will show you your new ship."

Accompanied by Abraham's representative, we left Madmun's villa in joyful spirits. Abdul Hamid could not stop talking about what had happened as we walked to the port. Deep in thought, I paid little attention. All I had done was lend my hand to a stranger in need. I had truly done nothing. I had only followed the law. Was this a reward from G-d? I was still considering all these questions when we reached Ahmed's dhow.

"What will you tell Ahmed?" Wallo asked.

"Forgive me, Wallo," I answered. "I have not thought about what to say. I am awed by the gift we received. Perhaps the words will come to me."

Ahmed was pleased to see us. "I have worried about you all. You asked me to wait, and so I have done. The season for a return to al-Misr is ending. Others may disagree, but I have been watching the clouds and believe storms will arise earlier this year. Will you stay in Aden, or shall we prepare to depart? Your father paid for a voyage in both directions. If you wish to stay, I will return to al-Yaman in a few months. Whatever you decide, you should do so soon."

I smiled. "We will return, Ahmed. But not in this vessel. We have secured another which is more suitable for our trade."

Ahmed did not know how to respond to this news and frowned. "I do not understand, Sayyid," he said. "You do not wish to sail with me?"

I continued to smile. "Oh, we do, just not in your dhow. You may sell it here at a good price. All is arranged."

Ahmed's frown deepened further. "Sayyid, you are joking with me. I have spent many years paying for my vessel, and now you want me to sell it? If I do obtain a reasonable price, purchasing another here, especially a larger one, will be impossible. Forgive me. You are making no sense, Sayyid."

Now I could not contain my laughter. "Ahmed, I am telling you. Your service will be well rewarded. You will keep the proceeds of the sale of your dhow, and we will make you a gift of a new vessel. In exchange, you will grant us free passage for ourselves and our cargo for ten sailings. Is this not fair?"

Ahmed rubbed his beard as he considered. "Truly, Sayyid, my dhow will be worth more here than in al-Misr, and it will certainly enhance my commerce if I have a larger vessel; but ten free sailings? That could take several years. Let me think."

Ahmed paced back and forth on the dock, deep in thought. Finally, he spoke again.

"Sayyid, you are granting me a great opportunity, that I admit, and I assure you of my gratitude. Can we limit our bargain not only to the number of sailings but also the time during which they occur?"

I began to answer, but Abdul Hamid interrupted. "My dear Ahmed. I understand your worry. We will make at least two sailings each year. Although we require preference, you will be free to engage in other voyages on your account. I believe you will profit from this arrangement. Come with us to inspect our new ship. You will not be disappointed."

Abdul Hamid was correct; Abraham's representative called for a small vessel to take us into the harbor. There, resting at anchor, was what the merchants called a *markab*. This vessel was twice the size of Ahmed's dhow and was newly built. Its wooden hull gleamed with fresh varnish. As he looked at the ship, Ahmed could not disguise his delight. "You have made me rich," he exclaimed. "I will grant you free passage for as long and as many sailings as you wish."

"Then we have a bargain," I declared. "You will now be a true *Nakhuda*, a shipmaster!"

Ahmed nodded his head in agreement and bowed low to me. "That I am," he said. "We will need more cargo. I need to hire more crew and labor to load what goods you purchase."

"That is not necessary, Nakhuda," said Abraham's representative. "This ship is already loaded with goods and is easy to sail. There is nothing you need to do but become familiar with it."

Ahmed was stunned by his good fortune. He did not know what to say. "Then we will depart soon, Sayyid. A ship of this size will not be attacked; we will not sail close to the coast. There is no need to join the Karim fleet. That will be to your advantage. Thanks be to Allah, we will arrive in al-Misr before the others, and your goods will fetch the best market prices."

For the next three days, Wallo and I rested at the home of Rabbi Madmun. Abdul Hamid organized the newly acquired makhzan and his place of abode. The days were spent learning more about the market and making plans for the next venture. Abraham suggested that I plan to import copper from his factory.

"Consider raw iron as well," he said. "It makes the best swords in the world. Even refurbished iron is valuable," he said. "The Fatimid would pay dearly for this product." The price can be as high as twenty dinars per bahar. And then there is kabbaba from Malabar. It is the finest quality of all. That product will fetch more than thirty-five dinars per bahar in Aden and much more in al-Misr. Your father's Collegantia will know better, of course. What you must do is think carefully. That is the secret to success!"

Each evening I spent time alone with Rabbi Madmun. I learned that the Rabbi was a follower of the Palestinian Rabbinical Academy, relocated now to al-Misr. At the same time, he was also the representative of the Babylonian Academy. This dual allegiance to quite different schools of Jewish thought raised many questions in my mind. Karaites rejected both teachings, and I had come to believe they were right. One evening, I asked Madmun about this issue.

"Joshua, all Jews in al-Yaman read the Torah," he said. "Small children can recite its words perfectly. My correspondents in the city of Fustat tell me that our diction and pronunciation of the holy words are better than anywhere else in the world. However, that does not make us Karaites. As you know, you could spend your entire life reading each word and still not fully understand them. That is why we have the oral tradition and the teachings of sages, who have devoted their lives to such study. G-d requires more of us than simply reading His words as given to Moses and the prophets."

"I still do not understand," I said. "How can you ascribe to two different opinions on the meaning of these words?"

Rabbi Madmun sighed. "It is not so simple," he said. "How do you think we will survive as G-d's chosen people? Western Christians have their Pope and his Bishops, who tell them what to believe. The Eastern Christians have their Patriarch. Muslims have their Caliph. Common people follow the dictates they are given. That is their strength. We Jews have no one like that. Worse, since our expulsion from Siyyon, our communities have been dispersed all over the world. We have lost our home, and thus G-d expects much more of us. How then shall we maintain our faith?"

I did not know and said as much to Madmun. It was true that there was no grand leader of the faith. It was true that the land of Israel had been lost to the forces of Amalek. What hope was there, I wondered?

"I see you understand the problem, Joshua; and I have an answer," said the Rabbi. "To survive, we must share a common tradition. We must follow the same laws regardless of where our communities lie. What would happen if each of us read the same words of the Torah and came to our own unique understanding? We would soon be driven apart, and all would be lost. Therefore, we have teachers and the Talmud. Yes, these teachers and our courts argue about the interpretation of G-d's laws, and yes, there is debate. Our faith evolves and grows. Together, through tradition, we remain one people in faith. Our fundamental beliefs are simple. One unique G-d exists, and we must pray only to Him. The words of the prophets are true. Of these prophets, Moses is the greatest. To Moses, the words of G-d were given and were written in the Mishna. The teachings recorded in the Babylonian and Yerushalayim Talmud are also to be believed and followed. Providing that we, as Jews, share these common beliefs, we do not need a Pope or a Caliph. We will be joined in faith regardless of where we live."

Remembering my studies in Qurtuba, I understood. However, I still had a question.

"Rabbi, I can accept what you say; but is it not our duty to regain our homeland, to free Yerushalayim from Amalek?"

"Indeed, it is," said Madmun. "However, it is only G-d that will decide when. We must maintain our faith and live our lives following the law. We must strive to perform our duties and responsibilities, based on our love for G-d, to the best of our ability. We must have faith in G-d's promise to us. Most importantly, we must remember that G-d's time is unlike ours. Have faith, Joshua."

I had little time to consider this advice. My first task was to faithfully perform my obligations to my father; thus, preparations for departure absorbed all my time. Provisions for the upcoming voyage had to be procured. Documents transferring the title of Abraham's vessel to Ahmed were drafted and signed. A plan for future business was developed with Abdul Hamid, and arrangements for his funding were made.

Finally, Wallo and I were ready to depart for al-Misr. Given the size of the new vessel, we would sail directly to Sawakin, on the western coast of the sea. We would then proceed to Aydhab and hire camels for the final journey to Iskandariyyah. On the morning of our departure, Abraham revisited us. He wished to speak directly to Wallo.

"I promised you a gift," he said as he handed Wallo a leather pouch. "You risked your life to save my own, dear friend. Keep this gift as a token of my thanks."

Wallo looked inside the bag and shook his head. "These cannot be real," he said as he showed me the contents. Inside the bag were many colored jewels that glistened in the sunlight. "I expected nothing," said Wallo. "What am I to do with these?"

"Oh, these jewels are certainly real, my friend. You can do anything you choose. You can purchase a home here, take a wife and become a merchant yourself. This is the least I can do for you," said Abraham.

Wallo stared at the stones. I could not contain myself. "You are rich, Wallo! The world is yours. What will you do? Do you wish to remain here?"

Wallo remained silent. "There is something else," said Abraham. "You lost your weapon defending me. A Jewish artisan of my acquaintance has made you another. Its blade is as good as anything made in Dimashq." With that remark, Abraham handed Wallo a short spear. Its shaft was exquisitely turned hardwood and its blade, forged of the finest metal, glistened in the sun. Seeing this, Wallo broke his silence.

"Sayyid, this is a beautiful instrument. I should defend you more often! I will pray to my god for your health and well-being. Thank you."

"Wallo, you have not answered my question," I said. "Will you stay here in Aden, or is there somewhere else you wish to go?"

Wallo furrowed his brows and shook his head. "No, Sayyid, I gave my word that I would accompany you on your travels. I am grateful for the generosity shown to me and will honor my promise. Who knows what will happen next?"

XV

REVELATION
The Christian year 1147

For the next two days, preparations for departure occupied all my time. Rabbi Madmun, true to his word, assisted Ahmed in the sale of his dhow, at a very favorable price. Ahmed deposited the proceeds with the Rabbi for safekeeping. I gave Abdul Hamid twenty dinars to cover expenses until the next shipment. I promised to send more funds when my father and his partner determined what goods were required. On the morning of our departure, I bid farewell to Abdul Hamid and Rabbi Madmun. I hoped to see them again and profusely thanked them both. We rowed into the harbor, boarded our new vessel, and set sail. The winds were fair, and we soon left Aden behind.

Given the spread of the markab's sail, the journey to Dahlak took only one week. There was no difficulty in passing through the dangerous reefs. A few smaller vessels were tied to the docks. None compared to our ship. As the Karim fleet had not arrived, prices for provisions were much less than we were charged on the outbound voyage. Ahmed insisted that our stay on the island be brief. He was concerned about a change in the weather.

From Dahlak, Ahmed sailed towards Sawakin. On the second day, black clouds began to form in the east ominously.

"A storm is coming," muttered Ahmed. "As I expected, it is coming early this year. It will strike before we reach Sawakin. Let us pray our ship is well built!"

It was not long before the winds grew stronger and the waves higher. Ahmed turned the vessel west, hoping to outrun the storm. His maneuver was to no avail. The wind began to howl through the ship's rigging, and the waves rose high. Some of them crashed on the deck. Wallo and I huddled in our cabin while the crew lashed themselves to the mast. It began to rain in torrents. Trembling with fear, I prayed to G-d for deliverance. All I had gained could be lost. Wallo shared my fear and started to chant in his language.

As suddenly as it began, the rain abated, but the wind grew stronger. I could see the great mast bend. Surely it would break, I thought. Ahmed shouted orders to his crew to lower the sail. As the crew began to comply with this order, the sail was torn loose. It flapped in the wind and tore along its seam. The coast now became visible, and it was much closer than expected. As the crew struggled to control the useless sail, Ahmed turned the vessel so that its bow was headed directly into the sandy shore of the coast. It was only a few moments before the ship's hull ground to a stop in the shallow water. The wind continued to blow, and the ship slipped sidewise. Waves continued to crash until the vessel finally rested on the shore itself. I was thankful that the ship's hull was held together not by nails, as was the custom in the Middle Sea, but by coir ropes that were daubed with grease. Otherwise, the ship would have been destroyed. There was nothing more we could do but wait for the storm to pass. Eventually, the winds died, and the clouds lifted. Now, under the afternoon sun, there was finally peace.

Ahmed and his crew inspected the ship, now stranded on the shore in the stillness following the storm. It was not difficult to see that the mainsail was torn and required repair.

"That is not the most serious difficulty," said Ahmed. "Our ship is deep in the sand. It will take all of us to move it into deeper water. We must not stay here as we are defenseless against thieves. Prepare to get wet."

For a long time, all of us pushed against the vessel's hull, attempting to move it. Our efforts were futile. The ship was heavy and buried deep in the sand. With sweat pouring down his face, Ahmed finally commanded those efforts to be halted.

"We will wait for the tide to change. Perhaps we will then have greater fortune. For now, we will work to repair the sail. There is nothing more we can do."

Wallo and I were relieved to rest from our exertions. But our respite did not last long. As we lay on the sand, drying our now waterlogged robes, one of the crew, pointing west, shouted a warning. "There are warriors on the grassy hill above us! Allah have mercy," he cried.

I looked in that direction and saw at least twenty warriors, all armed with spears, coming toward us. Wallo ran to the ship and retrieved his spear. I removed my sling, and Ahmed drew his sword. "Allah, save us," he whispered. "There are too many of them, and we have nowhere to run!"

A few moments later, the warriors encircled us. The leader, a man as black as night, motioned for us to put down our weapons. Wallo did not comply. Instead, he drew himself to full height and shook his new weapon at the man, who replied by shouting in his strange language. Afraid that Wallo's action could bring disaster upon us all, I shouted:

"Wallo, put down your weapon. We cannot fight so many. They will kill us all."

Wallo ignored my plea and again shook his spear at the leader, who now came closer with anger in his eyes. It was clear that Wallo had issued a challenge. I prayed to G-d and made my sling ready.

As Wallo and the warrior's leader came closer together, an older man, supported by a staff, appeared amongst the assailants. The older man shouted something, and Wallo responded. Whatever Wallo said caused the entire band of warriors to murmur amongst themselves until, finally, the old man knelt in the sand and bowed to Wallo. The rest of the warriors followed suit. Then, the old man stood and tearfully embraced Wallo.

I opened my mouth in wonder. "Wallo, what is happening?" I asked as I put down my sling.

"That is not my name, Sayyid. Wallo is the name of my clan. I was its leader, what we call a 'Luba,' until I was captured. The elder here was a great friend of my father. Thank your god that he recognized me. Our people hate the Muslims, and I doubt we would have been left alive."

I did not know what to say. For all this time, I had assumed that Wallo was an ordinary person who had the ill fortune to become enslaved.

"Forgive me, Wallo, or should I call you that? I never asked you about your origins. Once again, my assumptions were wrong. Now I owe you my life for the second time. I can never repay you, and please, I beg you, for the last time, not to call me Sayyid!"

Wallo smiled. "Then I will call you 'my friend'. You will never remember my true name, so do call me Wallo. I am used to it. I did not want the slavers to know who I was. That would have made things difficult. The evening is coming, and I must speak with my people. Tomorrow, we can all work together to move the ship."

Ahmed and his crew had observed this encounter in silence, without understanding what was happening. That we were still alive was all that mattered.

Wallo gathered his people at some distance from the ship and engaged in a lengthy discussion. Ahmed asked me what was happening.

"I do not know," I answered. "What will happen is a mystery. It seems that Wallo is a prince among these people. Let us camp here and wait."

It was almost dark when Wallo returned. Ahmed and his crew had built a fire and were huddled around it. Wallo was a changed man. He spoke with authority and carried himself with a newfound dignity.

"My people will help you release your vessel from the shore," he said. "Tonight, make yourselves as comfortable as you can. Do not worry. You are now under the protection of the Wallo."

I could not contain his curiosity. "Wallo, I beg you to tell us what has happened. Forgive me. Who are you? I do not understand."

Wallo sighed. "You ask who I am? That will take some time. Do you wish to hear my story?"

"Yes," I said. "There is nothing we can do this evening, and I want to understand."

His proper name, he said, was Moti Lencho, and he was the eldest son of the great chief of the Wallo clan of the Oromo people. Their home was in the highlands, far to the west. Muslims and Christians call them Galla, but this was an insult to the Oromo.

"The Christian monks to the north of our land claim that our people only recently arrived. That is not true," Wallo said. "The Christians wish to either convert us to their faith or drive us from the land. We have been here forever. We have our own faith and a long history. To our south and here on the coast, the Muslims dominate. They, too, wish to convert us or destroy us as a people. We live between two worlds."

"As do my people," I said, nodding my head in understanding. "But what happened to you, my friend?"

Wallo sighed and continued. "My father died when I was about fifteen years of age. His death came only a few days before we were to travel to the spring ceremony of Irreechaa, where we give thanks to our god, Waaqa. My mother and sister insisted that we join others of our clan in the pilgrimage to the sacred Lake Haresedi. We believe that after death, we are united with our loved ones. Thus, my mother said my father would want us to make the journey. So that is what we did. Of course, now that I was the leader of the Wallo, I could have said no, but I did not. We had only been walking for one day when we were attacked. Some of us fought, but too many of the enemy were there. When four of our men were killed, everyone knew that we were defeated. I had stayed back from the fighting to protect my mother and sister. One of the attackers, whom I assume was their chief, told us to put down our weapons. If we did, he swore, they would only take ten of us captive and let the others go. Otherwise, all of us would die. There was no choice. I put down my weapon and offered myself. Other men of my clan did this as well."

"Who were these attackers?" I asked. "Were they Muslims?"

"I do not know," said Wallo. "Bands like this sometimes raid our lands searching for men and women to be sold as slaves. It truly did not matter. We were now the victims."

"Did the raiders know who you were, Wallo?"

"No, my friend. I thought I could find a way to escape once our captors had freed my mother and sister and the others. If my captors knew I was the Luba, they would have known my value, and I would be closely guarded. There would be no chance of escape. As it happens, there was never an opportunity to free myself. Our captors bound us all with iron and led us north. We traveled for many days both by land and water until we finally reached al-Misr. It was a difficult journey; we were given only water and bread. We were traded to merchants in al-Qahirah and Iskandariyyah. As you know, I was eventually sold to your uncle. I learned your language and customs during my captivity and was treated kindly. But I was still a slave. You know the story after that. Every day, I thank Waaqa for my deliverance into your hands."

I had heard a story like this from my dear friend Blazh and shook my head in disgust.

"It does not seem right that human beings are bought and sold. I am sorry this happened to you, and I count my blessings that I could free you. You say you give thanks to 'Waaqa'. Who or what is that?"

Wallo smiled. "Joshua, we believe that long ago, my people's god, whom we call 'Waaqa,' created the first Oromo and his two wives, Barentu and Boranawas. All the clans of the Oromo people descend from these two women. Waaqa is our supreme being. I have watched your rituals. I have listened to your discussions. Waaqa is just and loving. He knows all and is everywhere, and His ways are a mystery. Is that not the same for the god you worship?" Turning to Ahmed, Wallo posed the same question.

I had never considered such a possibility, nor had Ahmed.

"Wallo, the Muslims and we Jews worship the same G-d," I said. "Both of us have many names for Him, and, from what you say, perhaps 'Waaqa' is another, and we all worship the same creator. There is only one. We must think about that. But you have not told me how your people came to find us here."

"The old man who recognized me is our Waaqeffanna, the same as what you call a Rabbi. He made the pilgrimage to see our prophet Abbaa Muudaa and was a great friend of my father. He has known me since I was a child. The Waaqeffanna told me that raiders from the south attacked one of our villages many days ago and took captives. The warriors you see here hunt for the raiders and intend to kill them. It is only by chance that they found us."

Once again, I wondered if it was only a matter of chance. The Oromo shared the challenge faced by

Jews. They, too, were caught between two enemies of their faith. The Oromo, too, were victims. That thought prompted another question.

"What do your priests tell you to do?" I asked.

Wallo grimaced. "Waaqeffanna tell us that Waaqa will protect us. We are to be patient even if it takes one hundred years. We will survive if we hold to our faith. Many of us believe we should fight. Our priests tell us that if we do so, we will lose. Our fate, we believe, is governed by Waaqa, and He is just."

I nodded my head in understanding. Was this not the same counsel as the Rabbis gave? I knew the Talmud claims that forces of fate do not govern the people of Israel. The will of G-d governs them. What is true, I had learned, is that prayer and living a good life following the law can change the outcomes of events, but G-d's ways are a mystery, and His time is not the same as ours. I needed to consider this further. Now it was essential to free the ship from the sand and continue our journey.

The following morning, Wallo and his clan added strength to Ahmed's crew and moved the ship to deeper waters. The sail had been repaired, and we were ready to depart.

I was surprised when Wallo remained standing on the shore. "It is time to go, my friend," I said. "Ahmed wishes to catch the favorable winds and continue the journey to Sawakin."

Wallo shook his head. "No, I must stay with my people, Joshua. I am the Luba. I will join my brothers here to search for the raiders. We will not see one another again. I will miss you, my friend."

I had tears in my eyes as I embraced Wallo. "I understand. You have your duties, as do I. I will never forget you. I owe you my life."

"And I owe mine to you," said Wallo. "There is something more. Take this. I have no need for it," he said as he handed his bag of gems to me.

"I cannot accept this," I exclaimed. "These are worth a fortune. Who knows when you might need such wealth?"

Wallo smiled. "Joshua, my lands and people provide everything I require. I have no need for what you consider wealth. Look at the grass, look at the trees, look at the beasts with whom we share the earth. Wives, children, and friends are all the riches a man needs. Where you are going, it is different. There is, however, something you can do for me."

"Anything you wish," I said.

"If you discover Oromo in captivity, free them from bondage. May Waaqa and your G-d protect and bless you." Wallo then turned away and climbed the grassy hill to join his clan. He did not look back.

XVI

RETURN TO ISKANDARIYYAH
The Christian year 1147

The voyage to Aydhab took two weeks. We stopped briefly at Sawakin to re-provision the ship. One week later, we reached our destination, and, this time, the port was almost empty of ships. Our vessel was the largest of them all. Once again, I found it necessary to pay taxes on the cargo. This time, I was careful to negotiate a proper amount.

Ahmed took me aside when the formalities had been completed. "You have done well, Sayyid. Now you must travel alone. Allah willing, I believe that you can do this without aid. I suggest you travel by camel to the city of Qus, on the great river an-Nil. There are two roads to follow. The best is what we call 'the Road of the Two Slaves.' You will find many pilgrims traveling to Aydhab, and the Fatimid authorities mount frequent patrols. Often merchants must leave their goods on the side of the road when their camels die. No one touches them. The journey is long, but you will be safe."

"How do I travel from Qus to Iskandariyyah?" I asked.

"I have a friend in Qus named Hassan, who owns several dhows. If you can give me a parchment, I will write a letter asking that he treat you well."

"But what about you, Ahmed?" I asked.

"I will honor my word to you, Sayyid. I will wait here for instructions regarding your next voyage to al-Yaman. I can make good commerce here until I receive your instructions. I will serve the needs of the pilgrims who wish to travel across the sea to the city of al-Jar. That traffic is bound for the holy city of Mecca and will be very profitable. My markab can take many more passengers than other vessels. Have no concern for me! Now we must find camels to take you across the desert to Qus."

With Ahmed's assistance, I located a merchant who provided the animals required to carry my goods across the desert to the great river an-Nil. At first, the camel master demanded twenty dinars for the service. I noticed that a camel train had only recently arrived from Al-Qahirah and was now waiting for a return journey. I pointed out that the Karim fleet would not arrive for at least two weeks. The merchant could either stay and earn nothing or transport my cargo and return as the fleet arrived. The camel master thought about this.

"You are right," he finally said. "I will reduce my price to ten dinars if you agree to provide me with new litters and saddles at your cost. The best are made in al-Yaman. That is fair trade, is it not?" I readily agreed. My trade skills were improving.

The journey through the desert to Qus took two weeks. Because the camel master had provided me with one of the new leather saddles, it was quite comfortable. This saddle was framed by supports on each corner, holding a canopy to protect the rider from the sun. I could sit in a reclining position and, if I wished fall asleep as I rode. The first few days of travel were difficult for the camels, given the many small ravines to be crossed. Each day, we stopped at a watering place. Usually, the water came from a deep hole dug in the sand, and was salty. Once, sweet-tasting water came from a spring in an oasis called Amran. At each stop, I met other merchants and pilgrims headed in the opposite direction. Evenings were spent sharing news, singing, and playing games. On this journey, I had time to reflect upon my good fortune and the lessons I had learned. Each day, I thanked G-d for my good fortune and for the friends I had made. My father would be pleased. Marriage with Hannah was now assured. I prayed for the well-being of Wallo and the Oromo people and gave thanks for what I had learned from this prince. I would, I swore, be faithful to my obligations and the law. Like the Oromo, tradition kept Jews together in the face of adversity, which I now know brought us all closer to G-d.

After days in the saddle, arriving in Qus was a blessing. The city was marked by busy markets, fine inns, and food stalls to serve the needs of travelers. Most were pilgrims bound for Mecca. Others were merchants from al-Misr and al-Maghrib, preparing to cross the desert to Aydhab. Qus was a meeting place for all. I spent the first night at a grand inn just outside the city and could bathe and enjoy a hot meal for the first time in days.

On the morning of the following day, I found Ahmed's friend, Hassan, at one of the many docks on the great river an-Nil. After the customary greetings, I handed Hassan Ahmed's letter.

He read the letter and laughed. "Ahmed tells me you are an honorable man and that he owes you his life and fortune. He instructs me to provide transport at a cost that will make me poor. Ahmed insists that I be content with whatever Allah provides. Greed, he reminds me, is evil! What choice do I have? I will transport your goods at no charge. I planned to send one of my ships to al-Qahirah empty, as I have cargo for al-Hind to load in that city. If you feel so inclined, you may pay the cost of feeding my crew on the journey. In addition, you must give me your word that you will give preference to my vessels for your trade. Is this acceptable?"

Once again, I was delighted and immediately accepted this bargain. We unloaded the camels and found enough space on the river dhow to hold all my goods. There was no cabin, but that was only a minor inconvenience. The journey to al- Qahirah lasted seventeen days. Along the way, there were numerous villages and towns on the banks of the river, and I visited several of them. Many had both mosques and Christian churches, and all were prosperous. One small city, called Manfalut, on the west bank of the river, was the center for trade in wheat. This grain, I was told, was the finest wheat in the world. I also visited massive temples, which the ancients had constructed long ago.

At the busy port of al-Qahirah, I hired another camel train to transport my goods to the Collegantia's makhzan in Iskandariyyah. There was a throng of travelers on the road, and our journey took almost one week. There were numerous inns on the road, which offered a place to rest for the night, and there was no danger from thieves. We reached Iskandariyyah in the evening. I decided to rest one more night and then proceed to my father's makhzan. Because I wished to meet my father in a more presentable condition, I bathed in a public hammam and purchased a new robe of fine gazz. When I met my father, I would be a changed man.

When I arrived at the makhzan, neither my father nor Abdullah was present. I had no difficulty, however, in convincing their superintendent to unload and store my goods. I was told that my father and his partner were entertaining a visitor from abroad and could be found at my father's home.

Around midday, I presented myself at my father's gate. When I saw my father with Abdullah, I hugged each of them. Tears of joy rolled down my cheeks.

"Forgive me for being so late, father," I said. "I have been supervising the unloading of our cargo at the makhzan. I smelled of camel and took the time to change my clothing. It has been too long! Are you well? And you, Abdullah, are getting older. I missed you. I am starving and in need of wine."

It was then I noticed another man. I opened my mouth in shock. "William, what are you doing here? I never thought to see you again!"

"That is a long story, Joshua, but God has provided an opportunity to be here and meet your family and my uncle. I have been waiting for you," he answered.

When the initial greetings were over, we all sat on cushions to enjoy a feast prepared for me. I could not devote time to the usual pleasantries accompanying such a meal. I was too excited. This time, I knew my father would be proud of me.

"I have done well," I announced. "When we have finished our meal, I will show you the cargo I have brought from the east. You will not be disappointed. I have established a grand makhzan in Aden, and our future is assured. There is no end to what products can be brought from that land."

I then turned to William and said, "I am happy to see you and want to hear everything about how it is that you have come here, but I want to show my father and dear Abdullah what I have brought. Tonight, or tomorrow, we can spend time together."

When I had satisfied my hunger, I insisted that everyone immediately walk to the makhzan. As we walked, I told my father and Abdullah I had brought twenty *adilah*, about ten camel loads of spices. When we arrived at their place of business, I grandly showed them the result of my labors.

"Look, father, there are sacks of cinnamon, al-Luban, azafran, zanjabil, and kabbaba. All these spices will fetch high prices in the market! I am the first to arrive with goods from al-Hind!"

My father frowned. "This is certainly a large quantity. What did it cost? Did you borrow funds?"

I smiled. "You gave me one thousand gold Dinars to purchase goods, did you not? All this cost five hundred. That is far less than what others pay. You know the price in the market. I think we will make three thousand Dinars. Does that not please you, father?"

My father grinned. Abdullah was shocked. "Indeed, you have done well, Joshua," said my father. "You have the balance of coin with you?"

"Of course, father. There is something more which may please you." I removed a small pouch from my robe and poured its contents onto a table. Glistening in the light of the makhzan, there were at least twenty stones. Some were deep blue. Some were blood red, and others were clear sparkling crystals. Each was the size of the nail on my thumb. "You know what these are and what they are worth," I said. "Does this bring more joy to your heart?"

Abdullah, close to tears, carefully examined the stones. Turning to my father and me, he shook his head in wonder and exclaimed, "Allah be praised. These are priceless! I am not certain, but the value of these stones is likely more than the output of our mill for al-sukkar in one year!"

My father opened his mouth in surprise. I glowed with pride. "Now, are you satisfied with me, father?" I asked innocently.

Instead of immediately responding, my father took me in his arms and wept. When he released me from his embrace, he said he had joyful news himself.

"I have good news for you, my son. The woman named Hannah, whom you described to me, is now in our city. She arrived with her father. You might wish to invite them to our home."

Now I was speechless. A range of emotions passed over my face before I asked, "Father, where can I find her?" My father gave me directions, and I begged to be excused so I could go to her.

"It is too late in the day, my son," he said. "You can go tomorrow. Now we must celebrate your success. We want to hear your story, and I am certain William would like to share his adventure with you. Let us go now to my home where we can talk in peace."

My father was correct, of course. It was too late, and it would be wrong not to devote time to talk. I did want to hear more from William. Knowing that Hannah was here was enough for now.

That evening, I related as much of my adventures as I could remember. It was fortunate that I had taken the time to keep written records. I would, I said, give them a copy of my manuscript when it was completed. I wanted to hear more from William, so I asked him to tell his tale.

"It is a long story," said William. "Is it not too late in the evening?"

I confirmed it was not too late and begged William to proceed. "I never thought to see you again, William. I have learned a great deal on my journey and expect that you have done the same."

"That is true," he said. "When you left, I, too, did not expect to see you again. I confess that I did not devote time to considering the story of your tragedies in al-Andalus. I had doubts you would ever find Hannah again. I thought it unlikely that her father would permit her to travel here, now that her brother was dead; may he rest in peace. Thank G-d I was wrong. Your condition was so poor that I had little faith I would hear anything from you. I was convinced your plans were doomed to failure. I have learned much, Joshua, and can see that all my assumptions were incorrect. Perhaps it would be helpful to tell you of my own experience."

We talked well into the night, and the following is what William related to me.

William's adventures began shortly after I departed Sicilia. Having taken so much time away from his duties at the palace to listen to my troubles in the land of Sepharad, William found himself far behind in his work. I knew he was an official, called a *Notarius Magistros*, but admitted that was the extent of my knowledge.

William pursed his lips, not certain how to begin.

"Joshua, officially, I serve under the authority of Sicilia's vice-chancellor. In fact, I report directly to Giorgos of Antioch. You may recall that Giorgos replaced our former emir, Christodulus, as the highest official in the land. Like Christodulus, my master was an Eastern Christian. Unlike his predecessor, however, Giorgos also commanded King Ruggiero's navy. Believe me, Joshua, Giorgos was a demanding taskmaster, but I admired him greatly. Before I continue," said William, "I assume you have not received news of the world on your journey. Is that correct?"

I admitted I was unaware of events and asked William to relate what he knew.

William nodded his head and continued.

"Then you should know that King Alfonso finally captured Lishbunah with the aid of crucesignati from England and elsewhere. You told me that many northerners had already joined the king, but their numbers were insufficient. That weakness changed after you left Sicilia. What transpired was that a fleet of over one hundred warships, en route to the Holy Land from Dartmouth in England, were driven into Portus Cale by a storm at sea. Alfonso convinced their leaders to aid him in capturing Lishbunah, in exchange for the rights of pillage and ransom from prisoners. The support provided by these additional warriors was sufficient to maintain a siege of over seventeen weeks before the city finally fell. Many crucesignati remained in Lishbunah, while others continued to the Levante."

I wondered what had happened to my friends in the city, but when I asked, William said he had no information to impart.

"I only know that the city is in Christian hands," he said. "But in my island of Sicilia, the spirit of conquest was also alive. The Eastern Christians in Constantinopolis contested our king's gains in Campania, Tunis, and elsewhere. You know they also covet the trade with al-Hind. Shortly after you departed, King Ruggiero decided to act. Giorgos brought this news to me himself. He commanded me to pack my belongings. I was to sail with him on a journey of retribution and conquest."

"Let me tell you, Joshua; I was shocked," said William. "Me, sailing to war? I am a practitioner of letters and law, not a mariner or a warrior. What was Giorgos thinking, I wondered? Giorgos just laughed at me. 'Are you afraid of adventure?' he asked. I can hear him now. 'Can you not swim? It is time you left your scrolls and manuscripts and saw some of the world'. I could not argue, of course. I sighed and asked where we were going. Giorgos answered my question with a smile. 'Our beloved king has decided that the Greeks should be taught a lesson,' he said. The emir reminded me that the Emperor in Constantinopolis had attempted to take our lands many times. Giorgos planned to take our navy to the Greek's doorstep and liberate a few of their possessions. He thought we might take Athens itself. It would, he assured me, be a lucrative venture."

Now I had a question. "But William, you told me that Giorgos is Greek. Had he no concern about fighting others of his faith?"

"That," said William, "is the way of the world. Giorgos told me that sometimes, we must sacrifice our personal interests for those of our kingdom. He then disclosed another goal that he had not shared with anyone."

William hesitated for a moment and looked into my eyes.

"I ask that you, Joshua, not disclose what I tell you."

"Of course," I said, and William continued.

"You see, the center of the gazz trade is in the cities of Corinth and Thebes. The rulers of Constantinopolis derive much of their wealth from that fabric. It is vital to them, both as a means of payment and for purposes of diplomacy. I had previously told the emir that I had learned something about those of the Jewish faith from you, and that was one reason he insisted upon my joining him. Georgios explained that it is the Jews in those cities who know the secrets of weaving gazz. Those of your faith developed the looms upon which gazz is woven and the dyes to color it. The emir intended to bring these Jews and their equipment to Sicilia, so as to dominate the trade."

I frowned when I heard this. "So, you, too, were planning to treat the Jews as chattel, William? You told me, and I saw for myself, that King Ruggiero gives members of my faith respect, but from what you say, we do not have the same rights as Christians. Thus, there is no difference between Sicilia and any other land. Is that not so?"

William nodded his head. He said he was ashamed to admit that fact.

"Joshua, believe me, I asked if the emir intended to offer the gazz weavers a choice, or did he plan to bring them here by force, as if they were slaves? I did not receive an adequate response, but in either event, I believed I could aid some of these people if I joined the expedition. Despite my misgivings, I had little choice but to agree to go. Although the emir's plans were secret, I did speak to my father and sought his permission."

"Did he agree?" I asked.

"It was not so simple," said William. "You see, my father was working with Roland at the hospice when I came to him. Roland listened to the report I gave to my father and then interjected his opinion. He gave my father no chance to respond. There will be battles, he said. I can recall his words. 'This is no peaceful holiday voyage through the Middle Sea. You have no training in arms, so what will you do? Defend yourself with your quill pen? What will a man of letters and law do on such a mission?' Roland did not wait for me to respond. 'Ahh,' he said. 'Here is what we will do. I will train you in the use of a sword. How much time do we have?' I told Roland I would depart in two weeks. I remember that Roland sighed deeply and said that two weeks would be insufficient to teach me anything. In that time, he could show me how to hold a sword but not to use it. He begged me to ask the emir for a delay."

"What did your father say?" I asked.

"I remember that my father listened to this exchange and agreed that there would be no time for me to learn the arts of war. That, he said, was something I would learn for myself. He said he would forbid this adventure if there were a choice. Nevertheless, he said, the king has called you to service, and his commands you must obey. My father decided that the least he and Roland could do was teach me how to provide basic care to the wounded. He asked that I request the emir to permit me to spend the next fortnight in the hospice so that I could gain instruction in medical arts. Let me tell you what happened. I learned a great deal."

XVII

WILLIAM'S TALE
Panormos, Kerkyra, Athina, Corinth and Iskandariyyah

Emir Giorgos granted William permission to study physician's arts with Roland and his father. For the next two weeks, William spent long hours learning how to clean and sew wounds, administer af-Yum and remove projectiles from the body without causing additional harm. Meanwhile, the emir collected his fleet of seventy war galleys with crews, warriors, and ten giant cogs to carry supplies. His navy largely consisted of Muslims, who had no qualms about fighting the Greek Christians, nor did they have any allegiance to the Pope. As always, there were a few priests assigned to accompany the expedition. These priests were of the Eastern Christian faith. When William asked why this was so, the emir explained that the Jews in the lands we intended to conquer would speak the Greek language. These Jews would, he said, know something of the Eastern faith, and perhaps, some would agree to conversion.

William departed on schedule and sailed south and east to the tip of the mainland. Although the seas were calm, he spent most of the time heaving his stomach over the rail. Because the cogs were slow, the first part of the journey took two days. From the peninsula's tip, it was another two-day sail to the island the Greeks called Kerkyra. All the ships anchored in the harbor. To any observer, it was a forbidding and formidable fleet. Although the army was excited at the prospect of pillaging the island, the emir did not give the order to disembark.

The emir called William to his side and pointed at the city. "William, there is no need for bloodshed here. I want you to go ashore and convince the city's governors that surrender is their wisest choice."

William took a deep breath. He had no experience in this sort of diplomacy. What if he failed to convince the governors to accede to the emir's demands? Would he not then be responsible for any deaths and destruction that followed? Giorgos saw the anxiety on his face and assured William that performing his task would be a valuable experience and that he, Giorgos, had faith in William's ability. All would be well, he declared.

Still trembling, William climbed into a waiting small boat. He was accompanied by only four knights, all in chain mail. As they rowed towards shore, William considered the words he would say. He knew that the Greeks in Constantinopolis imposed exorbitant taxes on the island's residents and correctly suspected that the populous chafed under that burden. He also knew that the island had suffered the consequence of invasion many times, and its citizens were well aware of the consequence of resistance. An idea came to him. As William came closer, he saw that the city had sent a delegation of dignitaries to the dock, with ten men carrying pikes. None wore mail; a local militia of some kind. When William landed, the dignitaries bowed and waited for him to speak.

Again, taking a deep breath and standing as straight and tall as possible, William greeted them in their language. "Peace be with you," he said. "I bring you greetings from Ruggiero, King of Sicilia. You see only a small part of his fleet in the harbor. We have come to liberate you from the oppression of Emperor Manuel Komnenos. You should not be under the thumb of Constantinopolis. We offer you the opportunity to become members of our alliance. I am confident that you will agree."

The oldest of the delegation stroked his white beard and angrily said:

"You say 'peace,' but you bring an invasion force. You suggest that we trade one ruler for another; perhaps the penalty for not doing so is destroying our island. Surely, this is not peace. What is it that you want from us?"

William decided to address this man with formality and granted him the highest Greek title that came to mind.

"Magistros, I understand your concern," he said. "I am authorized to make you an offer I know you will accept. We understand your plight and have our own issues with your Emperor Manuel.

If you can convince your council to ally with us and accept vassalage to our king, we will assess no taxes for two years and, thereafter, will reduce them to half of what you now pay. The emperor has left you undefended, has he not? You must fear pirates and Turks. Thus, if you agree, we will leave a contingent of one hundred of our soldiers to protect you and a *strategos* to govern them. Of course, you may practice your Greek faith in peace, and your monasteries may continue in their present form. My proposal is fair and reasonable. Discuss this with your people. I will wait here for your answer."

Having a fleet of seventy war vessels behind William in the harbor was helpful. Anyone would understand the implied threat. While he waited, William wondered if the emir would accept what he had just done. Giorgos would be angry that he had proposed an abatement of taxes and had promised that the island's population could continue to follow their Greek faith. William hoped the emir would see the value of arranging a peaceful acquisition of the island. Had he gone too far? The delegation gathered some distance away, and William could hear a loud argument. Finally, the delegation reached an agreement.

The man he had called Magistros returned, drew a deep breath, and said gravely, "I do not know your title, so forgive me for not addressing you properly. I, Alexios of Kerkyra, am the Kephale of this island. I am not a Magistros; that is now an empty title and one I do not deserve. My colleagues and I agree to your terms. We expect a written document to memorialize this compact. In exchange for a reduction in taxes, we will become vassals to your king and sever our ties to the court in Constantinopolis. I am certain that our Bishop will agree as well, providing your king provides us the protections promised."

William was pleased that an agreement had been reached so quickly. He wondered, however, what the emir would say. An idea occurred to him, and he decided to push his good fortune to the limit.

He confirmed that the Kephale's decision was wise and promised to prepare a formal document for signature. Then he decided to test his luck.

"There is another minor condition that I neglected to mention," he said. "While we are here in the port, we expect you to provide the necessary provisions for our ships and commit to paying for the cost of the troops we will provide. As you will not be subject to taxes for two years, I think this will not place an undue burden upon you."

Alexios raised his brows when he heard the additional condition so casually presented. There was no choice but to agree. The cost of provisioning the emir's ships and the expense of maintaining a garrison was, at least, far less than the heavy taxes now paid to the emperor.

William returned to his ship and explained what he had done to the emir. At first, Georgios was angry that William had given away so much merely to achieve a peaceful resolution. However, it was not long before the emir calmed enough to understand the logic. The acquisition of this island would cost nothing and would do grave harm to Sicilia's enemy. The troops from Sicilia would lose the opportunity to pillage the island, but no blood would be shed.

The raid on Athina was quite different from William's experience in Kerkyra. There he learned the horrors of war. A contingent of Greeks and a few Venetians defended the city and fought well, despite their small numbers. Georgios lost many troops in the engagement. Together with the priests, William did his best to apply the knowledge he had gained at the hospice. One of the cogs became a place for the wounded, and it was not long before the deck became slippery with blood. The screams and whimpers of the victims made it difficult to hear. A coppery smell permeated the air. The supply of gazz thread to sew gaping wounds dwindled quickly. The legs and arms of some of the combatants were virtually severed, and these were cut away. The stomachs of some soldiers, unprotected by mail, gaped open, and William could see the glistening white coils of their bowels. These poor souls smelled of excrement. Most cried in pain and fear. The severely wounded knew there was no hope for their survival on earth and called for the priests. William helped to wash superficial wounds with wine and seawater. He administered af-Yum to the most grievously injured but did not have enough. What William remembered with horror were those struck by Venetian arrows. Roland had demonstrated how to remove these missiles, but doing so was a hideous procedure. William found it impossible to draw out arrows without inflicting appalling pain. Many of those victims begged him to leave them to die.

That day, William and the priests performed their grim tasks until sundown. By that time, William was so tired that he could barely move, much less think. The priests wanted to throw the dead over the ship's side to make room for the wounded. William refused. If that were done, he said, the Muslim troops would rebel. In their faith, it is essential to bury the dead properly so that they may be transported to paradise. William thanked G-d that there had been no time to learn to fight. He was no warrior, nor would he ever be.

The fighting had been brutal; there was no holding back Giorgos' warriors when the city finally capitulated. For two days, they ravaged the city. Women were violated. Children and the elderly were not spared, and many were killed. Boats, laden with the spoils of war, returned to the cogs in a steady stream from the mainland. Gold, plate, jewels, and fine clothing were loaded into the holds. The emir was delighted with the result.

William, still in a state of shock, was appalled when Giorgos exclaimed, "Look at all we have gained from this, William. We have lost only a few of our number, and this adventure has brought wealth to our warriors and the king's treasury. The Greeks will not forget this lesson. Let us go to the city and see the sights. Now we can view the monuments of a great civilization!"

William had no interest in seeing anything. He wondered how anyone could smile, much less wander streets running with blood and despair. He told the emir that he would prefer to sleep and assist in caring for the remaining wounded.

A few days later, the fleet left Athina and sailed further into the Ionian Sea. The emir unleashed his warriors on several coastal villages and towns on the coast of Euboea and into the Gulf of Corinth, collecting plunder on the way. Giorgos had transformed on this voyage from an able and kind administrator to a ruthless warrior. No more troops were lost on these excursions, and the holds of the cogs became full with treasure. Finally, they reached the city of Corinth. There, said Giorgos, he would collect the gazz weavers and the looms he coveted.

Corinth had always been a source of copper. The city was famous throughout the world for this metal, but the emir had no interest in that. What he wanted were the Jewish dyers of gazz, who produced the product with the most significant value. William wondered how the emir intended to secure their cooperation, and his question was soon answered.

The city was undefended and was at the mercy of Giorgos' fleet. Another ship lay at anchor in the harbor, but it flew the colors of Genoa. That vessel would not interfere. William was ordered to meet the Jews in the city and convince them to come to Sicilia, where the emir promised they would be well rewarded for their skills. If the Jews agreed, no harm would come to them.

This time, when William boarded the boat to take him to shore, he was neither afraid nor concerned about his abilities. He had a more significant worry. He remembered all that I had told him. Was he not participating in the subjugation of those of the Jewish faith?

As expected, a delegation awaited William's arrival. William made the customary salutations and, to their surprise, asked to meet the Chief Rabbi. After some hesitation, one of the officials left the dock and soon returned with a white-bearded man carrying himself with great dignity. William was astonished when this man spoke in Arabic.

"You have asked to speak with me? I am Rabbi Da'ud." The Rabbi looked at the war fleet and, for a moment, William thought the Rabbi mumbled a prayer. "How can I be of service?" he asked.

William spoke as eloquently as possible. He had come, he said, to invite those of the rabbi's community who worked with gazz to join in a great enterprise in the Kingdom of Sicilia. There, said William, it was intended to establish the most important gazz industry in the world. The help of the rabbi's people would be most welcome. King Ruggiero would reward them well, and a great partnership would be built. The Kingdom of Sicilia, William declared, respects those of the Jewish faith, and, while under the King's care, the rabbi's people could practice their beliefs and follow their laws freely. "We are not like the Greeks," he said. William begged that his offer be accepted.

For a long time, Rabbi Da'ud said nothing. Finally, he spoke.

"Young man, our people have lived in this city since the time of the Romans. The man you call Saint Paul lived here and worked with our weavers to earn his bread. The Greeks remember this, and because of our skill in the art of dying and weaving gazz, we are permitted to own our ancestral land and live freely. You ask us to abandon our homes and privileges and travel to a place we do not know, where the future is uncertain. I see no advantage to us. Thank you for your offer, but I must refuse on behalf of my people."

Now William did not know what to do. The rabbi could see the warships. Their threat was obvious. William could not understand this man's obstinacy. He looked at the other officials and opened his hands in disbelief. These Jews should not doubt what could happen to their city if the offer was refused. William thought to give them time to convince the rabbi of the action that must be taken, so he stepped back and waited.

The sun was beginning to descend, and still, there was no response. William decided to return to his vessel and report to the emir all that had transpired. Giorgos received the news with fury.

"These people are fools," he shouted. "Do they not realize the peril of refusing our offer? At home, I must constantly deal with their complaints and stubbornness. The Jews are no different here. I still must take the Jews of Thebes, and there is no time to waste on this nonsense. Tomorrow I will send one hundred of our warriors to collect them. I will not tolerate disobedience!"

True to his word, Giorgos sent his troops to the city to gather the Jews and their equipment and bring them back to one of the cogs. Rather than going ashore, William watched from the rail as at least two hundred men, women, and children were carried back to the fleet. The wailing of these people carried clearly over the water, and tears began to well in William's eyes. He knew the Jewish artisans would be granted excellent compensation for their labors in Sicilia and find a welcoming community of Jews on our island, but this was their home. These Jews spoke Greek, not Arabic. Their new life would be difficult. Worst of all, they were being treated as captives. Later that day, William asked Giorgos what had happened to the Chief Rabbi.

"Oh, that obstinate man," said the emir. "I have no use for him or his daughter. All he does is stand in our way and complain. He is fortunate to escape with his life. Why do you care? In any case, I have another task for you. Do you see that ship in the harbor? I sent some of our soldiers to inspect it and found that the colors it shows are false. The vessel's captain must have seen who we were and tried to hide the truth. They are Venetians, and that city is in league with the Greeks. It is loaded with gazz and bound for Iskandariyyah. We have removed the crew and replaced them with our own. It will now go to its original destination, and the benefits of its cargo will accrue to our king. I cannot trust that mission to common sailors. I have no one else to send, and I know you will protect our interests when the goods are sold in the market. Gather your belongings. You will be the commander."

William's first inclination was to refuse the order. He was no merchant. Yes, he could write a binding agreement for trade and render an opinion on taking this ship under maritime and Roman law, but he had no experience acting as a commander of anything. The emir gave William no time to protest and waved him away. As William walked across the deck to collect his clothing and writing instruments, he realized that this would be an opportunity to meet his family in al-Misr and, if God willed it, meet me again.

When William stepped into the boat carrying him to the newly acquired cog, he ordered the helmsman to first row to the port. He had unfinished business. William's guilt for the forcible removal of the Jews weighed heavily on his mind. He wanted to beg forgiveness from the rabbi for what transpired. William was standing on the dock when the rabbi arrived and, at his side, was one of the most beautiful women he had ever seen. There was no time to wonder at this; the rabbi scowled as he addressed William from the dock.

"You were as good as your word, young man," said the rabbi. "Did you hear the despair of my people? Are you proud of what you have done? Your emir has thrown over a thousand years of history in the dirt, and for what? So that you can produce gazz in Sicilia and sell it to the rich? What more do you want from us?"

William remembered something that I had told him in Sicilia. "Forgiveness," he answered. William had not intended that the rabbi's people be taken by force. He asked that the rabbi remember the story of Moses. "Have faith that God will show you a new and better path," he said. "That you and your people are alive is what matters most. Is that not true?"

Rabbi Da'ud looked at William in surprise. "You are familiar with the Talmud?"

William explained that I, a dear friend, had instructed him in some tenets of the Jewish faith. William reminded the rabbi that the Talmud requires a transgressor to ask forgiveness from anyone he has harmed, and that is what he, William, was doing. Providing that a request for forgiveness was sincere, William argued, it would be wrong if that request was refused.

The woman whose appearance had so enthralled William looked at Rabbi Da'ud and raised her brows. The rabbi shrugged his shoulders and nodded his head. "Yes," he said. "You are correct. I must forgive you. However, other Jews are now being loaded on your ships, from whom you must also beg forgiveness. "

William protested that the plight of those Jews was not his doing. It was not his decision to force their removal from the city. The emir had ordered them to be taken. The Jews would, he argued, be treated well in Sicilia and rewarded for their labor, as King Ruggiero was known for his tolerance and goodwill. William then asked Rabbi Da'ud if there was anything more he could do.

"Without my people, my role is without meaning, "Da'ud responded. 'My daughter and I were just now discussing that subject. Perhaps we will travel to Thebes, where more of our faith exists.

William shook his head. He warned Rabbi Da'ud not to consider that option. Giorgos was planning to sail to that city and convince the weavers there to also come to Sicilia. The Jews in Thebes would suffer the same fate as those in Corinth.

A thought occurred to William. He said that he was traveling to Iskandariyyah, where there were many Jews. It is a place of learning. William suggested that Rabbi Da'ud would be most welcome there. He asked if Da'ud would consider taking such a step.

Rabbi Da'ud stroked his long white beard and considered William's words. Before he could say anything, his daughter spoke for the first time. Her voice was sweet and sounded like music.

"What is your name?" she asked softly.

Being addressed directly by this vision of heaven discomforted William, and he nervously introduced himself as William, a counselor to the emir. He wanted to say more, but words did not come to his mouth.

"Well then, William the Counselor, my name is Sophia, the daughter of the Chief Rabbi of Corinth. My father hesitates, as he wishes to do what is best for his flock. On his behalf, we will agree to travel with you. He will realize we have no choice if he thinks about our situation. As you said, perhaps we will find a better path."

William was surprised that this woman spoke for her father in this way. He noticed that Da'ud smiled coldly and then nodded his head.

"Young man, my daughter's true name is Chochma, our word for wisdom. The Greeks have translated that name as Sophia, which means the same. She is rarely wrong. We will travel with you."

William asked the rabbi and his daughter to collect their belongings. When they had done so, they rowed to the Venetian vessel that would become their home for the next two weeks. They sailed the following day. The crew was Muslim and was amenable to William's direction. For protection, the emir had assigned five skilled archers to accompany the vessel and ensured that the crew was armed. The cog was loaded with fine weavings, and William conducted a thorough inventory. The value of the cargo was extraordinary. By weight, gazz was more costly than any other commodity. William did not know what price it would fetch in al-Misr, but understood why the emir wanted him to go on this journey. Giorgos knew that William would do his best to carry out his duty.

Rabbi Da'ud remained silent for the first week of the voyage. He read his manuscripts and spent long hours gazing sadly at the sea. It was doubtful that he had truly forgiven William for the disaster that had befallen his people. William, however, forgot his concerns whenever he spoke with Sophia. During the long voyage, there were many opportunities to engage in conversation. Sophia continued to enthrall William not only with her beauty but her knowledge. William introduced her to the game of shatranj, which many of his friends played in Sicilia. Although Rabbi Da'ud was not interested in such a frivolous activity, Sophia learned it quickly. True to her name, she learned well, and William often found himself losing. Her victories only enhanced William's infatuation. At times, they just talked. Once William asked Sophia how it came to be that she and her father spoke Arabic.

"We lived for many years in Jaffa," she said. "My mother died when I was ten years of age, and my father spent years mourning. So sad was he that he could not practice his calling. The Franks made life difficult for us, and he decided that his only option was to leave our home and travel to Corinth, where there was a need for a Chief Rabbi. We made our home in that city until you came along. Now we must start our lives again in a new place."

William asked her if she had ever considered the possibility of traveling with the others to Sicilia.

"Not for one moment," she answered. "My father is convinced that we will be treated better by the

Muslims than by the Christians in the west, and I agree. We know the Jewish community in al-Misr is strong and enjoys numerous privileges, and we have heard only good news from that place."

From what I had told him, William doubted she was right but said nothing. He prayed that conditions in al-Misr might indeed be different from those in al-Andalus.

The voyage was uneventful. On occasion, sails were sighted in the distance. But because they sailed so far from the coast of the Levante, there was little danger.

It was not long before William realized that he was deeply in love. During the last week of their voyage, he seriously considered how to ask her father for his permission to marry Sophia.

On one of the rare occasions William spent with Rabbi Da'ud discussing the tenets of the Jewish faith, he asked for his opinion on marriage between Christians and Jews.

Da'ud looked at William and shook his head. "You are not asking me a theoretical question, William. I am no fool. I see what is happening between you and my daughter, and I am sad to say that a union of that kind is impossible."

William immediately protested. He told the rabbi that his grandfather, Thomas, had married a Muslim, and no harm was done. Why would a marriage between a Jewish woman and a Christian man be impossible?

"You are wrong, William," the rabbi said sadly. "Any child born of such a union would be a Jew. That is our law. Would your family accept this result? I doubt it."

Rabbi Da'ud looked out over the rail at the rolling waves. "Of course, you could always convert to our faith, and that would resolve the problem. Could you do that?"

William pondered his words, but before he could form a response, the Rabbi interjected.

"I will answer that question for you, William. You could not. For a Christian to convert to our faith, his intentions must be pure. Whatever you say, your conversion would not conform to the law. You would be taking such a step to marry my daughter, not because you honestly believe in the tenets of our faith. You would not be what we call a 'ger tzedek,' a righteous convert. Read the Book of Ruth, and you will understand."

William could not dispute Da'ud's argument. Another thought occurred to him, but before he could express it, the Rabbi continued.

"No, William, my daughter would never convert to your faith. Her beliefs are as strong as my own. If women could become rabbis, that is what she would be. I know she values your friendship and company, but that is the limit. Put your dreams aside, my boy. As you once told me, have faith that God will show you a new and better path."

William found it difficult to accept this judgment. The advice he had given so casually was hollow when turned on its head. He was still deep in thought and sadness when he heard the shout of the helmsman.

"There is the lighthouse," he cried. "We have arrived!"

XVIII

SUCCESS
Iskandariyyah
The Christian year 1148

It was very late at night when William completed his tale. I had not interrupted his narrative and could see from his face that he remained overcome with guilt about his role in forcibly transporting the Jews from Corinth. The only bright moment was when he talked about Sophia. When I finally went to my bed, I could not sleep. I had my own concerns.

Early in the morning, I rose before anyone else, donned my best robe, and walked to where my father had told me Hannah resided. Pacing in anticipation, I waited outside the gate until it was an appropriate time for me to request entry. During that time, which seemed forever, I rehearsed what I would say to her father. By the time I knocked on the gate, I was sweating profusely.

I need not have been so nervous. When I saw Hannah, it was as if we had only been apart for a few days. Her beauty, her smile was overwhelming, and it was everything I could do not to take her into my arms. Hannah's father greeted me as if we were long-lost friends, even though we had never met. Hannah must have told him everything. Our meeting was brief.

I virtually ran back to my father's home. I could not wait to tell William my news.

"Hannah will marry me," I shouted. "Her father has approved. I want you to meet her."

"What about your father?" William asked. "You told me she is a Karaite. Will he accept what you intend?"

"I will speak with him this morning. I am certain he will grant me his consent. I think my success in al-Hind was such that now I can do no wrong. Although he is a good Jew, he does not concern himself with the details of our faith. In any event, there is no prohibition on such a marriage here. We are not in al-Andalus!"

"Will you take her to Yerushalayim?" William asked.

"I have no plans to travel there now," I said. One day, perhaps; but not now. My father needs me and..." I did not complete my sentence. "And what?" William asked.

I thought about what I would say for a few moments. "William, all is different now," I said. "Now I must return to Hannah's home and tell her of my father's approval."

I was correct in my assumption that my father would approve of my plans. He quickly granted his assent and asked that I inform his partner Abdullah as well. He did have other requests.

"Joshua, I want William and Abdullah to attend and witness the marriage contract, the ketubah. I know they will happily accept that role, but I have another requirement you may not be so pleased with."

"Father, I can think of nothing you could ask that I would deny, "I said. "What is it that you wish?"

"I want you and your bride to travel with William to Sicilia. We expect one of our vessels to arrive at the port in about fourteen days. Thus, you will be leaving soon. Now that you will have a wife, I do not want you to make dangerous journeys to al-Yaman or al-Hind. The new trading route you have begun will enable us to ship more goods at lower prices to Christian lands, and Sicilia is the best intermediary. I want you to establish a trading house on that island and represent our interests. Given William's relationship with the emir and officials who manage the treasury, I am confident you will do well. Of course, we will need to have the ceremony performed quickly if you are to travel with William. Will you agree?"

I had already thought deeply about my plans. The lessons I learned in al-Yaman and on my journeys were fresh in my mind. I did not hesitate. "Yes," I said. I suddenly realized that I would need Hannah's consent as well. "Assuming that she agrees, of course. "

The wedding itself was a grand affair. Many of the city's Jewish community attended. Even Rabbi Da'ud and his daughter were present. William did his best not to look in their direction, but I saw that Sophia was accompanied by a fine-looking man, whom I assumed was Halfon ben Halevi, another Jewish merchant engaged in trade with al-Hind. It was unusual for a wedding like mine to be held so quickly. Custom dictated that the time between the betrothal and the final ceremony was at least one year. Our situation differed. Because of this, the Nagid himself had granted permission to dispense with that formal requirement. I did, however, follow one custom. The husband usually offers a ring of gold as a symbolic bride price. This time, the ring I gave to Hannah was not only made of gold but encased one of the brilliant crystal stones, called Almas, from my store of gems. It was worth a fortune! My wedding gift reminded me of the story of Abraham's marriage to Rebecca in the book of Genesis, when he showered his bride with treasure. How could I do less?

Hannah and I moved to my father's home that day. She readily agreed to travel to Sicilia and was excited at the prospect. She doubted that her father would want to join us as, already, he had made good friends among the Karaites in al-Misr and was making use of the extensive library. With Hannah's consent, I spent considerable time in the market while we waited for our ship. William asked me in what commerce I was engaged, that was more important than spending time with my new wife.

"I am freeing as many Oromo people as I can find," I answered. "I made a promise. I have spoken to my father and Abdullah, and both agree that my promise should be upheld. My father will provide whatever funds are required."

I told William that my task had proven to be challenging. Despite my inquiries, finding these people in the city was difficult.

William smiled. "I think you need my assistance. Have you been to the offices of the Quadi? The officials there will have a record for purposes of tax of all enslaved persons in the city. Let us go there now."

William was correct. The Fatimid rulers kept detailed records, and we could identify not only the slaves designated as Oromo but information regarding their masters. The official who provided access to the records demanded to know why we were searching for Oromo slaves. I told the functionary that we intended to purchase their freedom. The official was surprised at my words.

"You have enough wealth for such a purpose?" he inquired. "Why should anyone give up a slave? Your intention is doomed to failure. You are wasting my time."

William said, "Sayyid, perhaps you have forgotten the words of the holy Quran on this matter. Allah tells us that freeing a human being from slavery is one of the most praiseworthy acts that can be accomplished."

William stared into the eyes of the official. "Help us to perform our task. Your action will be meritorious in the eyes of Allah."

The official considered William's words for a few moments and finally agreed to assist us. With his help, we located almost forty Oromo slaves held captive in Iskandariyyah. William assisted me in negotiating the cost of their freedom. Some of the Oromo wished to remain in the city, but at least thirty expressed their desire to return to their homeland. I arranged for their transport, asking only that they tell Moti Lencho, the Luba of the Oromo, that I had faithfully discharged my obligation. The Oromo were free, I said, because of their Luba. I prayed that Wallo would learn what I had done.

In the few days before we departed, William also attended to his duties. As promised, Abdullah had sold William's cargo of gazz cloth. It totaled just over 1,000 dhira' al-'amal. William was unfamiliar with the measurements used in al-Misr, so when Abdullah explained that that unit was equal to the length of an average man's arm, William was amazed. Several buyers had made offers for the cloth, and Abdullah had accepted the highest bid. There had been what Abdullah described as insolent questions about the cargo from the Venetian merchants. Abdullah ignored them. 'It was none of my business or theirs to know the origin of the gazz," he declared.

William's cargo fetched over 5,100 gold dinars, about 20,000 Tari, the currency of Sicilia. That, William knew, would bring tears of joy to the emir, and it would cover the cost of the expedition to the Greeks. Everything gained from pillage would be pure profit to the kingdom.

Having nothing to occupy his time while waiting for our ship, William often visited the port to discover news of events outside Iskandariyyah. He already knew that the fall of Edessa to the Turks in 1147 had prompted Pope Eugene to dispatch an army, led by King Louis, to the Levant. The Turks had defeated this army on numerous occasions, due not only to their skill but because continuous disputes between the various factions of the Christian leadership weakened the king's army. When Abdullah learned of William's queries, he told William not to waste time collecting rumors.

"The ship we have been expecting has just arrived in the harbor. Its captain is the grandson of a former partner in our Collegantia and can answer your questions. His name is Rowan, the same as his grandfather, and you and Joshua should meet him."

The cog captained by Rowan flew the flag of Genoa and was easy to find at the dock. When William and I introduced ourselves, Rowan was delighted.

"My family and I owe much to your grandfathers," Roland said. "Because of them and their Collegantia, we gained our wealth and the twenty ships we now own. We can never repay the debt we owe. I will do anything I can for Abdullah and Elazar. Abdullah has told me that you will be my passenger on the voyage to Sicilia. What else can I do for you?"

When William told Rowan his story and the need to bring the latest news to emir Giorgos, Rowan smiled.

"If that is all you need, you have come to the right place. Only recently, we were in the port of Jaffa. Have you heard what happened to King Louis?"

William and I admitted ignorance, and Rowan then told us that the king had made an ill-advised decision to attack Dimashq and had been soundly defeated by the Turks."

I found this event interesting, but it had nothing to do with me. William, however, was concerned. "How did this happen?" he asked

Rowan shrugged his shoulders. "That depends upon your point of view, William. The armed pilgrims lost many of their numbers on their march through Antioch. The king had less interest in victory than in visiting Jerusalem as a pilgrim and made many errors. His qualifications as a leader in war were sadly lacking. You see, most of the Pope's army traveled overland. King Louis immediately ran into difficulty. The Turks burned all the crops on his route, his army was starving, and the king was forced to complete his journey by sea. That was good business for us; we were paid to dispatch a fleet to Adalia to carry his soldiers and horses to Antioch. The most grievous mistake was attacking Dimashq with too few troops. He was soundly defeated. Now the Turks hope to drive us all from the land and retake Jerusalem. Only God knows what will happen next."

I had the same question. I admit I was not unhappy with this news but kept my thoughts to myself. "You do not seem overly concerned, Rowan," I remarked. "What will happen to your trade?"

Rowan laughed. "We will be in excellent condition. These events are no tragedy for us. Now, we will have the opportunity to carry the king's army and horses back to their homeland and earn a great profit once again. This, I think, is sound commerce!"

Everything I knew confirmed it was wrong to earn profit from war or pillage. William had profited from the forced removal of the Jews from Levant. Surely, this was displeasing to G-d, but I was learning that is the way of the world. I did not voice my opinion.

"Will you return to the Levant?" I asked.

"No," said Rowan. "We will load sukkar and spices here and carry that to Sicilia. Abdullah said that you will join us. You and your new wife can use my quarters. You, William, will join me on deck."

Rowan paused and said softly, "I would advise we plan your departure quickly. There is a possibility of war between the Greeks and Sicilia."

William frowned at this news. Had the emir gone too far, he wondered?

Seeing the concern on my face, Rowan explained. "You know of Conrad who wishes to call himself Emperor of the Romans do you not?"

"Of course," William said. "He is the King of Coblenz and has claimed to be King of Italy."

"I fear you may hear more of Conrad before long," Rowan said. "King Conrad has responded to the Pope's call for a second armed pilgrimage and joined with King Louis. Conrad took a different route into the Levant and suffered many defeats. After Louis failed to take Dimashq, Conrad felt betrayed. He has now returned to Constantinopolis and his friend Emperor Manuel. I am certain he will seek some way to regain his prestige and satisfy his army. It is only logical that King Conrad will form an alliance with Manuel against King Ruggiero. Of course, I do not know if that will be the case. My instincts tell me otherwise. That is why we should depart as soon as we can."

William wondered what Giorgos would think of this. The emir had prodded a venomous snake, and that was never wise!

XIX

HOMECOMING
Iskandariyyah to Panormos
The Christian year 1148

After the long voyage across the Middle Sea, we arrived in Panormos in the fall of the Christian year 1148. A friend of William's father found a pleasant residence near the port for my new wife and me. It took only a few days to secure a large makhzan and establish a permanent place of business for the Collegantia. I was so engaged in establishing my home and new commerce on the island, I did not see William for some time. When we finally met, William had news of his own.

"The emir was pleased with me, Joshua. As you know, your family helped me to sell the gazz we acquired from the Venetians for twenty thousand Tari. The emir told me that sum would repay the entire cost of his attack on the Greeks. I have been granted a reward of three thousand Tari. That is enough for me to purchase a home of my own."

"That is good news," I said. "But you are not smiling. You should be very pleased. Is there a problem?"

"I am not certain," said William. "While we were in al-Misr, the emir led a fleet to Madhya, on the coast of Ifriqiya, and conquered that city. Then, he took the cities of Sfax and Sousa, incorporating both under the administration of King Ruggiero."

Now I was confused. "Bringing those lands under the control of Sicilia will only enhance your island's control of trade in the Middle Sea. I do not understand why this event concerns you."

William scowled. "You are correct but there is more. The Greeks and the Venetians are attempting to retake Kerkyra. If they succeed, Giorgos has sworn to drive them out again. This time, he says, he will take the battle all the way to Constantinopolis itself. He has commanded me to join him when he assembles his war fleet. I bring him luck, he says."

I was beginning to understand. The last thing William wished to do would be to join the emir on another military adventure. If I guessed correctly, he now wanted only to spend time with his family and settle into the routine of his regular duties

"William, can you refuse such a command?" I asked, "Surely, you have done enough."

"I am a servant of the court, Joshua. I have no choice in these matters. What I will refuse to do is enable the removal of any more Jews from their homes. It is true that the Jews we transported from Corinth have been welcomed into the community here. They are now engaged in constructing the first facility in Sicilia to produce fine woven gazz. That is good for King Ruggiero but those people are victims.

They lost their homes by force. Now they must learn a new language, new customs and build new lives. They were given no choice and I am responsible for their plight. My guilt weighs heavily upon me. I will not be a party to such a tragedy again, If the cost of my refusal is the loss of my position, then so be it."

"I admire your resolution, William but surely your refusal could be considered treason," I said. "Would you truly take such a risk?"

William nodded his head in the affirmative. "How can I stand before G-d if I am again a party to the enslavement of your people, Joshua. Of course, it may not be necessary for me to take such a step. You see, the emir is not in the best of health. If he becomes too ill to lead the war fleet then perhaps all will be well. If he dies, another will take his place. The most likely candidate is a man called Philip of Mahdia. He is a eunuch and a trusted advisor to the King. Philip is not qualified to lead such an expedition. I can only pray that I never am called upon to test my resolve."

Despite my prodding, William did not wish to pursue this discussion further. There was more news.

"Did you hear that Qurtuba has fallen?" he asked

"All of us have heard this," I said. "Even now, the Almohad are raising large armies in Ifriqiya, which will be sent to capture more cities in the land of Sepharad. Many Jews will leave. They will have no choice. Some will travel to al-Misr, and, once again, my people will be dispersed across the world."

"What about you and Hannah?" William asked. "Will you remain here? You said you would go to Yerushalayim. Does that remain your plan?"

I gave a deep sigh. "William, I will remain here," I said. "I have sent a message to my father requesting certain spices and other goods that will sell well. Your father's friend Aubert has provided me with a list of herbs required in the hospice and has entered a partnership with me. There is a grand Beth Knesset here where I can worship, and Hannah and I have already become acquainted with others of our faith. I am taking lessons once again from the Chief Rabbi. If G-d wills, Hannah and I will have children. Unless we are driven from here by the forces of Amalek, Sicilia will now be my home."

"But you swore to go to the holy city, did you not?" William asked. "King Louis and Emperor Conrad lost most of their armies. King Baldwin failed to conquer Dimashq after a long siege. I am convinced that his defeat will result in disaster and the loss of the Holy Land to the Muslims. Is this not the time to regain a place for the Jews?"

"William, I am from Sepharad," I said. "I believe the words of the prophet Obadiah. Our people shall return to Yerushalayim. That is G-d's promise. But He will decide when that will be, not me. If we do not return next year, then perhaps we will do so in the year following. Perhaps it will be my children, or theirs, that return. G-d's time is not our own. I know that now. For the present, I will live the best life I can and give thanks for the blessings I have received. I will follow tradition and the law. I will do what is right. That is all I can and must do."

To G-d be Glory

תהילה להיות לאלוהים

GLOSSARY

Adilah – (Arabic) one-half of a camel load

Aethiopia – (Greek) modern-day Ethiopia

Af-Yum – (Arabic) opium

Al-Andalus – (Arabic) Muslim Spain

Al-Bahr Al-Ahmar – (Arabic) the Red Sea

Al-Eaqrab – (Arabic) scorpion

Al-Hind – (Arabic) India

Al-Iskandariyyah – (Arabic) Alexandria, Egypt

Al-Luban – (Arabic) frankincense

Al-Maghribiyah – (Arabic) modern-day Morocco, literally "the West."

Al-Mas – (Arabic) Diamonds

Al-Misr – (Arabic) Egypt

Al - Murabit Almoravid – the ruling dynasty of al-Andalus and al-Maghribiyah

An-Nil – (Arabic) the Nile River

Al-Qahirah – (Arabic) Cairo, Egypt

Al-kitan – (Arabic) flax

Al-Quds – (Arabic) Jerusalem

Al-Shaam – (Arabic) Syria

Al-Sukkar – (Arabic) Sugar

Al-Tutili – Toledo, Spain

Al-Yaman – modern day Yemen

Arth al-Bortucal – (Arabic) Portugal

Ashurit – Hebrew script

Azafran – (Arabic) saffron

Bahar – a unit of weight in the India trade equal to approximately 300 lbs.

Bahr-i-Qulzum – (Arabic) Red Sea

Bezant (Old French) = ¼ oz. of gold or 3.22 oz. of silver or 46 English Pennies

Beth Midrash – a religious school for older youth

Beit Knesset – Synagogue (House of Worship) in Hebrew

Caliph – (Arabic) chief Muslim civil and religious leader

Cardamomum – (Latin) cardamom

Collegantia – (Latin) early form of joint-stock company

Commanda – (Latin) early form of a contractual trading enterprise

Constantinopolis – (Greek) modern-day Istanbul, Turkey

Crucesignatus – (Latin) an armed Christian pilgrim, a crusader.

Dimashq – (Arabic) Damascus

Dinar (Arabic) = 1.5 Bezant or 1 Al-Qahirah Bezant

Erythra Thalassa – (Greek) the Red Sea

Fatimid – the ruling dynasty of Aegyptus

Faufal – (Arabic) for betel nuts

Funduq – (Arabic) an enclosed compound used and owned by foreign merchants.

Gazz – (Arabic) silk

Hakim – (Arabic) physician

Hammam – (Arabic) bathhouse

Hashishi – (Arabic) an assassin, a member of the Hashishiyyin

Ifriqiya – (Arabic) modern-day Tunisia

Ishbilliyah – Saville, Spain

Iskandariyyah – (Arabic) Alexandria, Egypt

Jalabah – A type of Arab sailing vessel like a Dhow

Kalaripayattu – (Malayalam) the oldest Indian martial art

Kabbaba – black pepper

Kafur – (Arabic derived from Sanskrit) camphor.

Kephale – Byzantine title for a civil governor

Kerkyra – (Greek) Corfu

Levante – (Italian) the lands of the Middle East along the Mediterranean coast

Lishbunah – (Arabic al-Ushbuna) Lisbon, Portugal

Madrassa – (Arabic), an Islamic school

Markab – (Arabic/Hindi) is a large sailing vessel used in the India Trade

Makhzan – (Arabic) warehouse

Malaqah – Malaga, Spain

Merrakec – (Berber) modern-day Marrakech, Morocco

Moallim – (Arabic) teacher

Musta'rib – Mozarabic, the language of medieval Spain

Nakhuda – (Persian) Ship Master in the India Trade

Panormos – (Arabic) Palermo, Sicily

Qadi – (Arabic) judge of Islamic law

Quadis – (Arabic) Cadiz, Spain

Quarib – (Arabic) seagoing barge used to transport heavy cargo.

Qurtuba – (Arabic) Cordoba Spain

Qutun – (Arabic) Cotton

Sahib al-Suq – (Arabic) – Port Master

Sayyid – (Arabic) sir; milord

Sayyida – (Arabic) madam; lady

Shatranj – an early form of the game of chess

Sicilia – (Latin) Sicily

Siyyon – Zion

Suq – (Arabic) market

Tari – (Arabic) Sicilian coin worth about ¼ Dinar

Tamaziyt – the Berber language

Tulaytula – (Arabic) modern-day Toledo, Spain

Waraq – (Arabic) paper

Yerushalayim – Jerusalem

Yeshiva – religious school for the young

Zanjabil – (Arabic) ginger

FROM THE SAME AUTHOR

The Sugar Merchant

When Thomas's family is annihilated in a raid, his life changes forever. Wandering for days, starving and hopeless, he is rescued by a monk and is taken to live at the abbey of Eynsham. There he receives a curious education, training to be a scholar, a merchant, and a spy. His mission: to develop commerce in Muslim lands and dispatch vital information to the Holy See.

His perilous adventures during the 11th century's commercial revolution will take him far from his cloistered life to the great trading cities of Almeria, Amalfi, Alexandria, and Cairo.

Spanning the tumultuous medieval worlds of Judaism, Christianity, and Islam, *The Sugar Merchant,* is a tale of clashing cultures, massive economic change, and one man's determination to fulfil his destiny.

Praise for The Sugar Merchant:

Publishers Weekly: "This complex and fascinating portrait of medieval life will appeal to history devotees."

First Place – Chaucer Award for emerging new talent and outstanding works in pre-1750s historical fiction

Bronze Medal – The Coffee Pot Book Club Historical Fiction, The Early Medieval Period, Book of the Year Award

Finalist – Readers' Favorite, Christian Historical Fiction

The Travels of Ibn Thomas

Thoma, the son of Thomas, the Sugar Merchant, born in Egypt but raised in England, is sent to the famous Salernitan School to train as a physician in the early twelfth century. In Sicily, he saves the life of a prince and becomes a court physician. But disaster strikes; escaping from Sicily, he is captured by pirates, befriends an assassin, and is plunged into political and religious turmoil in the Holy Land following the first crusade.

The adventures of a man torn between religious and political loyalties, and embroiled in international conflict and intrigue, *The Travels of ibn Thomas*, the second book in the series that began with *The Sugar Merchant*, is a gripping story of one man's life, and a fascinating glimpse into the tumultuous twelfth century commercial and scientific revolution when the three Abrahamic faiths meet in both cooperation and deadly conflict.

Praise for the Travels of ibn Thomas:

Historical Novel Society – "for those fascinated by the religious friction in the time of the first crusades, *The Travels of Ibn Thomas* is an elucidating and recommended read."

Silver Medal – The *Coffee Pot Book Club Historical Fiction, The Early Medieval Period, Book of the Year Award*

First Prize – *Chaucer Award for emerging new talent and outstanding works in pre-1750s historical fiction.*

US Review of Books – *"Thomas will quickly become a hero to all readers, and this book will become one that they are likely to return to over and over again".*

Made in the USA
Monee, IL
10 May 2023